IT is New Year's Eve, and Captain James Dawn's shipmates are gathered in his house in Merrymeeting, Maine, to await the birth of a child. Wagers are laid, watches like silver turnips are gripped in bronzed fingers, and the stroke of midnight has ushered in the nineteenth century when word comes that young John Dawn is "off the ways."

With this rousing scene Mr. Coffin opens his new novel, a romance of American seafaring, and of Maine and the Dawn family in particular—a tale in which stirring incident and deeper meaning combine to bring a colorful epoch vividly to life and produce an epic of American living.

John Dawn, shipmaster and shipbuilder of Merrymeeting, is the central figure. Four generations of Dawns, however, pass through the story—all stalwart, proud, handsome men who had a way with ships and women. It is through their eyes that we see the early

raid on the settlement, the

im-

JOHN DAWN

THE MACMILLAN COMPANY
NEW YORK · BOSTON · CHICAGO · DALLAS
ATLANTA · SAN FRANCISCO

MACMILLAN & CO., LIMITED
LONDON · BOMBAY · CALCUTTA
MELBOURNE

THE MACMILLAN COMPANY
OF CANADA, LIMITED
TORONTO

JOHN DAWN

By
ROBERT P. TRISTRAM COFFIN

NEW YORK
THE MACMILLAN COMPANY
1936

Set up and electrotyped. Published September, 1936
First Printing.

SET UP BY BROWN BROTHERS LINOTYPERS
PRINTED IN THE UNITED STATES OF AMERICA
BY THE FERRIS PRINTING COMPANY

TO

FRANK COFFIN

MY BROTHER ALL HIS LIFE

and

ANDREW PENNELL

MY BROTHER FOR A DOZEN YEARS

BECAUSE THEY BOTH HAVE BOATS IN THEIR BLOOD

AND A LOT OF JOHN DAWN

JOHN DAWN

I

"WHAT do you make it, Fearing Upjohn?"

"It wants a quarter to midnight, Sir."

"And you, Davy Snow?"

"Sixteen and a half, Cap'n James. But my works would be spryer for a drop of whale oil, Liza says."

The man whose unpowdered blonde hair almost brushed the cross beams of the kitchen ceiling twirled the silver turnip he was dangling by its thick chain in his fingers.

"My timekeeper says eleven to, God blast me, and I'll swing if 'tisn't so!"

"Swing if you're a mind to, Cap'n—and it's likely the way you'll end—but I say your watch is fast. And I say your young-one is coming into this vale of tears before the century turns."

David Snow turned away from the tall man in the blue coat with silver buttons, and shook his wrinkled square face at the blazing coals. He shoved his hands under the tails of his coat and stood with his white silk stockings running fire.

"You've had your way in most things, Captain James. But you won't in this. You can't dictate to Providence. A woman's time is like the sea's tide, and it can't be put off. Not for you nor any man."

As if his words were coming true, there came a sudden

rumbling of furniture above, the fall of a chair, and women's excited voices.

Mr. Snow turned his face from the fire.

"What did I tell you?—What does that sound like?" And then he lowered his voice, as he went on, "And happen it be a girl-child, Master James, after all you've said all along? Happen it be a girl?"

"Davy Snow, you hear me! My young-one is to be a son. And he is not going to be birthed until the year 1800!"

"You had best swing the hands to your timekeeper, then. For I think the young-one is landed, bag and baggage."

"Betsy!—Betsy O'Reilly!—Ahoy, you up there. Betsy, you trollop!" Captain James Dawn's voice made the rafters quiver above his wide mouth.

"Yes, Cap'n James?" A female's voice came muffled down to them.

"Betsy, is my son off the ways yet?"

"No, Sir. Not yet. But Mistress Dawn is sore took. And it will be right soon now."

The master of the house swung on his friend, David Snow.

"I'll lay you ten silver dollars that my son, John Dawn, won't be born till the new century is here. Will you take me?"

"Take him! take him!" several male voices there piped up.

"I'm with the master on this," Fearing Upjohn called out in a shrill voice. "There ain't been man nor wind that ever could stand up to Jamie Dawn. Here's ten more dollars for you to cover, Davy. I'm with the master."

"And I'm with the Lord who orders such things," David shouted. "And there's my ten dollars!"

He shook out his long purse, and the coins rolled over the table among the tobacco pipes, flashed and clinked. One clattered to the floor.

"Time it," commanded Captain James. "Betsy," he bellowed, "you call down to me the instant it happens. I have a wager on it." He stood there, head and shoulders over them all in the tobacco smoke, holding his huge watch in his great fist. He was the only one whose hair was not white. He wore it natural. It shone golden in the firelight, drawn back and tied with a black silk ribbon.

The room fell silent, and the minutes ticked off.

"We'll have the young-one's wail in a moment," said David.

There was a dead silence above.

Fearing Upjohn could stand it no longer. He took a prodigious pinch of snuff. Tears filled his eyes. He choked, and then sneezed violently. His wig slipped to one side, and the ribbon hung over his ear. All the men burst out into laughter.

"Silence!" The fist of Captain James smote the table so that the thin crystal glasses hopped about. One tipped over and tinkled into splinters. A thread of dark liquid ran crazily over the polished mahogany and trickled down to the floor.

A man could hear a pin drop.

The tap-tap of the spilled wine.

A long spell of complete hush. The minutes were running away, ticked off on the captain's silver watch.

Then it came. A thin, weak cry.

"There she blows, Cap'n James! And I will trouble you for those dollars of yours."

David Snow's hand was out, with the deep lace around it.

"Betsy!"

A sob above.

"Betsy!—Damn ye!"

"Yes, Master." Very faint and muffled.

"Who made that noise?—Has he hove in sight yet?"

"N-no, Sir. That was me."

James Dawn folded up his friend's fingers for him and thrust his hand away.

"Don't you count your pullets till they be hatched, David."

The seconds went on ticking as before.

"It's 1800, by my watch," Captain James said, very quietly.

Mr. Snow shook his head. "Four minutes to go, blast ye, Cap'n Jamie."

All the others took in a deep breath. Fearing Upjohn seemed to be the only one breathing. He could not help it. They could all hear his breath going wildly out and in.

The doctor's voice broke out loudly upstairs.

"There! there!—Only a minute now, my dear."

"Betsy!"

"Yes, Sir."

"Any sign of him yet?"

"No."

A minute went by. Then more muffled calls above, and the sound of feet.

"Any signs of the little sinner yet?—Damn ye?"

"N-no, Sir. But he's about ready to come."

Another minute. Another burst of bustling.

"Can you see him yet, Betsy?"

"No, not yet."

The clock outside in the long hall began to chime. All the men turned and listened. It went on in peace and struck twelve.

Captain James Dawn put his watch into the fob in his trousers. He reached down and gathered in all the dollars that still lay on the table.

There was a shrill treble overhead.

"Oh, Master, I can see his head a-coming!"

"Gentlemen," said the captain in a calm, deep voice, "let us drink to 1800 and my son, John Dawn."

He poured them all out a glass of wine. His big hand did not tremble a hair's breadth as he steered the slender stream of red into glasses with stems fragile as a Maine sand-peep's legs.

They all raised their glasses.

"Oh, Sir! the handsomest little boy you ever laid eyes on!" Betsy's voice shrilled down.

"Gentlemen!—my son!"

II

"WAKE up, David Snow! and see what a bright, sunshiny year it is!"

The man with his wig all awry lifted his face from the table. There were wine stains on his cheeks. He rubbed his eyes with both fists. The room was foggy with blue tobacco smoke.

"Davy ahoy!—And a Happy New Year!"

A dozen men were flourishing their churchwardens over their soiled wigs.

"A Happy New Century, say I," said Captain Dawn.

He was standing with his back like a wide plank to the eight-foot back-log in the fireplace, and his great thighs were wide as a tie-up door. He was the only man still standing on his pins. He was fresh as a daisy. The frost-flower blue of the eyes of the Dawns made his eyes in his head snap like two cut stones.

"Top of the century to you, David! Eight o'clock, and an icy clear morning."

He was the only man there who had not had a wink. And he carried five good quarts of the best wine of the Dawn cellar under his belt. He was the only man there whose calves were not stockinged. His huge legs were cased in pearl-colored cloth to his thick ankles. He had been the first on Merrymeeting Bay to take up with the outlandish French fashion. He had a warm spot in the cockles of his heart for the rabble who had pulled down the Bastille. Forward-looking rapscallions, he called them. Citizens of the future. He was, too, he loved to boast. A nineteenth-century man. Independent as a hog on the ice. Kowtow to nobody. That was his religion. Take nobody's backwash. Any man good as a king!

"Is it day already?" queried the blinking Mr. Snow.

"A day and be damned! A day like a diamond. A day bright as one of your silver dollars! Look there, Davy, lad!"

The captain stepped over to a window and threw back the shutter. A light like a bushel of diamonds leaped into the room. The beam of it cut across the fogs of tobacco stench, and a grillwork of sunlight crisscrossed by the window sashes lay on the floor.

David Snow went to the window and blinked out. He had to keep his eyes half to.

"A Maine kind of morning!" roared Captain Dawn. "And they don't make them anywhere else. A sight for sore eyes, eh, Davy?" He smiled at his oldest friend. The sunlight showed up David's deep wrinkles around his narrow lips. "And you're looking as homely as a basket of eels!"

On the other side of the window the world was all splintered glass. The tall elms were crusted with ice to the last twig. Their branches bent over and touched and grew into the crusted snow. Every vine stem had a casing of crystal about it. Iced grasses shed a rosy lustre on the snow. It was like looking into a chandelier. The sky was dark blue and looked as if it would ring if a man so much as touched it with a fingernail. The low sun came across the glassy hills too splendid to look at. It was tipping the dark saw of the eastern spruces with flakes of flame. The whole earth was afire, with a cool blaze. A man could not bear to look up among the elm boughs, for they were full of the dust of rainbows. The only thing that was not transparent was the bay. But it was like a sheet of black diamonds. It faded as it went out uphill and joined the dark blue of the high Atlantic, stretched like a wall along this bright Maine coast.

"God!—what a day to be born!"

James Dawn brought his open hand down on the wine velvet of his friend's coat with a slap that made Davy's teeth rattle in his jaws. The dust flew in a cloud from the velvet cloth.

"A new world, old shellback! A century that will shelve us high and dry as the high-pooped tubs of the Spanish Main! That young-one of mine upstairs will be up to his struts in things you and I never dared to meddle in. He'll see lands we never saw and do great businesses on the waters of the world. A new world! Come, let's have a look! It's close in here. Let's have a whiff of 1800 air!"

The tall man stooped to the window frame, his thighs parted. He laid his hands on each side of the window sash. His hands were red and hairy as old anchors that have been much in the sea. His fingers were too large for the iron side-latch. He could not get a hold of it. "Damn my great gut! but she'll come!" There was an ominous cracking of wood.

"Easy there!—take it easy, Jamie, or you'll tear your blasted house up by the roots. Go easy, or you'll——"

"I want air, I tell ye!"

There was a great rending sound, and a jingle of glass. The window went up lacking two panes. Went to the top and stayed there. The air of the January morning came in like a great cool wave. The smoky room cleared. The logs on the hearth spluttered and flared up into sheets of gold. Hearth smoke and ashes eddied out, and the gray ashes drifted across the square tiles and the scrubbed floorboards.

James Dawn tore open his coat and unbuttoned his fawn waistcoat. Tore the gilt buttons from the holes. Two of the buttons plopped and shot the length of the room. The man stood there with his ruffed linen flapping in the wind.

"Ah!—ah!—ah!"

He flared his nostrils as a stallion might, took in a deep breath, and filled himself with morning and the new year.

"You'll catch your death a-cold, James Dawn. God made you such a fool!"

"The air is better than the wine. It is the air for a new man to breathe. My son's air!"

"It's getting colder than Providence here," shouted David Snow. "Shut the window down, in God's name. We'll all have the phthisic!"

"Who's got a window open?—Shut that window down!"

"Oh, are ye there, Constant? Have you rubbed the oakum out of your tarry eyes, boy?—You've been snoring like a porpoise, the night away."

"We have more sense than stand by an open window in a shrewd Winter wind, Captain Dawn," Constant Converse spoke up. "We ain't daft."

"You are all dumb-gutted men, and I'm righteous sorry to confess ye are friends of mine, damn ye! I with a new son to my name and wanting the morning in my bones and the sunlight!"

He stood there breathing hard. He was the best built man in the room full of men, taller and stronger than any. With the ruffles to his shirt rippling in the breeze that came in over the Atlantic, up out of Fundy's Bay and the Banks beyond. There wasn't a man-jack there but loved him better than the apple of his eye. Not a one of them but would have jumped into the icy ocean for him without a minute's notice. They had all been into the Antarctic with him more times than they could count on the fingers of their hands. Bending hell for leather on the hafts of the long sweeps, hot on the flukes of the square-headed sperm. Hearing the line sing out wicked as the world between them as the whale sounded. Working like barefooted devils, up to their armpits in blubber and blood as they cut up the kill by sooty lantern light. Tumbling like lost souls, alone and in empty vacancies of bitter ocean, under the wicked glitter of the Southern Cross.

"Fire-huggers! Old women in shawls! afraid of a little clean Winter!"

Through the window they could see the icy spars of the ship they had all sailed in, when the season came and they had put off their fine clothes and buckled down to whaling, the length of the world. To the bottom side of the world, where the white continents of ice cracked and groaned under the moon and the days went by like cold and terrible dreams. They'd have been down there now, if it hadn't been for Jamie's wanting to be home when his calf came, as he put it. That was why they were here hugging the fire. James Dawn knew that. Their ship was frozen fast in the ice which had made around their pier on Merrymeeting Bay. They had brought home the whale oil in tierces and tuns and hogsheads in her. They would be up in her rigging when the geese flew again. They would live on the narrow paths of round and slippery wood, in a house where life depended on thin ropes crisscrossing the empty sky, in a house of cobwebs that the gales came through, that made a wide arc across the clouds, a hundred feet above the white-topped waves.

"For God's sake, put that window down, or your son will suffer for it." David Snow was wide awake now at last. He sneezed a great sneeze, and his wig fell over his eyes.

A lusty squalling burst out above stairs.

"I told ye so, Jamie Dawn, I told ye!"

The face of the man at the window lit up more than ever. It shone with more than the January sunshine.

"Listen to that!—There's a man-child for you, my lads! There's a pair of lungs for you. Wait till you hear those lungs fill up with the Antarctic breeze! They'll make you buckle to your oars!"

"Betsy O'Reilly will be down here and tan your hide for you, Jamie, for cooling the house off on the baby," Constant Converse put in. "You mark me. She can't abide a draft, as you know."

"What say I up-end Betsy instead and tan her keel before the lot of ye all?"

All the men roared.

"It wouldn't be the first time, I warrant," cried Abel Winship. "I wager you've stood Betsy O'Reilly topsy-turvy more than once, if all I hear tell of be so."

"You mind the heat in your own breeches, Abel Winship. Betsy and I are nought but good friends."

"You two are nought, all right. And there's like to be one more son than Mistress Dawn knows about running about under this same roof before long."

The sunlight suddenly went out of James Dawn's eyes. They went dark.

"You keep your backstairs gossip to yourself, Mr. Winship. You keep to your petticoats, and I'll keep to mine."

"The pot calls the kettle black," Fearing Upjohn tittered in his high-pitched voice.

There was another big bellow of laughter.

"And is it Bedlam itself we are having this morning down here, I want ever to know?"

Betsy O'Reilly stood at the door. Her nightcap was keeled over to starboard, and she had thunder in her eyes.

"Sweet land of Erin! and is that a window open I see?"

"It's all right, Betsy, my darling. We are just airing out. Getting the fog out of our eyes. And how is the new captain above stairs?"

Betsy bounced across the room and smashed down the window.

"Your son is sitting on top of the morning, no thanks to you. And it's in his grave he will be surely, if you go breaking out all the windows in the house whatever."

Her sprigged muslin skirt brushed the toes of Captain Dawn's boots as she swept by him with her head tossing high and her cheeks like rosehips.

"Wait, Betsy." James Dawn's big hand went out and grasped the girl by the wrist. "We want the young sannup brought down here where we can look him over and see if he's ballasted right. We want to see the color of his eyes. You go fetch him down. There's a good girl. And that's to go on."

Before the maid could wrench away from him, the man leaned and planted a smack on Betsy's neck where it rounded out for her shoulder.

The girl spun about and fetched her master a slap with her hand that left a red welt on his cheek. Her eyes were glittering like huckleberries in her head.

"Will you keep your big paws to home, Cap'n Dawn? You'd better keep them to home. Ain't you ashamed, and you with a son and a wife upstairs!"

"The new father has the right to kiss the woman who brings him the tidings. Ain't it so, gentlemen?"

"You bet it is!—That's so, Betsy!" They all roared together.

"Well, it's no son of yours that will be being fetched down this morning. Arrah, and whatever would Dr. Shaw have to say to that?"

"Give Dr. Shaw my compliments." The voice of James Dawn had gone down deep in his chest and was grave. "And tell him to send my son down here at once."

The tone of the captain's voice cut the girl's mood like a snip of a shears. She bent her dark curls down and went straight out of the room.

"A neat piece of Erin," breathed Constant Converse.

"As pretty piece of baggage as a man will see in a month of Sundays," said Abel Winship.

The squalling above stairs died away. There were sounds of feet. Perhaps the low sound of a gentle voice. The voice of Dr. Shaw droned like a troubled bumble bee. Then the door opened at last, and Betsy O'Reilly came in with a bundle of pink and white coverlets in her plump arms.

The captain had the bundle out of her arms before she was off the threshold. He looked down into it, put down a paw and rummaged about.

"He's in here somewhere, I'll lay to that. I feel his heft. Where are you, Son?"

Betsy was hovering over the clothes. She drew back a quilt's corner, and made a quick little sound with her lips. Like the cluck of a hen.

James Dawn looked and looked. He did not move. He did not say a word. It was a long time that his eyes under his bushy brows stared upon the sight the girl had uncovered. All the men could see the shine in Captain Dawn's eyes. It was like the shine of cut diamonds. The man took a deep, slow breath at last.

Then he marched straight over to the door, threw it open, stepped out upon the crusted snow, and stood there in the full shine of the low sun. The sun's light was all over his blonde hair, and it fell full on the wrinkled face of the new-born child.

Betsy caught in her breath and threw her hands over her mouth to choke back her cry.

"The air of morning," James Dawn was saying, "the air of the Atlantic. Breathe it in, my Son. Take a good breath of it, for it is yours. It is yours all your life. And the new century belongs to you."

James Dawn's voice was quiet and low. Like a preacher's of a Sunday. All at once, as the two were there in the flooding sunshine, a small red fist came up and stayed aloft.

The man lifted his eyes to his friends. His eyes were full of the sun's fire.

"See! he takes hold of life hard! That's my son."

The little clenched hand fell out of sight. The captain came in and closed the door gently. He put the bundle back into the maid's arms. He went over to the mantel. There was a small panel there in the woodwork. He opened it and took out a pewter cup. It had a deep dent in its brim.

"Gentlemen," said James Dawn, "this cup has a story to it. I will tell you it. But first, let's fill it up and drink to my son."

He poured it full to the brim from the whisky flask on the table.

"The cup is called the Luck of the Dawns. You will see what it has on its side as it comes round."

Then the captain did a queer thing. He went over to the wall and took down his whaling iron. He held the wide head of it aloft. It was sharp as a quill at its point. He put the point into the liquor and stirred it three times around. He lifted the cup high into the sunbeam that slanted in through the window.

"I give you John Dawn, son of James!"

The captain drank from the cup and passed it on. Each man took it as it came along, raised it, and drank his drink.

"John Dawn! John Dawn!"

Each man looked at the mug as it passed through his hands. It had a rising sun on its side with beams which rayed up to the rim. And below the half-circle of the sun were the letters

J. DAWN.

III

THE trees were too bright to look at in the January morning. They were sheets of glass and threads of crystal. The sun shone full on their icy twigs and boughs, and they turned to pieces of rainbows and trembled with drops of melted gold. Every so often there was a sharp crack like the report of a pistol as a limb gave way under its weight of ice.

The kitchen was flooded with a strange, unearthly splendor. The pewter plates on the dresser caught it and became silver. The separate kernels in the ears of dried maize hung by braided husks among the rafters stood out like stones in a sunlit stream. The light had gone up even into the corners of the ceiling, and the dusty cobwebs there looked like black lace.

The door to the next room opened suddenly, and a white head appeared.

"A twelve-pound son you have, to start your family with!"

The doctor settled his square-rimmed spectacles on the bridge of his nose, and tugged his wig down over the cropped brown hair back of his left ear.

"Yes, a lusty son!—You should be a proud man this sunshiny day, Dawn."

"I am," said the man who had waited in the kitchen, "I am so."

"Well, the she-folks can look after the babe now. I must be off to Squire's. He is like to be having a shrewd nip of the gout this sharp, frosty morning."

" 'Tis a marvel to me you ever left Squire's gout and troubled yourself with the likes of us."

"That's a bold bit of folly to toss on your tongue, Sirrah. But it's like you to bite the hand that offers you bounty, pox on you!"

"I am not beholden to Squire for bounty, and you can tell him so for me. And there are your two guineas for this night's work."

The tall man flung the coins on the pine-board floor. They rolled to the doctor's feet.

"I am half a mind to kick your coins into the fire, Jake Dawn. Lud, you are wanton! You would not have a roof over your head if 'tweren't for the Squire and his ships, and the labor you have on them. He fills your crop with victuals, and this is the thanks he has of you."

"I earn my victuals with my sweat, and there would be no masts going out of Merrymeeting Bay, if I did not put my axe to the pines."

"The pines are Squire Trefethen's."

"The earth may be Squire Trefethen's. But I am not. Run now and tattle that to him as you tattle everything."

"You are a stiff-necked young jackanapes, and I will not waste words on you."

The doctor bent down and gathered up the gold pieces. He dusted them off with his handkerchief and put them into the pocket of his greatcoat. He fumbled under his big silver buttons, whipped out his snuff-box, applied a fierce pinch to each side of his nose, and flung the rest of the snuff into the air.

"I bid you good day, Sirrah!—a very good day!—Pox take you!"

"Pox take the two guineas!" shouted Jacob Dawn, "Lick-spit!" And he slammed the door so that it cracked the doctor's high heels.

The inner door swung open, and a woman came into the kitchen with a high armful of coverlets.

"I bring you Happy New Year and a fine son, Neighbor Dawn. A proper rogue it is! Please you, look!"

She rolled back the top covering.

The tall man leaned over. He took the whole bundle on his long arm.

"Ah, Maria, my son! I—I——"

He could not say a word more. He stood there quiet for a long time in the light of the sun. A bright drop trickled down his nose and fell into the warm nest he was holding.

"Lud! Lud! Master Dawn. You must not take it so sorely. 'Twill be but the first of many. You must not go baptizing your babe with tears. That is a bad omen. Here now!"

She took the child from the father.

"Tears at the first will bring tears at the last, as the old saying goes. Marry, come up!—And you a man in breeches!"

Jacob Dawn stood there with his right arm still

crooked as if he still held the infant. And he wept unabashed, his tears glistening in the sunlight.

There came a timid lifting at the latch.

Jacob swabbed at his eyes and dried them on the cuff of his gray homespun shirt.

"Come in!" cried Maria Orr.

A very small boy, in a three-cornered hat sizes too big for him, came in with his breath all around him. He was muffled to his eyes in a blue woolen scarf. He had a bundle under his arm.

"Why, bless me, if it isn't Davy Snow as ever was! Come in and shut the door, Davy, and don't bring in all the frost of the morning with you. What is it you want so bright and early this morning? Oh Lud! are the Indians coming?"

"Please, Mistress Orr, Squire sent me."

"Squire sent you?" Jacob Dawn came to himself with a shout.

"Yes, Sir. He give me this and said 'twas for the babe that was coming this day, and give me two silver pennies, and I wropped it so as not to nick it and legged it out and runned the whole way, and slipped down three times, and didn't nick it, and skinned my elbow, and here I be!"

"Well, well. And what might it be you have, David?"

"A cup, Sir—Oh, the prettiest cup you ever seed! Here it is, Mr. Dawn." He unwound the cloth coverings and put a shiny new pewter mug on the table. "And now please, Mr. Dawn, may I see him?"

"That you may, Davy," said Maria. "Come here."

"And how did you know it was a he, David Snow?" asked Jacob Dawn.

"Oh, I know'd. You wouldn't have a she-one.—Ain't it a he?—Oh, Mr. Dawn, is it a she-one?"

"As he a one as you be, David. He'll be knocking you down some fine day soon."

"Oh, la! Neighbor Dawn—what a master cup it is! Good enough for an earl to drink out of! Who would have thought it of Squire!"

"Yes," said Jacob Dawn, with a black look, "pewter—worth three pence in Portsmouth Town! And he eating off silver every meal of his life!"

"You mustn't look a gift horse in his teeth, Neighbor Dawn. No good ever comes of that. A gift is a gift, no matter whence it comes or what it be. If you can get blood out of a turnip, get it, says I."

"I want none of his cups!" roared the man. "I want none of Ronald Trefethen. He and his toplofty airs! As if he was George the King himself! King of all Merrymeeting!—He can take his cup back and be damned!"

The master of the cottage reached out and seized the pewter drinking mug and threw it across the room. It struck the pine dresser and bounced to the floor. Little David Snow's eyes were like saucers. His mouth came open, but he could not say a word.

"Oh, bad luck! bad luck!" moaned Mistress Orr. "Oh, but you are full of folly, Jake Dawn, to go throwing gifts all over the house. You'll live to see the day you will be sorry, mark me! You and your hot head. But the Dawns will be Dawns, and full of pepper to the end. Might as well look for a tiger to change his stripes. Lord ha' mercy!"

Maria clasped the baby to her ample bosom and tottered out of the room.

"Don't you like the cup, Mr. Dawn?" David Snow found the tongue in his head at last.

"I don't like the man who sent it, Davy."

"But wouldn't it do just as well for the baby? Squire sent it to him."

"That's so, David. Damme! that's so. It belongs to the baby."

The man went over and picked the piece of pewter up from the floor. He took it in his big hands and straightened out the dent in it best as he could. He held it and looked at it for a long time. It struck him suddenly that the boy was watching him. He fumbled in his breeches' pocket and brought forth a shining new coin.

"Here's thanking you for bringing the cup, Davy." He thrust the penny into the small lad's palm. "And his name is to be James. And I hope you will like him."

"Thank you, Sir." David's eyes were all lit up like a church. "And I better be going." The boy plucked his forelock and went out through the door quickly.

Jacob Dawn heard the boy's small feet pattering over the crust fainter and fainter.

He went over to his work bench and sat down. He got out a tool with a very sharp point to it. He tried it on the pine of the bench. Then he put the pewter mug down between his knees, held it there tight, and began to cut into it. He wrote in big capitals, J. DAWN. He looked at what he had done. Then he had a new idea. He drew a half-circle above the name and cut long rays up from its edge to the brim of the cup.

"And that's for the day coming. The day when Dawn puts out the light of Trefethen!"

He patted the silky surface of the metal, and set the mug back where he could see his rising sun. The grooves caught the light and made the thing look as if it were made of silver, after all.

Then Jacob got down the Family Bible from its little shelf at the side of the oven. He found his quill, and ground some ink. He moved his wrist in several grand flourishes to get ready. He dipped the tip and put the point to the blank page, and wrote in big scrolls of letters

James Dawn, Born In The Morning Of The New Year, 1751.

IV

JAMIE DAWN was walking like his father that sparkling September morning. Toes out and buttocks swinging. His breeches helped a lot. They were cut-me-downs of his father's, and there was as much of them fore as aft. Maria Orr said she had to look for Jamie's face, to see if he was going or coming. She had cut them down herself from his father's green homespun ones. She had gone on the principle of taking off only at the outside seams. The inner ones she had not touched, for the contours of the male being were beyond her. Maria had done most of the sewing and darning this Summer, for Mistress Dawn had been ill of a new baby. There were four boys now in the Dawn cabin. Like a flight of stairs, going down to the head in the cradle.

Jamie felt his place as the oldest. It was like being head of the family. He walked more like his father, too, because he had had hulled corn for breakfast this day, with sorghum. The first of the year's hulled corn. And tonight it would be beans. It was Saturday. Maria had put them in the earth oven, and Jamie had put the red-oak charcoal around them. They were cooking now, yellow-eyes his father and he had planted, and he had shooed the crows away from them all through June, until they had begun to crook their fingers up through the loam. His beans and his father's.

And he was carrying his father's dinner to him in his pocket. A half-loaf and a smoked herring. That made Jamie want to walk like his father, too.

The crows were acting odd today. They were not minding their own business. They were screaming a good deal in the woods back of Mast Landing. Must be a dead fox or something over there. His father said crows could scent meat ten miles away.

Jamie had seen this meadow that dipped to the blue water of Merrymeeting Bay full of men, many the time. When they were bringing down the peeled pine masts. One hundred feet long, without a twist to their grain, and hardly a knot in them. White as snow, and where their branches had been they had brown eyes. Who knew but what they could see out of them, when they stood up on decks far out at sea? The meadow was a wide one, for they had to have room to swing the masts around. Jamie had seen ten yoke of oxen chained to one, and all the Merrymeeting men bending and shoving with cant-dogs and crowbars.

His father was the tallest man of them all. He could lift as much as any two men there. It was his axe that had cut the logs at the ends, so you could see how many years old they were by the rings there. A ring for every year. Five hundred in one log, they had counted one day. It was Jamie's father who brought every one of the trees to the ground. He went through the forest filling it with thunder. You could hear the thunder at the house. Another mast starting on its travels, folks would say.

All the pines were going out to sea. Across the ocean which was two months across. Masts for the King's men-of-war. There was a broad arrow burnt into each one, near the butt end. That made them the King's. Jamie had seen a man burn the arrow in with a red-hot iron. He heated it in the coals. He spat on it to see if it was hot enough. If it was, the man's spit rolled off in a little ball. The iron made sparks when it went into the dry wood. Masts for the King!

The King had his hand on every straight and fine tree, Jamie's father said. He reached across the ocean and picked them out. Where his fingernail touched was an arrow. He laid his long arms on the backs of men he did not know. Men good as he was, said Jamie's father. The boy could not understand all of it. But his father's eyes got full of sparks of fire when he talked about it. Like the pine wood under the man's hot iron. The King had the best of everything. Had his silver ladle in every man's porridge. Taking the best hunks of porridge for himself, taking the food from men's mouths. No meal's meat, but the King was there, getting the best. So he could dress up his soldiers in scarlet and build ships that spat out thunder at the French. Some day, Jamie's father said, those tall masts were going to turn on the King, the Merrymeeting masts, and then he would get his going-home-a-crying.

The boy wondered how it would be. He had seen the white masts turn on the men in Mast Meadow. One day, one of them broke away from the cradle and came down the hill. A yoke of black oxen were right in the way. They lay on the ground afterwards with eyes like sunflowers and breathed hard through their noses till the man hit them on their heads with his axe. And the mast went over a man, too. He was white in the face, and he kept picking at nothing with both his hands. Jamie had seen him from between his father's legs. They did not use the axe on him. They took him away by the four corners of his father's coat. And two days afterwards there was a new grave on the hill. There had always been a stain on Jamie's father's coat. Maria never could get it out, even with lye.

The King had done that, Jamie's father said. With his heavy hand. There would come a day of reckoning. The King would have to pay for every drop of that blood on the coat.

The King's hand must be red as the hot iron. Jamie could not ever think of the King's hand without thinking of little sparks flying up from it in the broad daylight.

Squire Trefethen would have to answer for that spot, too. Jamie's father said so. He had put the claws in the King's hand.

The seven-year-old boy could see the white pillars of Squire Trefethen's big house from the field he was walking along. It was on the highest place along Merrymeeting Bay. So Ronald Trefethen could talk easy with God, his father said. Squire could pick the best, for the King had said all the meadows the men had cleared and all the forest behind were his. He had a sheepskin with it all written down to prove it, and the King had signed it. Jamie's house was Squire Trefethen's, and the charcoal around the beanpot. But Jamie's father was not. Not by a jugful. He never would be. And some day the big white house would fall, he said. Probably the same day the masts in the meadow turned on the King.

Jamie hoped not. He didn't want the house to fall, no matter if the masts did turn on somebody. He had been in that house. The pillars looked as if they held up the clouds, when you stood under them. He had only been in the kitchen. But he had peeked in through the door, when the cook was busy and wasn't minding him, and he had seen two boys no bigger than he was, black as charcoal all over their faces. Their hair was big as a bushel basket and fuzzy as moss. They had on white stockings and blue breeches, and gilt buckles twinkled on their shoes. They did not move an eyelash when he looked at them. But they were real, all right. And by and by a tall lady came through the door they were standing by. Her hair was white as the everlasting roses that grew in the pasture back of his own house. It was heaped up on her head like a crown. She had a dress on like strawberries and cream. She took Jamie's breath away. Then the cook came and shook her long ladle at Jamie, and he took to his heels and ran out of the house.

He ran face on into a slim boy with flashing black eyes in the yard. Jamie had seen him quite often in Merrymeeting, but never this close. He had never spoken to him. He didn't now. He brushed himself off and backed away from him. He knew who the boy was. It was Stephen Trefethen. He was about Jamie's size. He had been knocked off his feet, too. He got up and dusted his knees and backed away from Jamie. When he was back to the kitchen door, he ran his tongue out. Jamie wanted to pay him back for that, but the cook was looking out, and it was Stephen's own yard. So he had turned around and gone along on his business.

Jamie had seen the black boys again, sitting with folded arms, and all white, watery satin, on each side of the Trefethens' new coach. The coach had come all the way from Boston on a ship's deck. It even had mirrors in it, and naked babies with wings on their shoulders and not a sign of a diaper on them.

He had seen the lady again, too, inside the coach. But not much of her, for the coach kicked a sight of dust up with its wheels. They had built the coach a road, all around the hill and up in back of Mast Landing.

It was a day, this September one, like the glass goblet Maria Orr thought the world of. Clear as glass. Not a cloud blowing up from the woods where the masts grew. Not a cloud coming up from behind the blue hill of the sea. Not a breath of wind. The meadow was blue with the flowers that blossomed just ahead of the frost. The forest was all afire where the maples stood under the tall pines. Red and golden fire. Jamie could see it pouring up out of the maples. But there wasn't a sound of burning. The maples were burning, though, for his father had said just this morning that the maple trees were on fire with the Fall.

His father knew everything. He knew about ships and how they sailed in under the bottom of the world and still held on there upside down. How they went away from Maine and never turned round once and yet came back to it again. His father knew where the wild geese went when they darkened the sky in November. He knew what the wild pigeons that darkened the sun of Merrymeeting lived on. Where the rain and the hail and the snow came from. What fire was made of. And why it came on Fall.

His father knew more than Davy Snow, even. And Davy could read the newsletters that came up from Boston and Portsmouth, and had smoked his father's clay pipe, when his father was not looking, and tasted Jamaica rum.

Jamie could read the *Primer* himself. And he knew some of it by heart,

> "*Xerxes the Great Did Die,*
> *And so Must You and I.*"

and better still,

> "*The Dog Will Bite*
> *The Thief at Night.*"

Davy could read even Foxe's *Book of Martyrs*, and find out how they boiled men alive in oil.

It had been the Papists who did things to men like

that, so Jamie's father said. There had been Papists in the Trefethen family once upon a time, if you went far enough back. His father had told him that, too. Maybe, Papists and boys with black faces and white breeches went together, somehow.

Jamie's father made masts that crossed the sea. Jamie was going to cross the sea when he grew up. His father was going to build whole ships of his own, and Jamie was, too. He would sail his ships along the underside of the world and see for himself how it felt to sail head down that way.

Jamie's father knew more than the Indians.

Jamie had seen Indians many times. They sat down a lot, on their own legs, and talked down in their chests. If they could get it, they drank rum till they keeled over. They smelled the way bears smelled. They greased their brown bodies all over with bear fat. Folks said they did it to keep the mosquitoes off. They looked like harness. Like leather. Their skin didn't look as though it would feel like skin if you touched it. But they were awfully smart in the woods. Smart as lynxes. Eyes like lynxes', too.

They stole, if you didn't keep your eye on them, they were all light-fingered. They found sweet-grass where Davy and Jamie never could find it, right in Mast Meadow where the two boys played every day. They made baskets of it. They were here today and gone tomorrow. You couldn't trust them any farther than you could see them. They hated fat people. They were thin as rails themselves. They could live for a week on a rawhide string. It was feast or famine with them. They ate themselves sick when they had anything, and lived on wind pudding the rest of the time. They showed the white men how to put a fat alewife in each hill of maize, to make the cob long and full of kernels. They would give anything they had for a gun and powder. They carried a tomahawk and cut off the tops of people's heads to get the hair. But that was when the King told them to. Another King—not Jamie's. There were more Kings than one. There were Kings everywhere, and they were all a bad lot, so his father said.

There were lots of different Indians. Passamaquoddies, Pejepscots, Sacos, Abenakis. The Abenakis had stuck William Bibber's skin full of powder and then put pine splinters in him and set them afire, and he had been cooked alive. They had made Isaac Greene eat up his own nose and ears after they had cut them off with clamshells. They were bad, all of them. The only good Indians were the dead ones, his father said.

When they scalped you, they turned up a piece of the skin first, then they leaned down and took a hold of it with their teeth, and stripped your hair off at one pull. Old Nate Peabody had lost his hair and had lived to tell the tale. His head looked like a washerboard. Jamie had seen it.

Jamie had heard the Abenakis give the warwhoop. They had given it all night long. The night last Spring when they burned New Meadows, two miles away as the crow flies. Jamie had sat up to see the red glow of New Meadows on the western sky. It looked like morning coming up the wrong way. They could hear the war-whoops all that distance. Jamie had seen an Indian's scalp which Squire Trefethen's men had gotten that night. It looked like a black horse's tail.

He had seen the Merrymeeting boys standing sentinel next day. A small boy and a big boy, on top of a big stump, butts to butts. They stood there while their fathers scoured the woods for Redskins. Davy had stood up with Waitstill Doughty. Jamie was too small himself. The boys stood butts to butts to keep them wide awake. Why a boy's backsides on yours would keep you wide awake, Jamie could not understand. But they did.

Maria Orr had said the Lord's Prayer all night long.

Merrymeeting was too big a settlement for the Indians to attack.

A bald eagle was floating so high in the blue that he looked like a leaf with a spark of fire on it. The crickets were saying their prayers right out loud in the hot sun. It was so late in the year they sang by daylight.

There was nothing in the world so good as hulled corn. And baked beans. Except sitting on his father's knee and listening to stories, while the candles flickered blue and the owls called outside the house in the deep woods.

Maria didn't like candles burning blue. She saw winding-sheets in them. Maria was always looking for death, his father said, just around the corner.

Jamie came over a little rise and saw his father and Jeremiah Wigglesworth sawing away at their log on the edge of the woods. They were going back and forth, back and forth. One leaned at the other, and the other man leaned away from him. Then they changed places. One forward, one back. It made the boy think of the clock's pendulum measuring out the time. They kept at their work as Jamie came up.

His father was taller and wider through the shoulders than Jeremiah Wigglesworth. His back was toward his son. The boy was so close he could see the sweat down the seams of his father's small-clothes. And there was a dark stain of it right down between his shoulder blades in his brown shirt.

It happened all at once. James was not a dozen yards away. It was like a quick sigh. And his father did not come back from his shove. He stayed leaning forward toward Jeremiah Wigglesworth. And the boy saw Jeremiah's face. It was a little round face with small eyes. But now it was even rounder, and even the small eyes had gone round. His mouth had gone that way, too—round as O in the *Primer*. The man was staring at Jamie's father as though he was a stranger to him. He had looked up and found a man he did not know at the other end of his saw. And it frightened him.

Jamie wondered what his father had done to his face to make Jeremiah look like that. He looked hard at his father's back. There was something more to it than there had been a moment before. The something left a shadow on the beechnut brown of the shirt, in the bright sunlight. It was something a hand's breadth long. It had feathers at the end of it. And a darker stain than sweat had begun to spread out around it. The shadow was disappearing in it.

"Good God Almighty!"

Jeremiah Wigglesworth's voice was not like a man's. It was thin and shrill as a gray squirrel's chattering.

It was the last thing the man had to say. For there was another sigh. And he bent over his own short, round belly, working for dear life with both hands at another short stick with feathers on it. He got tired quickly, though. His knees slowly bent under him, and he went down into the grass among the singing crickets, his mouth more like an O than ever.

Jamie's father was still leaning at his log. But he had let go of the saw handle and had spread both hands out along the log to hold on.

He was still that way when Jamie got up to him. The boy grasped at the great body he loved. The man turned slowly, and he saw his face. His father could whisper still.

"Run!—run!—Jamie—run! . . . house!"

He crumpled up over Jamie, and his mouth poured blood. They went down together. The boy kissed him on the forehead with dry eyes. He would rather have stayed and died with him. But his father had given him his command.

James sprang away just as the lean shadow slanted at

him from the fringe of small firs. He ran like a young deer along the shadow of the woods. He knew better than take to the open meadow. He saw his chance. He dived into the thick firs, and raced on. The trees were small, and he could run blind. He heard the guttural grunting behind him. Like a horse with the heaves.

The boy ran till his ear drums were bursting. Down the little gully, over the creek where he had fished for mummie-chubs so often, into the birches. He doubled back then, keeping to the cove. The thatch and sea lavender whipped his legs. He heard nothing now but his thumping heart. He stopped, took a great breath, and plunged up the open hillside. He burst through a clump of alders, and the tall portico was before him.

The black-eyed boy was there in front of the door. He had gray gaiters on and a hunting crop in his hand. He came right up to see what Jamie wanted. But Jamie shouldered him out of the way and rushed past him into the house. The two blackamoors were at the door. They were like rag dolls with button eyes that could not close up, ever. They did not try to stop him. He burst into a vast room, upset a gilded chair, and half fell across a long table. An inkwell tipped over, and a stain spread out from it. Like that from his father. A man was at the other end of the table. His smooth wig was frosty with sunlight.

"The Indians!—my father—he—he—got killed! Call the men!—My mother and the children at the house!—Send them! Send men quick!"

The world spun around James. The wigged man was pulling a cord by the curtains. People appeared. People ran about. The Squire was shouting:

"To the road. Cover both sides of it. Ten of you to Mr. Leigh's. Five at the edge of Mast Meadow. Try to hold them there!"

Jamie's house was far beyond Nathan Leigh's. At the far corner of Mast Meadow. He lifted up his head and shouted as the room kept on turning around him:

"Send them to our house! Send them there! Mother and the babies—they—"

He heard Squire Trefethen's voice speaking as if a long ways off. "The Dawn house is lost. It is too far. You will do no good there. Save whom you can. Do as I bid you."

"You—you—damned—damned Tory! King's lick-spit, you! You—you—"

Blackness came over him. But the Squire's words were burnt forever into his small brain, like a scar left by a red-hot iron. Like the King's arrow. And the scar would grow as his brain grew, since that is the way of scars, and it would be there when he became a man and would be moving out at the corners of the world, by the white mountains of Antarctica.

James woke and felt around with his hands. It was dark where he was. He crawled around. It was some sort of an outbuilding he was in. There was straw. Maybe the blackamoors had carried him there. There were blackamoors, he remembered, two of them. Or maybe the black-eyed boy had carried him. He would find out, and if he had, he would kill him.

He got out of the building at last, but it was almost as dark outside. There were stars already. He was trying his best not to think. He was up on his feet and running, before the whole thing came back on him. His father's terrible whisper, so low and clear. He ran as the bee flies. The west had a glow of light in it. But that might be New Meadows burning again.

He knew the way in the dark. The cool air of the open meadow sucked around him. His feet hissed in the grass. His throat was drier than choke-pears ever had made it. Fear began deep at his spine and spread out all over him.

He knew what he would find.

Jamie stumbled and fell headlong over a log that ought not to be there. He felt it over in the darkness. It had a cap tied over its end. After a minute he knew it was Maria Orr. She had something in her arms. He touched it. Cold, too. It was the baby.

James got to his feet somehow and stumbled on.

The doorstone his father had brought from over across the bay was there. But the house was not behind it. Only just glowing embers shining up into the night. The cellar was full of red coals. He got down on the stone. He lay with his head hung over the heat a long, long time. His face burned, but he did not care about it. It was so hot, maybe that was why he could not shed tears.

All the others were there in the redness of the cellar.

He ought to cry. He ought to pull himself over the stone and go down there, too. But he thought of the scar on his mind. And he got up and went stumbling off another way.

Heat was near him again. There weren't any coals, though. That was strange. He bent over and felt of the strange thing.

It was the beanpot in the hole. He lifted the cover. The beans were done. The fragrance of them came up to him. He had not eaten since the hulled corn. He dipped into the dark warmth with both hands and ate till he could not eat any more.

He got up at last and wiped his hands on the grass. His fingers struck something. He felt it over. It was a cup of some kind. Metal. He ran his fingers along it, and they made out the rising sun. It was his own birthday mug. The Indians must have lost it from the things they had taken away from the house. Maybe they meant to melt it down for bullets.

James Dawn put his cup carefully away inside his shirt. It was the only thing he had left to remember his father by.

He would remember him by it. Till the time his brain went blank out.

V

It was bright as day, and the full moon rode along over the tops of the trees among the frosty stars. The light of it slipped alongside of James Dawn as he walked fast. It kept abreast of him on the crusted snow. The man was muffled to his sparkling blue eyes. His old breath was frozen into fringes along the upper edge of his muffler. His new breath made a little cloud behind him in the air. A snapping cold night! The bay boomed lonesomely now and then, as the rising tide lifted the ice on it and made it crack from side to side. It rolled like a Winter thunder under the clear moon. Another gray James Dawn walked with his feet joined to the man's feet. There was even the shadow of his breath on the white snow of the fields. Little pin points of snow dust here and there flashed and burned fiercely like hot, small sparks. Not a sound but the crunch of the walker's boots.

It was good to be alive and a man and have warm blood racing through a body under wool. And better to be a man who was going to be a husband this night, for the first time, and in a house of his own building.

The house was ready to be lived in. The candles were lit in it. And the bride carried in. The church business was over. James and his wife would be the first people to live in the house. It was new to living. But the cellar under it was not. The cellar was the cellar where the father of James Dawn had laid up stones and his mother had shelved her preserves. It was also the grave where his mother and his brothers' ashes had mingled with the ashes of the house over it. It was a grave. But a new life was going to spring from the grave tonight.

James had been bound to have it so. No one, not even his Molly, could get him to set his house anywhere else. It was the right thing. He had not had to think it over at all. Ever since that night when he had leaned over the hot embers that had been his father's home, James Dawn had gone straight along in a way that led to a new house on that cellar, on a way which seemed mapped out to him as sure as the stars.

Bright little candles so far overhead. Heat in them, and the things that were to come. Heat in him, and sons to climb up out of crawling babyhood and put their hands on tall trees and iron, and move them around the world, through storms, through sunshine, through life and death, to the end.

James had to favor his left leg as he walked, for he had a big bulge in his breeches' pocket there. It was the wedding gift of his best friend, David Snow. It was to be the next-best thing of all in James's house. After his own mug with the rising sun. It was the one thing he and his wife would have toward the beginning of the big house they would have over their heads one day. The only thing that wasn't a cottage thing. It was a gilt pitcher. It had wild swans on its sides, flying over trees not half the size they were. It was thc only big-wig possession David and Miriam Snow had had to their name. They loved it. The sun had risen and set by that pitcher. But it was the only thing that would do for Jamie on his bride-night.

"You are late getting home to your new wife, Dawn."

A man stepped out from the shadow cast by a giant oak tree by the path. His shadow joined James's on the snow crust. It was as long as his.

"Yes, I was late finishing up the mortising in your father's stern-post. But that's no affair of yours, Stephen Trefethen."

"Come, come, Dawn, don't get up on your high horse with me. I meant no offence. I was merely asking for manners' sake."

"Keep your manners for them as ask for them."

"That's no way to speak, on your wedding night. I bear you no hardness for the hard things you have said about my father and me. This night of all nights. You are a stubborn, narrow-headed man, James Dawn. But let the past bury the past. I want merely to wish you God-speed. And I am fetching here a wedding present to you and Molly. Here it is. You being in the mood you are, perhaps I had best deliver it now."

The young man put his hand into his fur coat and drew out a slim package. He reached it out in his hand James Dawn's way.

"I want no wedding gift from you or any of your breed, damn you!"

The bridegroom's hand shot out and hit the bundle.

The wrapping burst, and a shower of slender silver spoons twinkled into the snow.

"You damned upstart!—That's the way you treat a friendly gift, is it? Pox on you!—Well, take that, in place of the silver!"

Young Trefethen's mittened fist shot out and fetched a box on James's ear.

It was a light blow. But Dawn rocked on his heels and nearly fell backwards on account of the slippery footing. Then he swung, quick as a cat, and hit the other man with everything he had in him. His bare fist caught the shipbuilder's son on his teeth. Blood flowed dark in the moonlight and spattered on the snow.

"Have it back as good as you send!" said James Dawn.

They leaped at each other, then, like two hungry bobcats. Five years of ship's carpentry and swinging a sledge had made James Dawn's muscles like whalebone in a whip lash. But Stephen Trefethen had lived outdoors and used his arms, too, and he had held blooded horses in check and had sat them as they took hedges and culverts in the air of Autumn. They were almost equal in weight. It was a match.

They rocked, locked together, then leaped apart, and their fists flew. James got a tremendous blow over the eye. He struck Trefethen back so hard he made the teeth rattle in his head, and Trefethen went to his knees. James threw himself upon him. But Trefethen shot up to meet him with his lean body, got home at him in the wind, and James Dawn went flat on the snow.

There was a jingling of china. The wedding pitcher was broken. James felt the shards of it gouged deep into his thigh. He could have wept. But he sprang up at Stephen instead, caught him by the slack of his velveteen breeches, lifted him bodily, and then threw him flat. He was on him like a madman and beat him in the face till his blood was all over the snow. He felt the other give up. Stephen Trefethen's body grew suddenly slack. James got to his feet and stood there brushing the snow and the blood from his hands. He did not move from his place.

After a little, the other young man got up, too. He never said a word for some time. He brushed himself off just as James had done. He was in no hurry to go. He straightened his coat. He did not know what had beat him. He was still surprised over it. He did not know about the pitcher. He tried several times to say something. At last he did:

"You've got the best of it this time, Dawn. Some day, it may be different." He turned around and went away through the moonlight. He walked with a limp and signs of pain in him. He grew smaller and smaller on the white field till he was gone.

The silver teaspoons lay there gleaming. James Dawn put out his foot and kicked them carefully under the snow. He took out the pieces of his broken pitcher. His thigh was warm with the cut it had in it. He threw the shards after the spoons.

He went off down the path toward the edge of Mast

Meadow and the cottage windows lit up there. The night suddenly felt very cold to him. A sharp pain kept stabbing at his thigh.

James was glad when he got to the house, for the moonlight did not make him feel good any more. Molly kissed him, and then grew shy and went off to the kitchen to be by herself and see to things for his supper. James warmed himself fore and aft in front of the big fire. It was his pine knots burning there in the six-foot fireplace. It was his pine table, scoured white, with the blue plates shining on it. He had made the cupboard with the other dishes along its shelves. The bed was his in the room beyond. He had turned the legs out of maple and carved the posts on it with his jack-knife, and the mattress was stuffed with cornhusks he had raised. Molly had cut out the striped cloth for it and turned the seams. He wasn't beholden to the Trefethens for a single thing in the house. Most of the workmen of the Trefethens could not say that, when they got married.

"Jamie," his wife called, "come out and see what is here. It is a surprise."

The young master of the new house went out. It was six cottage chairs there, of shiny new maple, and pretty spoolings in their high backs.

"Who brought these here, Molly?"

"Why, who should it be but Squire himself. He came with them in the coach. He had on the loveliest velvet hat with lace all along the edges of it, and he came right in natural as could be, and when the men were bringing in the chairs, he made himself to home. He looked all around and admired everything you had done. You'd never have thought he was the Squire to see how he—"

"Mary! fetch me my axe!"

The tone of her husband's voice took all the wind out of the woman's sails. She went out into the woodshed and brought in the two-bladed tool he asked for. But tears were welling in her eyes. Her face was white.

"You know, Mary, how 'tis betwixt Squire and me and mine. You should not have allowed him to step foot in this house."

James heaved his axe up and brought it down on first one chair and then another. He splintered them apart with great blows. He notched the new pine floorboards in places. Molly watched him, quiet all through it, tears scalding her eyes. When he had finished, she found her tongue.

"It's a wicked thing you have gone and done, James Dawn. Cut fine chairs to pieces like that. No good will ever come of such folly. It is a wicked, wicked waste. 'Tis a wicked thing for you to go on hating the Trefethens as you do. Year in, year out. You would carry a grudge to the grave. You are a stubborn man, and you do not know which side your bread is buttered on. And we so poor and in want of everything! And they were my chairs as much as yours."

She burst into loud sobs.

"See here, Mary Dawn," her husband said, "wife of mine you are, and wife of mine you shall be all the days of your life. And while you live, don't you dare say a word again for the Trefethens. There is only hate in me for them. And I must ask you to remember that always. There is blood between that house and this. My mother's and my brothers' blood. I am going to live my life for the sake of paying the Trefethens back. And I am going to rise high until I have them under my feet!"

He gathered up the splintered legs of the chairs, carried them into the front room, and fed them piece after piece into the fire. The flames licked high and lit up the whole place like day.

It was a strange house-warming they were having. The new wife weeping to herself in her linsey-wool dress in the kitchen, not changing into her best one. The meal porridge she had dished out for her husband's wedding supper growing cold and untasted on the table. Her own bowl of it grew stone cold, too. There were no words back and forth between man and wife. The clock ticked, and an hour of their marriage flowed away.

Then cow-bells began to ring through the still, cold night outside, and horns blew. Voices and horns and bells came nearer and nearer. The little cottage was walled in by the sound. A mighty thumping came at the door, and the hinges began to creak.

"Open up your doors, Jamie Dawn! Open up your doors, and let your friends come in and put you into your wedding bed!"

The big voice of David Snow drowned out all the others. Women's shrill laughter mingled with the men's.

"Open, in the King's name!"

James went over and pushed the oak bar back in its slots.

All Merrymeeting came in. Davy and Miriam, and behind them, Fearing Upjohn and Constant Converse and their wives—all the young and middle-aged men who worked in the Trefethen shipyards with James. They made themselves at home around the fire. Each slipped his big bundle down into the heap on the table. They had two fiddlers along.

"Strike up the music!" roared Davy. "Give us *My Lady's Gone to Town.*"

The fiddles began to squeak.

"Have you no tongue in your head, Jamie Dawn? Or is it you are saving your breath for your wife?"

They all burst out laughing at that.

"Where is the lady of this house?—Molly Dawn, are you gone into your bed already and will give us no word of greeting? Marry, come out of bed! There's time enough coming for that!"

Everybody was calling and laughing.

Molly came in with shining eyes. She had found the way round to putting on her party dress, after all. All those having horns blew them in a great blast.

"Horns for Jamie and Molly!" shouted David. "And may they be the only horns to flourish in this place!"

"Amen!" all the men roared.

The music struck up with a mighty swing. David and

Miriam rounded up the crowd. James and Molly were pushed into the dance at the head of the leading figure. They all swung into action and went through their sets by fours and eights and sixteens. The women's wide skirts billowed out. The fire burned up brighter for the draft. The house was full of whirling movement and laughter. They swung into *The Battle of the Boyne.* David roared the figures out:

"Pass your true-love to your left! . . . Ring the roses, swing your posies! . . . Bow before the wind and bend! . . . Swing your true-love to her place! . . . Hawk fly out, and bird fly in!"

The new floor and the whole new house shook under them.

Then it was time to eat. The women opened up their bundles on the table. Slices of ham, Kennebec bloaters, smoked eels, cranberry jellies, and crab-apple tarts. There was a calf's-head cheese big as a bushel measure. And a small roasted pig with garlands of sausage wreathing him round, and two frost-bitten cranberries for his eyes. Long kitchen knives flashed. The tongues of the women were hung at their middles and loose at both ends. The men pulled on their long churchwardens between bites. The room was blue with tobacco smoke. There was a noble great demijohn of hard cider, and it went the rounds, each man wiping its mouth before he tipped it back on high and drank from it on the crook of his arm.

Healths were drunk to Jamie and Molly. Fifty years, a dozen children, fat always in the spider, and God save the King! A cake was unveiled, a three-decker, and candles were lit around it. Molly cut it across. It was as deep as her longest knife. Then it was apples and cheese and cider and more cider, till the men began to have to walk with their buckled toes set very wide apart.

"Bedtime for the bridegroom and bride! Bedtime, Jamie!"

David Snow led on the pack as they bundled the couple into the inner room. They did not stay for undressing. They tumbled the man and wife in, boots and stays and all between the sheets. The fiddlers sawed out *Greensleeves.* They tucked man and wife in up to their chins. A dozen new crazy-quilts were piled upon them by the women who had made them against this night. The men filled their noses with snuff and beat out jig tunes with their feet.

"Happy night, and no room for dreaming!" David Snow shouted out.

"Happy night! happy night! happy wedding night!"

"And a brace of bully boys!" sang out David.

They blew out the candles and tiptoed out. They hushed each other loudly out in the big room, found their cloaks and shawls, and went on the tips of their toes out into the frost and the moonlight.

The house fell silent. Only the clock ticked, and the embers snapped. The sound of fiddles and horns grew thinner and faded out into the quiet under the high stars.

James put his arm over the woman on the bed, above the cellar where the ashes of his people lay. And they were man and wife before they ever unloaded the wedding quilts from their high bed.

VI

THE drum went on as regular as a heartbeat. Rat-a-tat-tat, rat-a-tat-tat, right through the quiet of the Sabbath day. It was as fine a Spring day as you could find in a month of Sundays. Some lamb's wool clouds were scattered across the western sky, but the sun was out as bright as a drop of pitch on a spruce tree, and the dandelions made small bonfires by the thousands across the grass.

It was no day for a drum. Or a fife, either, for that matter. There was a fife going, too. All along the quiet of Mast Meadow. Merrymeeting people were boiling with anger.

Out on the bay, a smart little frigate stood up as pretty as a posie, her spotless sails hanging limp in the calm. She was all ready to go, when the work was done and the breeze, always around the corner of a Maine May morning, should say the word. She had the blue flag with the royal cross on her mast. A mast that had been grown right here on Merrymeeting, most likely.

It was the Squire's doing. The big house on the hill was open house today. The frigate was loading Squire Trefethen's seasoned pine into her hold. Squire's scows were going back and forth to her. The lumber was for Boston and the new buildings going up there to house the redcoated soldiers from oversea, thick as hasty pudding now in that Yankee town.

It was enough to make a man's blood boil.

There was blood on the young new grass out Lexington and Concord way. The news of it had come up to Merrymeeting last week. Houses for the soldiers of a tyrant King.

It wouldn't have been so bad, if it hadn't been for the redcoats right here, with their white straps making big crosses on their backs and chests, looking like hornets and playing fife and drum on a Sunday. They might have loaded their lumber in without soldiers to rile people up.

The fine, new Trefethen ship, the *Margaretta*, lifted her spars high among the trees at Trefethen's wharf.

Decent people were all bound for church. Men who would load lumber on a Sunday were men whom you could trust to suck eggs. There weren't many Merrymeeting men who would do it, but there were some. They were hard at it. They were so few, it would take them a longer time to get the cargo in. But they'd do it by sundown. And the eight silly, senseless men in red and shiny buttons were marching up and down, big as Billy-Be-Damned, beside every drag load of boards that went from the Trefethen yards to the dock. They weren't giving the men a hand. Oh, no, they were too good for that. They just went along and swayed their tails to show off the four silver buttons on them there. They had an officer with them, too, if you please, looking like a walking flower-bed, and redder than red. Lucky for them the Snow bull was in the bull-pen and not out there in Mast Meadow. The officer's hat caught its lace in the birches every time he went under them.

The people were all in church at last. It was hard getting all the boys in, on account of the soldiers down below. The preacher was praying. The windows were wide open, and the smell of the new grass came in. And the noise of the drum, too.

"O merciful and mighty God, give us patience to endure like men and possess ourselves in meekness in these times of peril and confusion. Give us strength to undergo all our calamities, and grant us wisdom to do the right as thou givest us light to see it. Help our poor, suffering kinsmen in the south in the midst of invasion and dissension. Thy will be done! Blessed are the peacemakers, for they—"

"Men of Merrymeeting!"

The man's voice cut like a sword through the droning of Parson Harris. Everybody turned and stretched up his neck in the tall white pews.

It was young Jamie Dawn, and his eyes were full of blue sparkles of fire.

"We are mumbling and praying here while our trees are being loaded for Boston, to make houses for the murderers of our kin. For red-handed hirelings of the tyrant of England! Their hands are smoking with our blood!"

Nothing like this had ever happened in the white Merrymeeting house of peace before.

"If we are men, let us go down to our bay and take our good pine from them and drive the redcoats and the ships of the tyrant from our coast. The time has come. The wind that blows up from Boston is full of murder. Falmouth has set up a Liberty Pole. Are we less than the men of Falmouth?"

And Jamie Dawn with a young wife and an infant son to think of! Parson Harris was trying his best to get his people's ears. But his voice was thin and old.

"My people! my people!—Think what you do. The house of God must not be profaned. Listen to me, my people!"

"Let the preachers and the old men hug the house. We who have guts in us ought to do something to show we are men."

Men were standing up in the pews and shouting. Women were gathering in their small children to their arms. One woman had fainted.

"Jamie! Jamie!—remember our baby!" Molly Dawn was crying.

A roar had begun among the men. Young man after young man sprang from the pews and joined James Dawn at the back of the church. Old men pleaded and tried to hold their sons in their places. Davy Snow was there beside James, and Fearing Upjohn, Constant Converse, and Will Haggard. A dozen men were there in no time.

"Down with King George! Down with the Trefethens!"

There were a score shouting now.

"You are a firebrand, James Dawn." The preacher's voice was shrill as a sand-peep's. "You Dawns have always had the name of being troublesome and fractious. You have borne Squire a grudge all your life. You are always making trouble. You—"

"A pole! a pole!—Run up a pole!"

It was like the trampling of twenty wild colts. All the young men were gone from the building at once. All the other men and the women and children poured out, too.

James Dawn and Fearing Upjohn and David Snow were staggering up the hill under the weight of a long spar they had taken from the Trefethen yard hard by. Fifteen or sixteen other young men rushed down and gave them a hand with it. They all came up stumbling and sweating in the sun, their Sunday-go-to-meeting clothes all soiled and awry. Somebody had fetched a shovel and was digging a hole right in the churchyard green.

"A cap!—we must have a Liberty Cap!"

Everybody was shouting all at once. The morning was full of shouting.

Miriam Snow upped her wide skirts and tore a great piece of cloth out of her red petticoat right before all of them there. She looped it, tied it into a knot with her fingers going like mad. It looked something like a cap. James Dawn put it on the spar's end. Then he put his shoulder to the burden. All the youths buckled to it with him. They lifted and stepped the pole into the hole that had been dug. Then everybody threw his cap into the air and danced around the upright spar like wild Indians.

The drumbeat at the landing had stopped.

"Everybody go for his gun! Get your guns and come back here!"

Dawn was giving his orders like a commander-in-chief. All the men broke out of the circle of dancing, and each made a bee line for his house. Mary Dawn ran down the hill after her husband. She could not keep him in sight. All the old men and the women and children ran. The preacher was the only one left on the top of the hill. His white hairs glistened in the sunlight.

"God have mercy on us!"

He was still there bareheaded as the red hornets came up swarming.

"The old psalm-singing trouble-maker!"

"They've all run home, but the old 'un."

"Knock him in the head!"

They jostled and pushed old Parson Harris. He went over on all fours.

A soldier knelt over his body. He leveled his long piece, struck the spark in the pan, and fired at the nearest house. The bullet went singing through the May air. The others went for the pole. They slanted it over, wrenched at it, and tugged at it. It went over slow. But it came down with a big thud at last. The officer spitted the red cap as it fell. He lifted it on his shining sword, threw it aloft, and cut it into three pieces.

Parson Harris could not get his second knee off the turf. The redcoat behind him assisted him by taking a great handful of his fine black breeches where they fulled out at the rear. He never got the preacher up. There was something sudden that buzzed like a bee. The red-coat joined Parson Harris on his knees. He coughed out blood red as the cloth on his arms, all over his hands. He looked at it in utter surprise. First one hand and then the other. Then he quietly went forward and put his face down deep in the grass.

Another soldier clapped both hands to his ears and ran. He had never done a thing like this in all his twenty-eight bright years before. He could not stop his legs going. Then he tried to get over a great pit in the earth that wasn't there, but crumpled and went down into it, black over his eyes.

"Well, I'll be damned!—Down flat on your bellies! the rebels are coming!"

The officer and the other six redcoated soldiers threw themselves prone. A wicked little furrow ran suddenly along the grassed turf in front of them. One of the soldiers spat calmly at it as it went past him three inches away. He coolly worked his piece up to his breastbone and took a long sight along it. He fired down the hill. A bush below lifted its top up, and that part of it became a man. The man went out a little way into the open, and then fell and turned over. His legs went on working for a long time.

"Got the rat in the guts."

The soldier spat again carelessly. But then he got up, too, big as life, and walked a step or two. But his knees kept going sidewise, and he sat down hard. He spat a third time. And he sat there doing nothing but thinking.

"Into the church! And make it lively!"

The officer and the four soldiers got up all at once. Four of the five got through the door. The other did not make it. He keeled over and began to scream.

David Snow came from one direction and James Dawn from another. They closed on the building and threw themselves flat against the walls. A third man came up to join them. But Will Haggard never got there. A window pane jingled, and he went down like a sack of cornmeal. But then a dozen others came over the ridge pell-mell. Just as they were coming, James Dawn ran to the door and fired into the church. There was a yell there. James leaped one side, and David, just behind him, fired into the door, too. The man outside was still yelling. Then the two men rushed in, James ahead.

There were two men left standing inside there. David fetched one of them a terrible blow over the head with his unloaded musket held full length. James took the other. It was the officer. James got both arms down over his shoulders and pinioned them so he could not get home with his sword. Except in the calf of Jamie's leg. He sawed away there like a good fellow, and spoiled Jamie's only pair of silk stockings with blood. That got Jamie very angry, and he bent the man up until the bright buttons popped on him and flew off and lay glittering all over the floor. One after another, they popped off. The two of them scuffled on their feet. The man was tough as a rawhide, a regular fox-hunter of a man. But Jamie was good and mad about his stocking. He bent the soldier up so his corded breeches flared apart and split from stem to stern and showed an unsoldierly triangle of white between the big young man's backsides. James gave a last heave, and turned the lieutenant completely over in the air and brought him down heels and head on the punkin-pine floor. When the officer got up, he was done. His sword was taken out of his hands. He was willing to go along quietly.

James picked up a *Bible* that lay open on the floor by the door. He dusted it off and put it carefully back into a pew. He was sorry afterwards, when he thought about it, for not looking to see what text it was open at.

The church bell was ringing as if it had gone crazy. Two men were at the rope that came down through the floor of the belfry. They went up with it as it sprang back through their hands, and came down with it again full weight. They were using their feet on the whitewashed walls, to get a better purchase. Outside, the hilltop was swarming with men carrying their squirrel guns. One had brought his raccoon hound along. They had straightened out the soldier who had screamed so hard so he didn't make any more noise. They had bandaged him around his thigh. And they had got the soldier who was thinking out on the grass up on a rude litter. He was still thinking there. The two Merrymeeting men were placed side by side on the ground next to the graveyard. Will Haggard was beyond all worrying about anything any more. So was the other. The five dead redcoats were all toes to toes in another spot.

The Liberty Pole was back in place. And a piece of the red petticoat back on it for a cap.

New young men were coming over the fields from the distant farms. Some men of middle age, too. The bell clanged on and on. The preacher had been kneeling there very quiet all through it. He got up now and dusted the dust off his knees.

"God be with you and bless you!"

Of a sudden, there was a great tearing sound, and dust came out of the church roof in a vast shower, and a gaping hole showed among the shingles. Out on the bay, a puff of peaceful-looking white cotton hung at the frigate's side.

"The sons of bastards!" said Parson Harris. That was all he could trust himself to say.

"Down the hill, all hands!" James said, as he went on bandaging up his own leg. "And we'll meet back of the logs in the Trefethen shipyard."

The men poured down the hill, the preacher with them. Only the dead were left on the hill. There was another ball of cotton out on the bay by the frigate, and the church steeple had a jagged tear in it. But the red cap still hung on the pole up there.

The scows had disappeared from the bay.

When the Merrymeeting men got to the log pile, they found all the lumber men huddled there.

"Are you with us or against us?" James Dawn demanded of the wide-eyed workmen of the Squire.

"They are with you, and so am I."

Stephen Trefethen appeared out of nowhere. He was carrying a beautiful musket across his right arm. He leaped down from the logs and joined them.

"What will your father say to this?" Young Dawn found his tongue at last.

"What he will. He has gone to join the King's men on the frigate, anyway. He and I are on different sides of this fence. I'm for Liberty and the rights of man."

All of Jamie's men burst into cheers.

But Jamie was quiet. It came on him that he would rather have had Stephen Trefethen on the British man-of-war this day than have a hundred good soldiers by his side. Still, he had to swallow his bitterness and eat his proud tongue.

Everybody was overjoyed to welcome the young master from the hill. Everybody but James. Half the joy had gone out of the war he had begun.

"What are you going to do now, James Dawn?" Stephen Trefethen asked.

"Fit up your father's *Margaretta* and go out and capture the British frigate and your father," answered Jamie calmly.

"Almighty God!" ejaculated Parson Harris. "Haven't you done enough for one day?"

All the men cheered again.

VII

"How many guns does the King's ship carry?"

"The *Adamant* has eight cannon," Stephen Trefethen spoke up. "I counted them."

"And we have five on Merrymeeting Head, in the fort."

"But those guns aren't ours. The King's men are standing to them."

"They will be ours," said James Dawn quietly. "We'll rush them after it begins to dusk."

"What good will they do us, I should like to know?" shrilled Fearing Upjohn. "Unless to get our crowns broken in the taking of them. What good's a lot of guns?"

"Why, to fit up the *Margaretta*, you numbskull, and go out and engage the *Adamant* and take her."

"She's alive with his Majesty's seamen," put in David Snow. "I'm for giving her a hot dish of chowder from the shore and making her skedaddle."

"Don't be a zany, Davy Snow. A gun on a deck is worth two on the shore. Any day in the week. You know that. And, anyway, the *Adamant* could get away, if we made it too hot for her, with all our good pine in her for the butchers in Boston. We'll have to sail her down and board her. I'm going to have that lumber, if it takes a leg. I'm glad the wind is holding down, for she can never get out of Merrymeeting Bay while it does. I'm going to board that ship."

"I'm with you," said Stephen.

The day was far spent. The sun was tipping the spruces of Merrymeeting Point. A lovely path of trembling gold came across the water to the men who were huddled among the timbers of the Trefethen shipyard. There were a few small clouds drifting by like wild swans going home to the south. They had sun on their bellies.

"There'll be a full moon, and that's what I fear most," said young Trefethen.

" 'Twill make it all the better for us to see to work our cutlasses on the *Adamant's* deck," answered Dawn. "We'll have the fort's guns aboard the *Margaretta* before it's light enough to show the men on the frigate what we're up to."

It was as quiet as a church. The *Adamant* had been as quiet as a lamb ever since those two shots. The people out there must have seen the people leave the hill, and they left the church steeple alone. No boat had come from her to the fort. They were waiting for nightfall and the wind that the flood tide was sure to bring, to fetch their sailors in from the fort, what soldiers might be left, and depart with what lumber they had already stowed.

The sun dipped into the dark trees, and the golden carpet rolled up off the waves. A heron slanted over the bay in a slow, graceful flight. The bright Maine light washed all at once out of the world, and things began to grow dusky incredibly fast.

Every man-jack in Merrymeeting but Squire Trefethen was huddled under the pile of logs. They had on every kind of a hat and every color of breeches there could be. And they had every kind of a weapon. Muskets long as a man, axes, adzes, scythes cut down, pig-stickers, hay knives, cleavers, spits sharpened on grindstones. Some of them even carried awls for the want of something better.

Parson Harris was on hand, and he still had his Sunday breeches on. He carried a hammer in one hand, and his *Bible* in the other.

Far off, in the thatch back of Mast Meadow, a marsh-hen coughed mournfully.

"It's time," said James Dawn.

"Let us kneel down and pray," said Parson Harris.

They all went to their knees.

"O Father of mankind, sinew our young men's arms as thou didst sinew the arms of the men of Gideon. Give us the victory this night!"

It was the shortest prayer Merrymeeting Bay had heard since the Christians first came to its shores. The shortest of Parson Harris's life.

"And remember, men," added the parson as they rose, "our battle cry, 'The Lord of Hosts!' That was the cry that overthrew another British tyrant, the Second Charles, in my great-grandfather's day. A century ago. At Worcester in England. The Lord of Hosts be with you!"

James led the way. He crawled like the Indians all

Americans had learned to be in the last century, since they were first Americans. He crawled like a snake on his belly through the black-grass and thatch roots. He cut his knees and hands on the crinkled mussel shells bedded there. The others came after. They crawled toward the spit where the fort showed vague in the afterglow. Stephen Trefethen and David Snow came next after Jamie. All the others trailed behind.

James came to the crest of the last beaver dam. He waited there till all the others had come up. Now against the last glow of the sunset sky they could make out two sailors passing back and forth.

"You take one, David Snow, and I'll take the other." James raised his musket.

Stephen Trefethen felt his heart leap up and then fall like lead. He lowered his fine piece. He could hit a squirrel's eye even in such a tricky light.

"When we fire, all of you spring and go in," Dawn hissed. "Now!"

Two spurts of fire leaped from the beaver dam and after them leaped fifty dusky shapes. A marsh-hen flew off, filling the night with screams to curdle the blood.

There was hell for a moment at the fort's side. Something came down past James like a flail and crushed in the head of a man behind him, like an old pumpkin. David sprang and finished off the flailer with his deer knife in the ribs. Stabs of hot lightning were all among them. But mostly it was bitter, quiet work in the dark of the inside of the fort. Close fighting, terrible deep taking-in of breaths, muffled curses as blows got home. Men's knees against men's arms and shoulders. Grunts. And evil dampness on bodies as the starch went out of them suddenly and they grew still.

It was over in a short while. Ten live sailors were trussed up neck and heels, neatly, and five dead or wounded ones lay with them. Two of the attackers would never attack again. They lay there with boot toes up, and men stumbled over them. The men of Merrymeeting dared strike no flint. They had to go at the gun lashings and trunnions in the pitch blackness. Ropes were dragged in and adjusted somehow. They had all five cannon off their places at last and down the glacis of the fort. All hands manned the ropes then and dragged the heavy iron things on the fir poles they were lashed to. Through the muck, over beaver dams, splashing into the pools they could not see in the gloom.

The ship had been still as the grave all through the set-to. But the rifle flashes must have given the trouble away. For now a cannon went off, and a ball went whistling over the heads of the muddy men. Then another ball threw the black muck of the marsh up into their faces. One struck the fort itself like a giant thunderclap. Bits of stone spattered the pools.

The Merrymeeting men sweat blood and worked in perfect quiet. The dusk was dusk no longer. A rim of silver had come up over the eastern wall of spruces. The moon was well clear of the trees by the time the men had the guns under the piles of lumber.

A boat had put off from the *Adamant.* They could see it pull swiftly abreast of the fort. There came a hail from it, as the oars rested. But there was no answer from the stone walls. The rowers did not like the look of things. For after a moment the boat rowed away back toward the frigate.

The Merrymeetingites rested for a minute, and the parson carried a jug of spring water around to them all. He had lost his hat. The moon lay bright on the silver of his hair. His face was black from the bog. So were all the faces there. James had ordered them all to dip their hands in the black muck and smear their foreheads and cheeks. They looked like a band of negroes in the night. Only their eyeballs glittered with the moon.

They had the alders along the beach for cover while they were slinging the guns and hoisting them up over the *Margaretta's* side. There had to be blocks and lashings improvised in the dim light. Some of the men were sent back to the fort for the cases of powder and the balls. It took two hours, and the moon was riding high by the time they were nicely in place along the deck of the Trefethen ship. The men had to crawl about on all fours while at work, so there should be no chance of the man-of-war's seeing them picked out by the radiance of the moon.

A good breeze was coming up, the waves lapped the *Margaretta's* sides. The *Adamant,* they could see, had all her sails unfurled and was getting ready to move out of a dark bay where queer things happened, sounds of fighting flared up and then died down quickly and mysteriously, and no one could see what had taken place. It was a good place to stand well clear of till the morning.

"All right, men, jump to the clews! Into the yards, and shake out her sails!" James Dawn was standing up at last.

The men had the sails out in a hundred shakes of a lamb's tail. The wind caught them, and they began to belly out in the moonlight. The *Margaretta* leaned away from the pier, and got under way, with a moonlit bone in her pretty mouth.

The British ship was slanting away down the bay like a good one, she was tacking for the open sea. She had too much canvas for the *Margaretta*.

"Davy Snow," called out James Dawn, "stand to one of the port guns, and when I go about, fetch me her mainmast down!"

After a minute, James spun the wheel about. The *Margaretta* went over low and then shot ahead, eased up and righted herself. David waited a long time at the piece. The moonlight caught the sheets of the British boat and turned them and her spars to silver. Just at that moment there came a flash of fire and a great sound, and something struck the *Margaretta's* bow just abaft the boom. She slewed in the water and quivered in all her timbers. Splinters of her wood came singing back like maddened bumble bees and went over David and James and away into the night. One man on the deck had gone down, both hands clapped to his eyes, and dark stains came out through his white fingers and laced them across.

"Take your time, Davy."

The man was still crouched over the gun. He moved his two hands to tell the men behind him when to take up or let out on the tackling which traversed the piece. The man beside him held the slow-match ready.

Another flash and thunder, and something went over them like a galloping horse breathing hard.

David dropped his two hands. The man thrust down the forked iron with smoking rags at its end. A cloud of fire opened at their ship's side and turned into half a bayful of smoke. One square of silver on the sky ahead crumpled into nothing and many silver threads with it.

"Pretty close, David. You got the yard and spoiled one sail for them. Here! you take the wheel, and keep her on this tack."

James Dawn helped them shove in the powder sack, ram it home, roll in the shot, and ram the rags down on it to keep it from rolling out of the muzzle when the ship rolled in the waves. James waited till the deck pitched his way and started on its down-roll. Then he yelled, the linstock came down, and another flower of red and white fire blossomed at their deck's edge. And the tallest piece of silver tracery went down there ahead of them, and the three squares of silver left on it vanished from sight.

All the men of Merrymeeting except the one with his hands on his eyes let out a roar. They got a mighty thump amidships themselves, but they kept on cheering.

After that, the *Margaretta* gained on the Britisher fast. The *Adamant* went about. As she did so, her whole side became a sheet of fire. One of the *Margaretta's* mizzen yards came booming down to the deck and a vast mass of torn canvas with it. Five or six men sprang aloft to get the torn sail clear of the others.

The *Margaretta* was hit again and again. But James was back at the wheel, and he kept her headed as close into the west wind as he could and still make speed, and he made her very slim to the cannon of the Britisher. The iron missiles had made kindling of the port rail and ploughed up the deck into tall splinters. A man was lying in the midst of them, flat on his face on the deck. His bowels showed below his jacket and glittered evilly in the light of the high moon. Another man had been hit hard, and he was crawling along the deck with his hands alone, for his legs were no use to him. All five of the *Margaretta's* guns were barking now. The men worked them as fast as they could. They swabbed them out with the dripping gun-swabs to cool them off, rammed the powder and the iron pellets home, the wadding on top, and fired. The Britishers were hitting them two times to their one. The air was full of splinters that had come out of them. They sounded like a swarm of maddened yellow-jackets. The men had thrown their coats over the rail to keep the splinters down, but there were plenty of them flying.

David was doing up his head where a piece of the deck had cut a great gash and his scalp was sagging open like a mouth. The parson was carrying buckets of water from gun to gun and dousing the water on the guns to cool them. Between the yells of the men and the roar of the cannon he kept shouting at the top of his lungs, "The Lord of Hosts!" Stephen Trefethen had taken a dead gunner's place. He was getting home oftenest of all of them in the hull ahead. They were so close now that they could see the wood in the enemy blossom into splinters every time they made a hit.

The forward one of the portside guns was loaded too soon. The whole thing reared up, let out a bellow like a bull, bunioned out, and burst. The two men at it were shattered into bits. A huge gap showed in the rail where it had been. The arm of a man fell at James Dawn's feet at the stern.

A man came running aft shouting that they had been hit below water and were filling.

James Dawn set his teeth and kept on after the *Adamant*. They were very close now. The *Adamant's* wake showed ruffling and silvery under the *Margaretta's* bows.

"Stand by to board!" yelled James. "It is our only chance!"

The flash of the Britisher's guns scorched the cheeks of the men of Merrymeeting and singed their hair. The

Britisher was going to go about, to get clear and shake them. James held his course, but he widened his legs, ready.

A terrible blow hit them forward. Their foremast tottered, leaned, crashed. Down came fore-royal, fore-gallant, topsail and mainsail, in a smother of white doom. The moon was eclipsed with the wreckage. A more terrible blow hit them amidship. A hot shot hit them, and smoke began to pour through the broken planking that yawed apart under James's feet.

The British man-of-war straightened up, and what sails she had left on her eased in. She began to swing about to pass them to the starboard.

"Now!" shouted James.

He put his helm over and followed the *Adamant*. He ran his jib-boom fair and full into her foremast shrouds until the *Margaretta's* nose brought up and buried itself in her timbers. Every man went to his knees as they struck. Then they all sprang up with knives, axes, and squirrel guns and surged forward.

"The Lord of Hosts!" shrieked Parson Harris, and threw his broad-axe at the men in British blue swarming under the *Margaretta's* prow. One of them went down.

It was James and David and Stephen Trefethen who hurtled down first upon the British deck. The others rained down after them. James came down upon three blue men, and they all went in a knot to the deck. But he and two others got up again, and the two cut at him with their cutlasses. One fetched a slash that would have made two of him, but James was out from under it like quicksilver, and the blade whistled to the planking. The man lost his balance. Before he could right himself, James had got home with a long thrust at the other man. He grinned wide at James in the moonlight, and then crumpled at the knees. The sailor who had notched the planks with his cutlass came at him again. He was all blade, this way and that. James had to look lively to meet all of the blades there were in the air coming at his head and shoulders. The air was full of sparks. But the man swung once too often and too far, and James Dawn slashed him open from ear to chin, and that settled it.

A tall and wiry fellow came at him with his point steady and still. This was a cooler customer. James found out in a second that this one could fence. James was not going to fence, himself, for James knew it was bad for the eyes. So he saw his chance and put all the brute strength he could into it, and cut the man's muscle in his upper arm. His fencing was over for the night. He staggered back into the moonlight, and James was able to get a good look at him. He might have known. It was Squire Trefethen. He had dropped his weapon and leaned on the shrouds and bled.

"That," said James Dawn, "squares us."

Another Britisher boarded James. He was a thick and tough one, but Dawn got him swapping cuts low down, and then went home overhead to the thick bone above his ear. And that one was through. But it seemed as if twenty men had come out of that single one as he fell.

They closed on James Dawn from three sides. He backed to a hatchway and tried to keep them off. There were so many points that some of them got him here and there. Terrible smartings at elbows and shoulders he had. One ear was partly cut through, and it scalded him unmercifully. But he kept on swinging.

Busy as he was, James could see a dozen things going on around him out of the corners of his eyes. Dark knots of men wound together like crazed eels in an eel-pot. Men sprawled on the deck. But plenty more on their pins. A sailor's head lay almost at his feet, with its eyes open. James found himself wondering where the fellow's body could be. He could not keep the ring of men away much longer.

"The Lord of Hosts!"

A body hurtled out of nowhere into the midst of James's assailants. It was Davy Snow, and he was using a borrowed cutlass like a scythe. Muskets began to crack around James. Stephen Trefethen hove into sight with a pistol smoking in his left hand and a cutlass swinging in his right. He cut down two of the men left around James. James himself fetched one man who had been slicing his elbows a blow over the skull that would have felled an ox. The skull felt like a pumpkin as he went through. There were only two Britishers left. They turned tail and ran with their butts wide. One of them tripped and put up both hands for mercy. The other went headlong into the sea.

A vast light, not of the moon, was shining on the

Adamant's quarter to starboard. James looked up and saw that it was the *Margaretta* all high flames. The water was lit up like day. A dozen heads were bobbing on the waves. He could see their white faces and the dark holes of their mouths belching out firelit water.

David and Fearing were cheering and waving their weapons. They were tugging at a rope on the only mast left standing. The flag of England came down. David took it and brought it aft and put it in James's hand. It was no time to be fooling with flags. James was tying up what places he could on himself with strips of his shirt. He drew the knots tight with his teeth.

"Cut the *Margaretta's* boom away, and let her go!" he called out between knots. "Look lively!"

The Merrymeeting men went to work with axes and pieces of iron. They got clear of the boom of the poor *Margaretta* at last. She floated away in a vast cloud of sparks and heeled over burning.

Stephen Trefethen was nowhere to be seen.

"Davy Snow, you old egg-sucker, we've gone and captured a British man-of-war!"

Failing Upjohn hit David Snow a tremendous slap across the shoulders.

A few other men were talking here and there. But mostly it was very quiet there on the stained deck of the *Adamant.* The wounded groaned, now and then. And the moon rode full, high and lovely overhead in the night.

James found Stephen Trefethen at last. He was

bandaging up his father's arm. The Squire was not saying anything. He was not even looking at his son. His eyes were on the dim edge of the sea. His wig was gone from his head. He seemed a much smaller man without it. James Dawn could not know what was passing through the Squire's head, but he could tell by his eyes that it was something that was like the end of pride. If he could ever have been sorry for him, it would have been this May night under the moon.

VIII

"Beware, my gentle, pretty pigeon,
To leave the haven of thy nest!
Should the cruel hawk o'ertake thee,
'Twould break the heart in this fond breast."

JAMIE DAWN was letting his big voice out on the wide Atlantic. He was feeling good, and he wanted the Banks and Fundy to know about it. He had a right to feel good, a right to sing. The timbers that creaked under him as his ship rose to the oily swells were his, every one. And the two other spanking fine ships that followed him, port and starboard, were his, too. One of them, the taller one with three masts, had been his Majesty King George the Third's, the day before yesterday. But now she had a few holes in her hull that a few weeks in Merrymeeting and hammers would heal, and the sailors who wore their hair in pigtails under their wide sailor hats and drank limejuice were stowed safely below—some of the bully ones who still had trouble in them, in irons—and all was in apple pie order. And there would be six ships of his in Merrymeeting harbor, when he got home with the new pigeon he had whistled to with his cannon.

James's cannon were good ones. They had been made in Bristol, and they all had a fine crown and G. R. under it stamped in the metal of their breeches. He was adding to his fine collection every year. If the war lasted long enough, he'd fill Merrymeeting with ships. But, still, ever since the French fleets had come west, the plums were getting harder to find. He had to go farther to find one each time.

The new ship had been rechristened the *Continental Congress,* and Davy Snow put in command. A much better name, when all was done, than the *Alligator.*

What wind there was came out of the southeast, and James was sailing on a bee line for home. All his sails were broken out, except the fore and main-royals. If Fearing Upjohn, off to port there, did not put on his main and mizzen-gallants pretty soon, he would be left in the lurch. The royals were a little too much in this roll, but the gallants were another story altogether. Fearing always had the name of being too damned cautious.

The sea was the same color as the air. James could not make out any horizon at all. He was rolling through a glass globe with no up and no down to it. In that tricky light, in the month of November, you could see anything you were looking for. A brace of British frigates hot as hell after you, for instance. Ships that weren't there, or an iceberg that maybe was really five hundred miles away. A cape where no cape should be. Thinking of icebergs made James notice that it had grown colder. It was fixing for to kick up a blow, maybe, before another night rolled round. He'd be in Merrymeeting, safe and sound, with Molly, before then.

A man might see his grandmother on such a day. His

grandmother going past his bows in a washtub. A ship might be suddenly right on your port bow and aiming her sharp nose at your ribs.

He was a made man. He could leave his two-by-four cottage and build himself a bigger house than old Ronald Trefethen ever dared to. Spank on the highest hill on the whole of Merrymeeting Bay. He owned the highest hill of them all. Higher than the Trefethens'. A house with a cupola and everything. He had the money to build it. He had gone up like a pine these eight years. He had done it all by himself, no thanks to anybody. He had a son to step into his shoes on three-masters a few years more. Too bad it was only one son. He should have had more. A man couldn't have too many of them. Best not to have all his eggs in one basket. Well, Molly was a young woman still. He would have to see to that.

Queer, James thought, old Ronald Trefethen's going off to Halifax and never coming back. He had gone with the other Tories down there. His son Stephen would have the old place all to himself, when he got back from knocking around with Johnnie Paul Jones on the other side of the Atlantic and got acquainted with the young daughter his wife had left him, in Portsmouth. Strange his marrying down there. Maybe he thought there was nobody good enough in Merrymeeting. Well, his wife was dead and gone now, and Stephen would have to bring his child home and have to look to the raising of her. James wondered what she looked like. Somebody who had seen her in Portsmouth said she was smart and pretty. Stephen would find it hard sledding. A lot of the money had gone to Halifax. The war had finished the yards. Stephen would have to hustle. James had heard talk of Stephen's being hard up. It would be a come-down for him. Oh well, times changed. New men went up, and the old big-wigs went down. Up and down, it was the way of the world.

Yes, a man might see ships all around him, just about to ram him and cut him in two. Ships so near he could make out the names in gilt letters under a bowsprit. The *Harpswell*, for instance.

By God!—It was a ship, and that was the name—and she was going to hit him! She was only three lengths away, and coming the Old Boy knew how with those slack threadbare sails. And nobody on her decks at all to take a hail. God damn! The *Harpswell* was going to hit him!

Captain Dawn threw every ounce of strength he owned on his wheel. His jib-boom swung round forty-five degrees on the gray. He braced himself for the blow and the splintering that would follow. He bellowed like a bull, in the hope of making someone hear him on the *Harpswell*. He was too late. She was going to shove her rotten old boom right into him, right where he stood. He leaned away with horror in his eyes and waited for the ripping of his mizzensail.

And then he tried to scream and couldn't get a sound

out of his mouth. For the *Harpswell* wasn't there any more. Not the sign of a mast or hull or spar. Nothing. Just a cold draft of air that swept round him suddenly as if somebody had opened a door into the north, and had closed it up again quick.

A sailor was coming running toward him through the vast ocean silence.

"What is it, Sir?" the man asked. "Did you speak to me?"

Captain Dawn brushed the back of his hand over his bushy brows. He swallowed twice, to wet his whistle.

"No, Dan Toothaker. I didn't speak. Not to you. It's nothing. Nothing. Just clearing my pipes a bit of the mist. Can't a man shout on his own ship? Take the wheel a bit. I need a dash of brandy."

"Aye, Sir."

James Dawn went below, closed the cabin door, poured out five fingers of spirits, and swallowed it at one gulp.

The *Harpswell*. An odd name.

He'd be remembering that name. And seeing it, likely, in his dreams.

Things like that couldn't happen in broad daylight. Not to a well man. There weren't any such things.

He turned in early that night.

When he woke up, the ship was plunging like a horse going home and close to his stable. He went up on deck. The gray had broken up into gray mountains in the sky, falling in a terrific landslide down into the northwest. And Mark Island Monument was at the foot of the clouds, and behind that beckoning finger thrust up through the sea was the dim frieze that would be the hills back of Merrymeeting and home.

Two hours later, not a soul there on the wharf had a smile on his face as Captain James leaped down the plank to tell them the good news. His landsmen were acting queer. They were all huddled at the farther end of the pier. One of them only came forward and touched his cap. It was Constant Converse.

"I have bad news, Jamie Dawn. Bad news for you."

"What is it?—Speak up and tell me like a man." Then, taking a good look at Converse's long face, "Is it about my son?"

"Yes, your son."

"What!—is he ailing?"

"He is dead."

James Dawn leaned against the pile and grew twenty years older in a moment.

"How did he—did he die?" His voice was small as a child's.

"Burned to death. Burned in his bed. In the dead of night. The house went. They think as how someone might have put hot coals in the cellar. The fire broke out there first, they said. They are sure about that. It began in the cellar. Coals in the cellar. Hot coals."

"Yes, I saw that cellar. Full of hot coals. In the dark. It was—it was—" James Dawn had closed his eyes and seemed to be speaking to himself. "It was the Indians' doing." His voice trailed off.

Then he jerked himself back and was terribly wide awake.

"But that was when I was a boy, years ago!—Hot coals in the cellar?—why, that is crazy talk! It's—it's—" His voice trailed off again. Then he spoke slowly and quietly at last:

"What night was it?"

"Last night, Sir."

"Yes, it would be." He had closed his eyes again. He could see it as plain as day. A mighty ship without a soul on her deck.

"What about Molly?"

"She—she went, too. Trying to save the lad, she was. Bad burns. She lived two hours. But she was past helping."

"So I am without a wife and without a son, Constant Converse. Just as you say. So I am."

James did not say anything more, to anybody. He went across the wharf Ronald Trefethen had built and he had taken over, under the dark bridge of the sail loft, out again into the daylight, and climbed the hill with his new years upon him.

People in Maine had always had the saying that it was tempting Providence to build on an old cellar where a house had been burned. Sayings people had weren't made up out of whole cloth. There were long years of living behind them, and much sadness. Where heat had been in stones, the stones got the habit of heat, maybe

He met no man. The bleak, raw day was empty

around him. No sun came through the clouds. Sunlight was rare and brief in Maine, in November. He was all alone in the world save for the wild and hurrying clouds. A few raindrops slanted down. All alone as he had been from the time he was a small boy.

James stood at the edge of the place at last. There was smoke still going up out of it. Some few pieces of furniture had been saved from the flames. The brown bowl Molly had served him his porridge in, the wedding night when he did not feel like eating and she wept in the kitchen. A few other odds and ends strewn about on the sodden grass. Heaps of clothing. He had not remembered Molly had saved that wedding-night dress. Fresh as when she first put it on. She had not had many bright dresses, Molly. She might have had. He could have afforded them.

The man saw something that caught the dull light from the sky. He stirred it with his foot. Then he bent down and picked the thing up. A child's cup. With a name on it. His cup, marked J. DAWN.

He put it in his pocket. Then he set his teeth together in his head, turned, and went on up the hills that were to be climbed, ahead.

IX

THE wind was moaning around the eaves as only a Maine wind could do. Full of voices far off and half of them forgotten. Full of voices from inside a man himself—voices he had not known were there. It was like that in October nights. Rain beat at the windows. The Trefethens had brought the glass from England. In their own ships. It was the Trefethens' way. They had brought their own gravestones over, too. No such fine stone carving on this side. Weeping willow trees cut as fine as the finest lace. A Death-Cherub with bared and even teeth and feathered wings. They wanted the best, the Trefethens. They always had the best.

Old Peter Trefethen, Stephen's grandfather, had even brought back a lead coffin to lie in, when his time should come. He had seen enough of the damp. He wanted to sleep dry when he slept last.

The glass was in a bad way. A glazier ought to be put to work on the panes. They rattled and creaked. Many of them were cracked already at the corners. The paint was gone at the cracked places. At this rate, some of the panes would soon fall out. Swallows would sweep in, in the Spring of the year, and nest on the mantels. After that, all the weather and ruin came in.

A house ought to have a man around it all the time.

It ought not to be left by itself. You noticed such things as paint gone along the window sashes, in the Fall of the year. It was the right time.

Too big a house for one servant and one child. And a girl-child, too. That made it worse. Such a big house needed many people in it, year in, year out.

The wall paper was mildewed and stained from the rain. This room was bare. There was little enough furniture now to go around all the rooms. Broken pieces of chairs did for kindling a small fire in the grate. The ashes of a chair whirled around under the October night wind in the chimney flue. An October wind always found its way down chimneys. The chairs old Squire Trefethen had wasted on his wedding could be used here, in these rooms. A man ought to be careful not to build a house too big for his children to fill. Empty rooms could do bad things to a family.

Men gathered great fortunes and great strength, and then wars came and times changed. And all was shrunken and small and scattered away.

James Dawn could not be sure if the man on the bed behind him was saying something or not, the wind howled so around the eaves.

He had better make sure. He got up and went over to the canopied bed and bent down. It was not much of a man there. Hardly more than a ridge under the faded counterpane. That was what wars could do.

"What is it you are saying, Stephen?"

The face on the pillow turned up to Dawn's. The lips had hard work to cover up the teeth, and the eyes of the man were deep back in his head.

"Marjorie . . . Marjorie. . . . It's Marjorie," the lips moved and whispered.

"Yes, Marjorie. I know, she is all right. She is asleep long hours ago."

"Marjorie. I—I am worried. About her. In days to come."

"I know. I will take care of her. Good care of her. I have told you that over and over. Now you rest. You ought to sleep and rest."

"Marjorie. I want you—you and she . . . I want you to promise. . . . You and she——"

"What is it you want me to do, Stephen?"

James Dawn's eyes were wide with what he was foreboding. He put his head close down to the laboring breath of the man who had come home thus from glory and long years of tossing on the sea, and the great guns going hour after hour.

"Marry—want you to—you and Marjorie. When she grows up. . . . Marry."

James was sure he had heard right. He stood up with his eyes fixed on the flickering candle flame. He stood still as a statue. The years crumpled all together. He was a small boy peeking into a large room and seeing a tall lady in a dress like something a boy would dream. A small homespun boy, holding his breath and looking past the powdered blackamoors at a lady like an apple flower.

James put back his head, and his eyes filled with light.

Then he bent down to the man, and moisture he had not had in the corners of his eyes for many, many years glistened in the corners of them now.

"I am sorry, Stephen Trefethen—sorry about—about the silver teaspoons. In the snow. That night you wanted to be friends. That night I was married."

The man under the bedding seemed to be trying to do something with his hands. James Dawn turned back the covers quickly. The withered hand came out to him, trembling. James took it in his and held it with all his strength.

"I promise, Stephen Trefethen. I promise. I will keep my word. I will marry your Marjorie." He spoke loudly in the windy room, so that the man would be sure to hear him. "I will make up for the hate and pride I have had toward you and yours. I will make up for it. There is only peace between you and me. And I will have a son who is as much Trefethen as Dawn. I swear I will. He will do what neither of us could do. He will have the strength of Dawn and Trefethen together. I swear before God."

The hand in his tautened in every wasted fibre. It wasn't the fever in the man's eyes that made them shine so. It was love. Love such as only a man can have for a man. And peace.

The tall man with the unpowdered hair went back to his chair by the dead fireplace and the ashes that the wind whirled there.

The wind outside was beginning to die away. After a long while, the night was silent as the house, except for the lapping of the waves the wind had stirred up on Merrymeeting, at the foot of the hill.

X

"MARJORIE!"

The big man's voice was lowered to a tender, small whisper. He came across the great room to the great Trefethen bed, in the January sunlight that was like a roomful of the bright dust of diamonds. He seemed to shed the Winter sunshine from his hair and his shoulders as he came. The floor was paved for him by the golden squares of the small panes which lay there where they had fallen from the radiant world of ice outdoors.

"Happy New Year, Marjorie! Happy 1800! And what a boy it is!"

"Oh, Jamie! Jamie!" The thin voice quavered from the canopied bed. "I am so thankful it—it—it is a he! You wanted a he-child so!"

"I was sure of it, Marjorie. There are—there are things that—that have to happen the way they do. I was sure."

"Yes," Marjorie said slowly and quietly, "I think you were sure of it before ever I was born. Before you had learned to stand and go by yourself. You were sure of it before there was ever any time. Before the stars were set in the sky! You are sure of everything, Jamie. You have had your way with all men. With me."

"It was a pleasant way, though."

"Yes, pleasant the way smooth iron is pleasant. You

are a hard man, Jamie. Hard as your own whaling iron. I hope your son will be like you, for I know it would break your heart if he were not."

"It's a hard new world, Marjorie, he is coming into this bright January morning. He is coming into a new century. His ships will have to be taller in the mast than mine ever were. They will have to carry greater canvas than mine ever did."

"And haven't you any little piece of pride in me, Jamie? in my part in this January night? The Trefethen people did fine things, too."

For his answer, the man went over to the bed and knelt down on one knee and kissed his wife's forehead. He remained there by the bedside.

"Oh, Jamie, Jamie!" The wife put out her hand and stroked her husband's hair. "You were so rough with your tongue last night. You shamed me so with your carryings-on and shouting up the stairs. Shouting things to make a woman blush. You made poor Betsy O'Reilly blush. You nearly put her out of her wits."

"That is not far to go, with Betsy. But she is a merry, lovable soul, and a man has to be merry with the likes of her."

"Merry?—Jamie, you know the girl dotes on you. She worships the ground you walk on. You ought not to make her blush. Don't ever do a thing to shame poor Betsy. Please, Jamie."

"Why all this rigmarole about Betsy and her liking me?"

"Fie! Jamie, you know what I mean. I have ears. I hear the talk people make. About you and her. . . . But you are a man, Jamie, and you are your own master, as all men are. And the women must close their eyes."

The woman turned her face to the pillow. Her husband knew she was weeping.

"Come, come, Marjorie! You are not yourself. You must not let trifles and old women's gossip upset you so, like this. You have a fine new baby. This is no way to act on the morning of a new century. On the morning you have birthed me a son!"

"And you have named the child," the wife put up her tear-stained face again, "with never a by-your-leave to me. It is a plain name, John is, a very plain name. And you know I cannot abide plain names. I wanted it to be Roger. Or at least Richard."

"The Dawns are plain people, and plain names become them best. Roger!—'tis a fop's name. A silken dandy of a name. My son has hard work ahead of him. And he must have a hard, short name that people can say in a breath. In a gale between two waves of the ocean, when many men's lives may depend on what the master will do. A short name on a ship. John is the name I wanted."

"Why not your own, then? James is better than John."

"James is my own name. My son must not stand still in my shoes. He will have to face the new, and he must have a new name. Besides, John begins with J."

"What has that to do with it?"

"It's a long story, Marjorie. And if I told it all, I might open an old wound which has been a scar for many years. There is bitterness in the tale. The old bitterness between your people and mine. That is all past now. I can tell you this, though. The first son of the Dawns must have a J at the front of his name. It has been so for three generations of us, and it must be so for all the generations that will come. And that is so because of a cup. A cup that was Trefethen's and now is Dawn's. See, here it is, and I have brought it up to my man-child."

James held up the pewter mug.

"Trefethen's?—Why, 'tis but a drab, mean thing, my Jamie. Why all this pother about it?"

"It is more precious than silver. It is the Luck of the Dawns. My father cut my initial on it, which was also his own. It has lived through fire and blood. It has been in the hands of the red devils of the forest, in the old days. Fire and blood and death! Now it shall go to my son, and he will keep it through the days when he will stand up and sweat blood and spill blood, maybe. He will pass it on to the first of his name. It shall go across the years as the sign and seal of our strength. For we are a strong family, and we will have our way with ships and sea, with men and the world."

"You speak always as if you were God, James Dawn. It is not fitten for any man to speak so. Men are not the orderers of their lives. Not even the strong ones like you. There is a Providence above, and he shapes the years as they go by. He will not have slighting words said of him. You make me afraid with your talk. It is—it is like blasphemy."

"That thing you call Providence is a little coward's word men roll on their tongues when they are hurt bad and cannot get up on their feet again."

"Hush! It is a holy thing you blaspheme. You have always been an arch rebel and a free thinker, James Dawn. You hold with doctrines that are new and strange and full of stubbornness."

"The doctrines that shook the yoke of the tyrant from our necks!"

"Oh, deeper doctrines than those men talk of in assemblies. Doctrines of the free thinkers of France who spat on their King and their Queen and their God."

"I will not have that name said in my house. You know that."

"No. Save in an oath, James Dawn. You call upon that name in curses. Don't you know that you recognize its power when you use it in a curse?"

"I may be free thinker and atheist, but I am master here."

"This house had God in it when it was the Trefethens'!"

"It had devils in it, too, then. But it has only Dawns now. But there, I won't quarrel, and I won't talk philosophy on my son's birthday. And you are tired, Marjorie. You must not hurt yourself with standing up to me as it is always your humor to do. Wait till you are well, before you speak the Trefethen tongue to me."

"I cannot abide in patience when you say things that may hurt my babe. You will not suffer alone. You and yours as well will suffer from the blasphemy you speak."

She buried her face again, away from the sunlight that slanted across the bed like a golden arm thrust into the room. After a little, she stopped shaking at her shoulders and leapt up with stained cheeks.

"Haven't you had proof enough that it isn't safe to think as you do?—Your—your other son—in that burning house, and she, your——"

"Marjorie!" James Dawn's face was white, but his voice was quiet. "Say not another word!"

The new mother drooped her head.

"I am sorry, Jamie."

"I forgive you."

"But you might have let me have James instead of John!"

"There! there!—I have better things to do than quarrel over a name. See, I have the cup here for my son. Uncover him and let me give it to him!"

"Why, Jamie, so small a mite can never hold such a thing," she answered. "See how small his hands are. They are like the buds on rosebushes."

But she threw back the coverlet billowed high at her right side.

"We shall see."

Captain Dawn put the cup down beside the little fists. The coldness of it made the baby's two hands stir. He did not open his wrinkled eyes. But he caught an enormous breath in and held it. And then of a sudden both small hands came open for the very first time in the world for him, and they closed side by side on the edge of the pewter cup.

"See! I told you so! He lays hold on the thing as he will lay hold on life!"

The man smote his wide hands together, stood up, and threw his head back in the sunshine.

"That's my son!—I would know him among a thousand! John Dawn!"

The woman had to smile, and from smiling it was a sudden way to tears. Gentle tears rolled down along her cheeks.

"He holds fast to the rising sun my father cut!" cried James. "The rising sun!—You talk of Providence! As if Providence you talk of could hold a candle to the great Providence we call the sun. There is the shaper of our strength! The sun that reaches down with his hands through the clouds, even far on the desolate sea, and smoothes the waters for sailors and keeps them in their way. With his everlasting hands!"

James Dawn stood over the man-child he had begotten. Over the wife he had taken from a great house that had belonged to his enemies. He stood up in the house where his enemies had come to birth and death. He held his head high in the light of the January sun.

XI

JOHNDY DAWN was up first over the ship's rail. Johnry O'Reilly clambered after. But he couldn't quite make it. There was a bit too much of him at the middle. So back John Dawn came and pushed him. He seized the boy under his breeches and lifted by his two butts. When his playmate was almost over, he downed head, butted him at the seat, and boosted him over. Then the two of them scuttled across the deck as fast as their stout browned legs could fly. Johndy ahead, and Johnry behind. It was always that way. Johndy always in the lead.

People in Merrymeeting called them Johndy and Johnry for short. They were as alike in their husky eleven-year-old bodies as two boys could be. Like peas from the same pod, Easter Toothaker and the other men said, with a broad smile. But not in their faces. Johnry's face was round and as calm as the harvest moon, and his eyes had nothing but smiles in them as he followed his leader into mischief. But Johndy's head went up high over his ears, his ears stuck out like a Maine beanpot's handles, his eyes were full of quicksilver, sudden lightning, the blue of frost-flowers, and the Old Boy. Mostly the Old Boy, Jim Doughty said, as he chased him away from the spar he had been testing his jack-knife on.

Yes, you couldn't pry them apart with a crowbar. They were only three months apart in age. They had grown up together through babyhood into boyhood. Ever since Johndy's mother had died of the brother he should have had to play with him, he had made Johnry his brother. And Captain James Dawn let Betsy O'Reilly's boy live at the big house he had intended to fill full of sons, and he smiled to see the boy make himself at home there. The two children were like David and Jonathan. If the captain scolded one, he had to scold the other. And if he laid on upon Johndy's backsides, as he did once or twice a day, Johnry did not rest till he had done something and he got his own breeches dusted, too. What deviltry one did not think up, the other did. Betsy moaned that her boy would come to no good, being brought up like a gentleman's son. But James said for her not to be a goose, and let the lad alone. And Betsy gave up. She got married to Daniel Holbrook pretty soon after the boys got old enough to shin an apple tree, anyway, and left the big house. And when she began to have a lot of regular children, one a year or so, she was quite as well pleased to have her Johnry up there on the hill. Where he belonged, when you came to think of it.

She shouldn't have gone to work and named her son John, if she hadn't wanted to have him stick to his John, James Dawn roared. It was all her own fault.

Johndy ran over the deck of the *Marjorie*, and Johnry took after him. He kept his eyes on the two patches at Johndy's tail and sailed after. Johnry had exactly the same kind of patches on him. All from the same piece of homespun. The two of them had the kind of butts that were hard on breeches, and they were forever coming through. Johndy threw himself up over the side of the ship's longboat. Johnry climbed after him. They threw themselves on all fours and crept under the canvas covering, breathing like two young woodchucks.

Nobody had seen them. They lay quiet, fitted close together like two peas in a peascod, breathing hard and saying nothing. They heard the men downing their tools and getting ready to knock off work for the day. Hammers and saws rattled down upon the timbers of the new forecastle. The boys could hear the men talking. They took in every word. There were some new words they had not heard before today.

"Hell's hinges! Jim Doughty!—Get your herring boxes out of the way of my hammer, or I'll make toe-jam out of them!"

"Oh, you will, will you?—Well, it'll be the last time you swing a hammer, by Christ!"

"God rot your guts!"

"I'll fetch you over the head so hard, East Toothaker, you'll waddle like a duck all the rest of your life."

"Oh, go straddle yourself!"

"I don't have to, East Toothaker. You think you're pretty big, don't you, with the women and all."

"The women think so."

"Well, I can tell you, you won't make no headway with some women I know of."

"What ones, for instance?"

"I ain't naming no names."

"You got a pretty nice woman yourself, Jim. Better keep your eye peeled."

"I ain't losing no beauty sleep over my Peggy. You'd have to be a lots longer man than you be to get on the sunny side of *her*."

"Maybe so. Maybe not."

"What do you mean by that?"

"Just what I said. If the old ram's cap fits you, put it on."

"You know I don't stomach no joke like that, Easter Toothaker. I'm apt to take this hammer and sink it in your knob to the eye."

"And what'd I be doing all that time?—You don't need to get upitty, Jim. You ain't the only husband that may get knobs on his head."

"I ask you to lay off that talk!"

"All right, Jim. Have it your way. What the miller don't see, he don't believe. Me and you are good friends."

The men got friendly again and talked about women. Not Peggy Doughty, but women as a whole. This was what the boys had been waiting for. They lay there all ears. Jim Doughty and Easter Toothaker—he had been born on that day and so got his name from it—were two of the boys' special friends in the James Dawn Yard. The boys had heard them mention women before, but they'd never heard them go on like this. They did not miss a word. There were a lot of things they had to guess at. But they were both good guessers. From women, the men went to the master builder.

"Yes, Siree, Jamie Dawn, he knows how to get on the good side of a smock, best of any man that warms a pair of breeches. He's the cock of the roost in Merrymeeting."

"It's God's truth. They all come round when Jamie treads on his wing to them."

"Those twins of his, Jim, are Jamie Dawn all over again. And Johndy and Johnry will make the feathers fly when they get their spurs on them."

"Bet your bottom they will."

The men finished stowing their tools. Their voices went farther and farther off, into silence.

Johnry took a deep, long breath and looked at Johndy in the dim light under the tarpaulin.

"What did East mean by calling me and you twins, Johndy?"

"Why, 'cause we are, Johnry. We have the same Pap."

"Well, I'll be hornswoggled!"

"You little lunkhead!—Whose Pap did you think was your Pap?"

Having settled that, Johndy threw his leg over the gunwale of the boat and climbed down and shook the shavings out of his breeches. The other boy came tumbling out on the deck after him.

"Golly, Johnry, they've left two of the sails hanging. It'll be easy as pie. Pap would give Jim and East hell if he knew."

The men had been patching the canvas, and the fore

and main-topsails were left sagging idle in the windless evening.

They had planned this adventure for weeks. That is, Johndy had. He did all their planning. First, he led Johnry down into the master's cabin.

"There's your bunk," he said, pointing to the first mate's, "and this one's mine." And he threw himself out full length on his father's place. "And you'll make them both up every morning."

Johndy showed the first mate all the gadgets there he had never been allowed to handle. They dropped one of the sextants, and it didn't work nearly so well afterwards. There was a big bottle full of spirits in the little cubby hole over the captain's berth. Johndy took it down and took a good swig of it. He passed it over to Johnry as he began the job of swallowing his mouthful of it. It was quite a job. He did it a little at a time. He got it all down. But Johnry coughed a big cough and spat all of his out on the quilts.

"You ought not to waste good liquor like that, Johnry," the captain said sternly. But the captain put the bottle back and did not take any more.

Then they went forward and had a look at the men's quarters.

"Too bad we couldn't ask Jim and Easter to come along with us."

"We'll get along all right by ourselves, Johnry. They would have blabbed right off. They would have run right off and told Pappy."

They went to the galley and mixed up some flapjack flour the way they had seen the cook do it on the last trip they'd been on. Johnry got the stuff down the front of his breeches.

"We'll cook that up later, after we've got sea room."

Johndy led the way to the hold. They went down the rope like two monkeys, hand over hand, among the empty whale-oil tierces.

"Pap will be surprised."

"Hell's hinges!—you bet your bottom he will!"

They shinned up again. When they got to the deck, they went bent double, so nobody would see them from the shore. They had saved the best for the last. They went to the wheel. They tugged at the lashings. They could not budge them. Johndy whipped out his knife and cut them. They practiced turning the wheel. It took the two of them to roll it.

It was beginning to dusk. A light was twinkling up home on the hill at one of the windows. But there was no sign they had been missed. They stayed out all hours, sometimes, when they felt like it.

The bay was growing very big and quiet around them. The stars were beginning to come out. They were sprinkling the air with sparkles, they were sprinkling the bay. There wasn't a breath of wind.

"God rot the wind's guts!—If'n it don't come up pretty soon!"

"Course it will, Johnry. You never see a night like

this, on the ebb, that didn't breed up a blow. We'll get it before long, when the tide turns."

The stars were thick as the daisies in a Maine meadow now, all over the sky. The two boys lay back and looked at them for a long time.

"There's the North Star up there."

"How can you tell, Johndy?"

"'Cause the rim of the Dipper points at it—blockhead! You've heard our Pap say so."

"Stars are pretty far off, ain't they?"

"A hell of a ways. Pap says some of them could go spank out, and he not know a thing about it all the time he was going after whale down under, getting his big bellyful of whale, and coming back along up home. That might be two years."

"Don't tell fibs, Johndy. When you knock over a tallow-dip, it goes out all at once. And a star would, too, God damn it!"

"That shows how much you know, you little sannup. You don't know beans when the bag's open. The stars' light takes a whale of a time going out. The going out has a hell of a long ways to go."

The spokes of the pilot's wheel made a vast dark cobweb between them and the starry sky.

"Do you suppose we can spin the wheel over all right, Johndy? Do you think we can handle her?"

"Of course, we can. We'll work the wheel together. We'll climb it and put all the guts we've got into it."

They stood still again for a long time without saying anything. The wide and high sky had gotten into their minds. They were on the edge of something vast and silent, and they knew it, and it made them quiet for once. The gentle sounds of the rising tide lapped the sides of their father's whaler. A wind was on the way somewhere, a good ways off still, but it was coming. They could feel the coolness and freshness to the air. They would soon be sliding over into places as new to them as the lonely reaches washed by the foam of the stars above.

"What are you fixing for to do, Johndy? After we get out—out there?"

"Oh, we'll find some kind of cargo or other. I don't think we could handle whales. We'll get a cargo. We'll get men to help us stow it. Everybody knows our Pappy, everywhere."

"We'll be coming back here?"

"Sure as sunrise. We belong here, Johnry. We're Maine people. There'll be a good lot of ships that me and you will have to build here, when our times comes and we wear long trousers like our Pappy. Shouldn't wonder if we built more sailing boats than Pap ever built in all his born days. We won't bother with whales and oil and small pickings like that. Not money enough in them. We'll sail our ships out to India and New York and London and Singapore and all those places. And you and me will live on the fat of the land, Johnry. We'll get married like Jim and Easter and do like them, and have all the sons to boss around we want. We'll make them toe the mark, too. We'll fill a brig full of them and make sailors of the whole lot together. We'll make them stand round and shin up into the yards. And we'll have houses with cupolas all over them. We'll have everything ship-shape and Bristol fashion!"

But just now the night was full of unknown things, strange and far off as the stars. A low whistling was beginning to come up from nowhere. It hung above them in the forest of dim spars over their heads, high and mighty and wide in the night. The idle sails began to belly out a little. The hawsers forward tautened, and the piles of the wharf groaned as the ship put her weight on her cables and leaned away from the shore, trying her strength. The wind was coming, and it was coming from the north. The right way for them. Johndy howled for joy.

"Time we was getting under way, Johnry. Look alive!"

Johndy led the way. They ran for the foremast. They went up like two quick little cats in the dark forest of lines aloft, as they had seen the men do. They went out together on the yards. The knots were too hard for them to untie. But Johndy had his jack-knife along. He cut them. They heard the vast whisperings of the loosened sails as they fell out of sight and unrolled below them. The ship began to strain harder at her lashings, and the piles of the wharf creaked. Great things they had started were beginning to go to work under their feet. They worked side by side. They scrambled from the foremast, and went for the main. They knew they had to be spry. The whisperings were beginning to be gigantic hissings and sharp reports. They couldn't do anything with the mainsail.

"I guess we've got enough sail out," said Johndy. He had to shout loudly to his mate to make him hear. "Let's cut her loose and get under way."

They dropped down through the lines to the deck. Side by side, they ran for the ropes that made the ship fast. There was no casting them off. They were hawsers as big through as their wrists, and the strain had made iron of them.

"The hatchet in the cook's galley, Johnry! There's a smart fellow!"

Johnry groped his way to the galley and found it. He took it to the captain. The captain took five or six hacks at the bow line. It ravelled out, gave suddenly with a sound of a hundred bumble bees going over, and the whole night and the whole world began to turn with them on a mighty circle. The stars moved over the boys' heads. They ran astern, and Johndy chopped at the other lashing. He did not get it off till they had fetched up sharp. The whole pier trembled. Johndy got home a good last blow, and this time it was a thousand bees that went away into the night. The dark world they were on brushed along the piles. Tremendous thumpings came up to them from the ship's sides below. The dim point, with its firs black as lace against the starlit sky, was moving past them and going north toward the Dipper.

Things were beginning to happen overhead. Vast sighs and fierce turnings of lines on seasoned, smooth wood. It was too dark for the boys to make out what was happening. But Johndy worked this rope and that, and the sounds changed their tune here and there. Johnry gave a hand. They worked till their breath was gone. They took up on every rope they could find. The sails began to work hard. A noise of waters began to come up from under their bows. All at once, the ship leaned over with them, and all the stars leaned with her, and they all stayed there at a slant.

They both cried out with joy and grappled with each other in a tight hug, as they always did when they were excited. They pummelled each other's muscles and caught in their breath. They sprang apart and hurried over the slanted deck, shortening their starboard legs as they rushed to the wheel. The great thing was on the go, it rolled down this way and back that. They sprang for it. It minded them no more than an ox wheel minds the Autumn leaves. It went on with its rhythms, back and forth, back and forth. The spokes caught them in the wind as they fought for them. But Johndy kept at it. He got right upon the thing. He shouted to the other boy to come, too. They got on to the trick of throwing their weight on the spokes when they were at the dead low point, just before the up-swing. They got so they could hold it pretty well there until the vast power hidden in it let up suddenly, and they had a breathing space until it began again.

They had to work like Trojans, looking alive three times a minute, straining their four sturdy legs till they ached all over. The stars were right where they had been, scattered among the spars and yard-arms, but the starlit bay was slipping from under their high ship. Gradually there began to be a new motion. The deck boards pushed slowly up, and the boys' knees creaked and bent as they rose. Then their legs straightened, and the whole world went beautifully downhill into a velvet nothing. There began to be these steady hills under them, one after another.

"We are getting out, Johnry!—Feel those old swells!"

They went on wrestling with the wheel. Their arms and hands and legs grew numb. They couldn't say much to each other, they were so busy in the dark. After a time, the stars grew to be a part of the great swing of the swells, and the swells became a part of them. They did not think about much, or say anything at all.

"Don't you dare to go to sleep, Johnry!—Come to there! Look alive!"

But it got harder and harder to shout each time. Johndy was whispering at last.

Johndy felt something warm on his cheek. His eyes snapped open. He sat up. It was the sun. Big and coppery red, right at his elbow on the edge of the long waves. The boy rubbed his eyes to see it there. Then he remembered and swung round. Johnry was curled up sound asleep on the deck. The wheel of the *Marjorie* was solemnly turning over and back, over and back, before the boy's eyes. Johndy looked ahead. Nothing but the endless and uneasy hills on the sky. He looked astern, and could see nothing but more of the uneasy hills, peaking up, sliding off, against the empty blue. Three of the sails were bellied out white in the light of the morning. But the fore-upper-topsail was bundled together in great wallops and was only half at work. The main-topsail, though, was big as a house and working like Kingdom Come. They had enough canvas broken out to take them along all right.

They were off at last, as they had planned it for months and months! The boy leaned over and took hold of Johnry and shook him till he woke up.

"We're under way, Johnry! We're out of sight of land. Look out and see where we are. And then you'd better look smart and go down and cook those flapjacks!"

Johnry sat up and looked around him in amazement. Then he got up and tried his pins.

"I'll be God damned!" he said.

When he got his pins under him, he ran off and started up the fire in the galley.

They ate fifteen flapjacks apiece. They didn't taste exactly right. Johnry had forgotten something or other in the mixing. But the boys were good and hungry and didn't mind so much.

After breakfast, they got aloft and tried to let out the main-royal. They didn't need it, but they had never let one out, and they wanted to see it go. They were so high up, they didn't dare to look down. The royal was too much for them. They came back down. They were flying now, it seemed. They didn't worry any more about the wheel's rolling back and forth there by itself. It had done it all night, and it might as well go on doing it. They had plenty of sea room now. Johndy was all for breaking out the mizzenmast canvas. But Johnry, who had a lot of blisters on his hand from the trip to the main royal, thought they had all the sail they needed out. They sat down on the deck and toasted their shins in the sunshine. Johnry discovered he had some marbles in his pocket. The ship's motion made them roll crazily, but that made it all the more fun. They rolled marbles for an hour, till most of the glass alleys had gone overboard.

They ate again when the sun was where Johndy said meant noon. Johnry fried some salt pork scraps. They tasted wonderful with what flapjacks had been left over from breakfast. After eating, they took a nap on the warm deck. They woke up feeling like the American eagle.

The sun was almost down, and the waves were running molten gold between them and the sun, when Johnry spied it astern. A ship with all three masts loaded with sails golden in the low sun. They stared at her for a long time, without saying a word. She was coming their way. She was gaining on them fast. They looked at each other.

"Pap!"

They ran for the mizzenmast and leaped into the

yards. They tried to get the clews loosened. But it was different work from that last night on the quiet bay. The ship rolled under them like a thing alive, and they had hard work to hold on by the skin of their teeth. They were too much in a hurry. They slashed the wrong lines. One whole spar fell to the deck in a tangle of rigging. Lines jammed. They swore at each other and worked at cross purposes. The ship following them was well up on their port quarter. It was no use. They felt like crying. They slipped back to the deck with one sail they had shaken out flapping crazily and yawing this way and that.

They could read the gilt name on the prow of their pursuer at last. The *Merrymeeting*. And they could see Pap shaking his big fist at them from the stern by the wheel. They looked at each other. They swallowed hard, and could not say a word.

The *Merrymeeting* came up to them as they wallowed and lost speed, sliding off first this way, then that. Easter Toothaker came aboard them with a coil of rope in one tremendous leap. The *Merrymeeting* was made fast. Many men swarmed over the rail and took charge. The boys stood near their wheel and never moved.

"Well!" said Jim Doughty, coming up where they were, "if you was my lads, I'd take this leather belt out of my trousers and lay it onto your backstruts till your eyeballs jingled!"

"Damme if I wouldn't, too," said East Toothaker. "I'd let your breeches down and tan you till you couldn't tell your bottoms from leather."

"But being as they're not your lads"—it was Captain James speaking—he had come aboard the *Marjorie* at last—"you won't do anything of the kind. I won't have a hand laid to their bottoms. I won't let anybody touch them. Look at those sails the little sannups have got out up there, pretty as a picture. Boys, I'm proud of ye! Here! come to your Pap!"

He bent down and caught each of them by the slack of the breeches, swung them aloft together, and set each of them on his wide shoulders.

"Lads, I am prouder of you than I probably'll ever be again in my life!—I'd rather have what you have done than a thousand new dollars in my pocket!"

XII

THE long clouds stretched from somewhere under the gray ocean to the nor'ard up over the whole sky and down in under the ocean to the south. Overhead, they had great sags in them. They seemed almost touching the masts of the *James Dawn* as the ship slanted forward sullenly in the sullen furrows of the lead-gray sea, rolled and slanted backward again. There was nothing but gray waste, overhead, underneath.

"I'm not the man to go out of my way and ask for bad luck. It was bad enough your going out of your way to give this ship a he-name, Jamie, without being out here on the Banks when you know the *Warspite* is combing them for Yankees. But then, you were ever a fool for taking a risk, James."

"And you were always a fool for having your whine when you were happiest, Davy Snow. You know you are enjoying this more than I am this minute."

"And bringing the two boys along. Tchk! tchk!"

"They are in long trousers and have all the growth they will ever have, the great lubbers! They are fourteen years old. Time they were getting some bumps to toughen them up. And you know as well as I do, we couldn't have made those boys of ours stay home if we'd tied them with hawsers! You know that. Bumps'll do them good."

"Bumps, is it?—They'll get their bellyful of them if the *Warspite* runs afoul of us! Forty-five guns to our twenty! You ought to let your trousers down and have it laid on you till you'd have to stand up to your grub. And I'd like to be the fellow to swing the cat!"

"Go ahead. But you will have to let your own down and let me swing the cat on you, for you helped me plan the whole trip."

"But I didn't plan on going after any first-class Lime-juicer! That is your idea. I was after the small fry. Like the two we got off Grand Manan two months ago. Why couldn't you stay inshore, Jamie Dawn?"

"And you was the one, Davy Snow, that had the pin-worms till we got out here!"

Fearing Upjohn had come up behind the captain and the first mate as they wrangled.

"You go below and bag your head, Upjohnny, and keep out of other people's business! I'm telling the captain we are all too old to be knocking around out here halfway across the Atlantic, and looking for trouble. Trouble is bad for the eyes. You just go mind your own P's and Q's. You go below!"

"I will not. I'm an officer, too, on this tub. And I'll have my ladle in the soup as much as any of you. If you had listened to me in the first place, we'd be snug in Fundy now, with a neat little Halifax merchantman in tow. But you two were after bigger game. One of you is as bad as the other. You two lunkheads!"

"I won't be called a lunkhead by the second officer,

Captain Dawn. I won't be called any such names. I won't put up with it!"

"Mr. Snow, you *are* a lunkhead," said Captain James.

"And that goes for you yourself, Sir, too."

Mr. Snow walked aft fuming like a kettle of fat.

A sailor came rolling along, hitching up his best blue trousers.

"Here! Toothaker!" Captain Dawn bellowed.

"Aye, Sir."

"Send my two louts up here at once. I want them to have a go at the wheel."

"You mean your two sons, Sir?"

"Who the Sam Hill did you think I meant? What other louts are there on the ship?"

"Why, there's Jim Doughty for one. And Davy Snow for another. There's lots of them. There's so many——"

"Close your homely face, Toothaker, before I break it with a handspike. Go do what I tell you."

Easter Toothaker grinned a wide grin and ambled off.

"Nothing like a little discipline on a ship, Mr. Snow."

"Nothing," said the first officer.

The day began to close in all at once. The gray clouds seemed to press in from four sides of them and from overhead. By the time Johndy and Johnry got on deck, the sea was going unreal.

"Suppose you take the wheel for a spell, Johndy. Keep her pointed no'theast-by-east, and don't let her slip off by a handsbreadth. Johnry, you stand by to take her when Johndy's hour is up."

The two boys crouched to the job. They were as tall as James Dawn, and heavier through their hulls. Big in their hands and shoulders as he was. But their elbows and hands sometimes got in their own way as his never did. Johndy gripped the grips of the great wheel and kept it steady as a vise. Captain Dawn threw back his square head and took a deep breath of Atlantic air. He set his shoulders back in pride.

"And where might that ship have been keeping herself all this time?"

John Dawn's voice was like a sudden bell striking a clean blow with its tongue in the middle of the quiet evening.

"A ship?"

Both James Dawn and John O'Reilly spoke at the same time and with the same astonishment.

"Three points to our starboard. Coming down on us fast."

"By God, yes!" shouted John O'Reilly. "Hard a port, Johndy, or she'll cut our innards open!"

But Captain Dawn stood there without so much as a gasp as he looked at what was coming. All the pride had crumbled out of his shoulders. They sagged like an old man's. His hands hung like lead at his sides. His eyes were the color of the fading clouds.

The captain's son had straddled out his widest and had thrown all his young heft upon the wheel. Their bow went round slow and sure, in a beautiful arc. It went round till they were heading almost the same way as the approaching vessel. Overhead tremendous creakings told what was going on among the great sails. The voices of surprised sailors came down to them indistinct in the dusk from the crow's nest. There were sounds of running feet below deck.

"You don't need to do that," Captain Dawn's voice was low and flat and monotonous. "She will be gone in a moment. Her name is the *Harpswell.*"

Sure enough, it was. As she came alongside near enough for the boys to make out her name, there it was, written in faded gold, the *Harpswell*. And there wasn't a soul on her deck or on her masts. The boys took a huge breath together and held it. The ship's sails were gray and old, and the color of the clouds. No wonder they had not seen her coming sooner. Not a soul on deck. Not a sign of life.

"Now she will go. Look!"

Just as their father said it, the ship alongside seemed to collapse. She was there, and then she was not there at all. Nothing but gray waves where she had been. And an icy streak of air came over them, like that in the lee of an iceberg.

"Well, I'll be hornswoggled!" breathed John O'Reilly.

"You knew the ship, Sir?—You knew her name?"

"Yes, Son. I know the thing well. Put her back on her course."

John Dawn swung the *James Dawn's* nose back to no'theast-by-east.

"I'll be back with you in a moment."

James Dawn went below. When he came back, he had something in his hands.

"Here, Johndy, this belongs to you. I meant to give it to you long ago. It is time I did now. It was yours before you were born—born or thought of. It belongs to the son you will have. I want you to take it now. Keep it. Keep it and give it to your first son. It belongs to him. And to his son. Take it."

The boy put out his free hand, wondering. His father put the thing into it. It was a cup. John could hardly make it out in the failing light. A pewter cup with something that looked like a sun carven on it.

The captain did not have any more to say. He stood there for a moment very still, while his son waited for him to explain.

John made out letters on the thing, J. DAWN.

"Your first son's name," James Dawn said suddenly, "should begin with a J."

The man turned on his heels. It seemed to Johndy suddenly that his father looked like a very old man. Then his father went down to his cabin and the night.

The night came upon the two boys from every quarter of the sea. John O'Reilly lit up the binnacle lamp. John Dawn kept the wheel steady in his big hands and steered away into the midst of night. Neither one of them could find anything to say to the other. The cup was like a weight of lead in John Dawn's trouser pocket.

The dawn was rifting the clouds when the sound woke

every mother's son on the *James Dawn.* A sound, and then the second sound as a yard crashed on the deck.

"There she is, gentlemen," said Captain Dawn, as he got to the deck with the first and second mates at his heels. "H. M. S. *Warspite.* And we are going to have a heavy morning's work."

Where he pointed, they could make out the tall sails of a man-of-war, all light with the first light of day, and the crosses of St. George and St. Andrew at her mizzen. As they looked, there came a blossom of yellow flame on her hull, then another boom, and then another great sigh high up over them, among their sails. A piece of spar with white rags of sailcloth on it came down at their feet.

"Look alive, everybody! look alive! Clear the decks, and stand to the guns!"

The hull of the *James Dawn* began to hum instantly like an enormous beehive. A trumpet blew and blew. Men shouted, feet pounded. And above all the sound of voices and feet, the voice of David Snow rose:

"I told you so! Jamie. I told you so!"

The gun deck was a bedlam. Men were stripping to their waists and rubbing their bodies slippery out of the vats of grease, so the powder blasts would not bite into the skin. Guns were being unlashed and wheeled into position. Men were ramming great gobs of tallow down their black throats. Buckets were being passed up full of water from the half-hogsheads near the bows. Hammocks were being lashed along the rails of the ship to keep the splinters from flying. Braziers for hot shot and pincers for handling them were being put in place. Powder lines were forming, and men getting their sacks ready.

Easter Toothaker and Jim Doughty were standing with arms folded across their tattooed chests and bellowing at everybody. They were gunners, and they were saving their strength. Their work would come later. Jim had the whole American flag with all nineteen stars on it on his hairy right arm. But Easter had a lady-love—like no Merrymeeting lady-love that ever was—bare as a flounder on his. She had curves the other men swore could not be true on any woman in their ken. But Easter said he'd break the man's head who said he had not known one or two such and seen curves like them on those ladies.

Davy Snow was ordering Fearing Upjohn and Constant Converse around like a good fellow. He was being nasty nice in his politeness. That was a sure sign to look out for him.

"Mr. Upjohn, if you don't mind, the guns on the port are three rounds of ball short.

"If you'd tie the rammers to your swabbers' wrists, Mr. Converse, they might be able to hold them and not drop them so often. Have them put some guts into their work! Good Lord!—They handle those things too lady-like for words! I want those men to go at things as if they meant it. I want only two-fisted male brutes on my ship!"

"Your ship?" snorted Constant. "The only ship you ever owned was a mudscow on the Merrymeeting flats. Your ship!"

"Close your ugly face up, and keep it closed, Mr. Converse. I want your men to take hold of those rammers as though they meant to break them!"

There was a terrific crack, and one of the rammers flew into bits. The men had cramped it on purpose. They were furious. Everybody was swearing till the deck was a blue fog.

"Heavy-handedness will never get you anywhere, Mr. Converse. Send the men that broke that rammer to the powder magazine, and let them snuff ashes down there.

"Are your men getting ready for a tea party, Mr. Upjohn? Are you crocheting a nightie, or is this a sea fight?"

A tub of grog was brought out and set exactly amidships, so there should be no partiality as between port and starboard fighters. The tension eased. All hands cheered when the grog was brought up. A dipper full of grog was served out to every mother's son on both sides.

John Dawn and John O'Reilly came bounding down the companionway side by side. They had been told off as liaison men between the wheel and the guns.

"Have the starboard guns ready, Mr. Snow!" shouted John Dawn.

"We are going to give them a broadside!" yelled O'Reilly.

"Load to starboard!"

Ten men ran forward with powder bags and shoved them down the gun muzzles. Ten rammers rammed them home, and leaped back out of the way. Ten pairs of men with balls slung in canvas hammocks between them then ran forward and rolled the pellets in. They shoved the waddings in on top of the balls. The guns swung around as one, ambled forward, and stuck their black snouts through the ports. The gunners sank on one knee and signalled for the men at the breech to traverse the pieces by means of the tackles. Ten men stood up at the touch-holes with their linstocks reeking and dropping blazing oiled rags.

A tremendous something struck the *James Dawn* amidships, between wind and water. A column of spray rose straight up and blotted out everything by the middle ports.

"Got us in the guts," said Fearing Upjohn calmly.

"Yes, we'll be shipping a bit of brine there soon, if you ask me," answered David Snow.

The smoke and the spume cleared slowly away.

John O'Reilly had planted himself at the foot of the stairs. John Dawn's stout legs showed against the morning sky at the top of the companion way. The men below were taut as oiled springs. David Snow waited with his arm up.

A great yellow squash blossom burst into bloom in the midst of the ten starboard guns. After it came a noise of twelve million brass kettles being knocked galley-west. Pieces of things screamed like invisible wildcats between decks, and bits of the oaken planks overhead came down in white splinters. Where one gun had been was a jagged bunion of twisted iron and a few smouldering rags. A man's head with muscles on it like roots on a radish lay quietly in the middle of the deck. It opened its eyes and mouth once, wide. Then the eyes snapped to. But the mouth stayed open.

"By God!" said Easter Toothaker solemnly, "they got the tub of grog!"

They had. The whole thing had crumpled in on itself in a litter of crazed staves, and the silky liquid was going across the deck in four wide streams.

"Well, blast them for that!" added Jim Doughty.

"More grog here!" said Mr. Snow very cheerfully.

Some portside men went to fetch it.

A man beside a good gun was on all fours. He seemed to be looking for something not to be found. He had a discouraged look on his face. Then he began to make a funny chirrupping sound like a sick sparrow. Another man bent over him and took the smoking linstock from his hand. The man on all fours did not mind. He went on looking, and suddenly buried his whole face in the splinters before him.

John Dawn's legs snapped together on the sky like a pair of pincers. Then his face loomed in sight with both eyes blazing like live coals.

"Fire!"

"Fire!" echoed John O'Reilly.

"Fi-er!" yelled David Snow, and his big hand smote his thigh.

Nine linstocks came down as one, and the nine good cannon bounced back in one lightning leap, and left a whole wall of fire beyond the ports. The ship staggered sidewise. The smoking guns ran back almost to the center of the deck.

"Continue firing!" John Dawn shouted down.

The men swarmed on the guns like frenzied, greased snakes. They swung them around. The guns were stuffed. The guns ran forward to the ports again, men pushing them from behind. They let out another wall of flame, and back they all lunged, men and all.

The noise was like being cooped up in a thundercloud.

Up on deck, John Dawn could see five men at the swivel gun, astern, firing under his father's eye. Between roars below and beyond, he heard his father's deep voice:

"—Men bunched by the mizzenmast——"

A long flash of fire by his father's knees. And the knot of men on the Britisher was not there any more at all.

They were close up on the *Warspite* now. The British man-of-war was alive with flashes from stem to stern. She looked like a corn-popper at white heat, and the flowers of popcorn were blossoming all along her. A brisk breeze was behind the *James Dawn*, and the ship was closing on the enemy fast. The British boat had no intention of running for it, either. She was pulling toward them on their starboard quarter now and pouring the iron into them.

A crack came that made John Dawn's teeth rattle in his head, and their fore-royal and all the upper foremast came down on the deck in a mass of rags and kindling. A thousand church bells were ringing in young Dawn's ears. His mouth was full of sulphur and dry as a cork leg. The deck under him was a box full of fire and fog. What bothered him most was the dust. He had never known a ship at sea could be so full of dust. It came into his nose and mouth and his eyes, and choked and blinded him.

The deck bulged up in a dozen big bunions of splintered wood. They were catching it. The Britishers were getting in two blows to their one. John's father brought his nose around right in the face and eyes of them, and then the other side of the *James Dawn* got busy. Long red tongues stabbed out from the ship's side. The smoke rolled out like a thundercloud, and both ships were lost from sight except for the stabs of the guns. The men on the *James Dawn* fired by the flashes of the British cannon. Then the smoke lifted again, and there was the British ship almost within a stone's throw.

The Limejuicer was catching hell aplenty, John could see that. Her mizzen was gone over her side, and men were swarming on it like bees over a broken beehive. Her forward deck was littered with dead sailors and tangles of rigging. She was smoking in two places, bad.

But the *James Dawn* was smoking in more places than John could count. Half of their sails were sagging masses of rags, and their rigging snarled like an unwound skein of yarn. They had only four sails whole. That was enough to keep them going, with this stout breeze behind them. They were headed straight at the *Warspite*, and catching it heavier every foot they closed in. Four blows to one, now. Most of their guns were silenced below. There were just a few stabs of flame here and there, keeping up the fight. The Limejuicer was all for coming close, but she wasn't coming too close. She was running on a tack that would keep her parallel to the *James Dawn*. She was counting on finishing her enemy without giving him a chance to board.

John's father beckoned him to his side. The noise on their ship was terrific. The captain put his cupped hand to John's ear.

"Go below and tell them to prepare to board. We are going to board her. It's our best chance."

John Dawn flew to the companion way. Just behind him, the after hatch lifted up and flaked apart into maddened yellow-jackets which disappeared into nothing. He went down the sagging stairs three at a time in a yellow dust cloud. As he reached the gun deck, one of the cannon on the port side blew up. John was hurled flat on his face. Men lay hurt and moaning all around him. In the mists he could see two men dousing a gun with pails of water to cool it down. Faces like negroes' leered and yelled everywhere in the terrible dusk that had come on since he last looked down here between decks. The heavy leg of a man was slanted across him, without any body to it. John thrust the thing off and got to his feet.

Fearing Upjohn was sitting on a water bucket with the white bones of his right leg sticking out through his trouser leg, where his knee should have been. He was holding a man up in his arms. John saw that it was Davy Snow. Davy's face was all chalk. His coat was dabbled with blood. He was hurt all over. John bent down to him.

"Wonderful," Davy was saying as he mopped the blood out of his gray hair and eyebrows, "wonderful fight, Johndy! Wouldn't have missed this for Timbuktu! Miriam'll be glad to—to hear what a—a—nice fight we had. Your Daddy will tell—will tell—her what——"

He slumped forward in Fearing's arms.

"Davy's gone," Fearing Upjohn whispered fiercely, "gone dead on us. What your father'll ever do without Davy I don't know."

"You are hurt, too, Fearing," said John.

"Oh, a scratch—a scratch or two."

The gun they had been dousing with black water blew up also. The second tub of grog rose on its bottom and came down over John and Fearing and the body of Davy Snow. The staves lay spread out like a fan. John tried to stand but kept slipping back to the drenched deck. He took hold of something and got on his feet at last. Only one gun was left firing. He couldn't see who was working it.

"Stand by to board!" he yelled. "Cutlasses and pistols! Going to board her!"

Two black faces grinned close to his in the smoke. John made out East Toothaker and Jim Doughty. But John's heart was heavy for not seeing the one he sought.

"Aye, Johndy, we are with you!"

Then Johnry was also suddenly there by John Dawn with a shining cutlass. John's heart leaped for joy. Johnry was safe!

As the smoke rifted a little, John Dawn made out Constant Converse rallying up what men were left and bawling to the men in the powder hold below, to come up.

They all crowded up the broken stairs. The deck below heaved up all of a sudden as they left it, and a golden explosion filled the abandoned gun ports. They felt the heat of it on their backs. John looked down. Where Fearing Upjohn and David Snow had been was nothing but a yawning hole trimmed with bright fire above the place where the powder had been stored. Goodbye, Davy and Fearing! His father would be mad as a setting hen to hear of this.

They stumbled through a wildwood of shattered yards and sails, toward the bow.

"Bit off more'n we could chew, this time," said Converse.

"We've got another bite left," John answered.

"Two or three," chimed in East Toothaker. "I'm going to slice me a steak or two off some British bastard."

"Don't fool away your time with cutlasses, boys!"

Constant yelled. "Here! Here are irons for you!" He tossed down a sheaf of whaling harpoons and stuck them up in the planking at the feet of Jim and East and the two Johns. They gathered the irons in.

The royals of the Britisher were towering high over their port in the smoke. All the rest of the ship was lost in the mist of the guns. Only red flashes showed here and there like steady lightnings.

Something came over John Dawn.

"Quick! Johnry, quick!" he said as he seized his brother by the shoulder. "Pap!—He may need us to help him ram her. Let's go aft."

He turned and raced through the ruins of the upper deck, and Johnry raced shoulder to shoulder with him. They got there just in time to see the stern planks lift up behind their father and see their father silhouetted against the terrible flash of flame that followed.

"Pap!" John Dawn shouted in horror. "Pap!"

The man was still standing when they got to him. But it struck John Dawn that his father was not tall as he had always seen him. He was low at the wheel. His huge hands held the spokes at the opposite sides, but his shoulders were as low as his hands. He was holding to the wheel for dear life.

"Take her, Johndy. She's yours now." John Dawn heard every word in spite of the roaring British guns. "Take the wheel. Right abaft the quarterdeck. Run deep—boom—your boom into wreckage there. Deep—deep——"

John had his father in his arms. All the strength the boy had known and trusted in all his life was ebbing out of the body he hugged to him. The body he loved. "Johnry! quick! Our Pap!—Our father is——"

And the other twin was beside John Dawn and holding fast to the man. The two of them felt the damp warmth lessening in their arms. The square head with its graying hairs eased itself down on Johndy's shoulder. James Dawn's eyes were filled with a beautiful smile.

"Good boys!" It was hardly a whisper. "Good boys—sons!"

So their father died between them, as their ship ran on in the smoke, in the course their father had set his wheel to, toward the British man-of-war.

It was Johndy who unclasped his arms from the dead man first. He leaped and got the rolling wheel. He bent to it with all he had in him.

"The damned butchers!"

He steered straight at the mass of wreckage of the British mizzen trailing in the sea through a rift in the smoke. He struck, and his boom went deep into the mass of sail and splintered wood like a pitchfork into a rotten pumpkin. His prow cut deep into the British rail and held. John let go the wheel, snatched up cutlass and harpoon, and followed on John O'Reilly's heels as he dove forward into the smoke. The ship's deck was hot to his feet as he sped the length of it, and every crack was belching smoke. He overtook his brother.

They leapt together into the tangle of men where the

survivors of the *James Dawn* had boarded en masse. The Yankees stood together, shoulder to shoulder, every man left who was able to move, and they moved like a wave along the British deck. Thirty-odd men, but they had their harpoons out in front of them, making lightning flashes in the smoke that swept forward with them from their own burning ship. They were blackened with powder, and their skins were filled with the yellow splinters of their own Maine pine. Their ship was done for, and every man-jack there knew he had to win another to go home to Maine with a deck under him. They cut and hacked and slashed, and they went on. They swept down the Britishers and roared ahead along the deck.

John Dawn spitted a blue sailor with his harpoon. But he had struck so hard that his weapon had gone into the planking, and he couldn't get it out. He had to leave it there, for the wall of his friends behind pushed him on. He whirled his cutlass over his head and went with them.

The harpoons did terrible business in the tangles of Britishers who stood up to them there. Johndy cut right and left and felt his blade hit everywhere. But new and sudden and unseen things came among the Yankees. There were spatters of flame from every side. Johndy's friends went down by twos and threes, and the feel of their shoulders tight to his was gone. He had more elbow room to swing his blade in. As he swung it back and forth, he saw Jim Doughty go down from a blow of a linstock from behind. It was odd, but he noticed things around him as though he was not fighting at all but only looking on. He saw a sailor's clasp knife lying on the deck with letters cut into the horn of its haft. A man's head was bobbing like an apple at Hallowe'en in the tub of grog by the mainmast. John Dawn could see how he and his friends were ending. East Toothaker was felled by a missile of some kind that came hurtling heavily through the air. Johnry got a slash from a cutlass on his left arm, slipped, and plunged headlong along the boards out of sight, holding his cutlass upright still in his right hand. Three or four men were still standing. Then they were all down but one beside him. It was Constant Converse. Strange that a man well along in years should outlast the young ones! Constant had his harpoon still, and he was handling it like quicksilver. Johndy remembered hearing his father say that Constant's harpoon was worth any other two when a squarehead was blowing ahead of a boat. Johndy could hear the harpoon whistle through the air. That was funny. Then he suddenly realized that all the sound of cannon had stopped. Just the click of his cutlass and the whistle of Constant's whaling iron. It seemed a long, long time. And it was deadly quiet.

John Dawn's foot slipped on the bloodstained planking. His head struck the wood with a great star of light and a small, inconsequential sound. But a haze came on him, and in the midst of the haze he heard a gun go. Constant Converse came spinning blind toward him, crumpled up, and came down on him with all his weight.

"There's a live one under the dead one. Finish him

off." John Dawn heard the words in a detached sort of way. "Pull that one off and get the other."

"Hold up there!—Why, it's only a lad!"

Hands were on him, and he was jerked to his feet.

"Spitting young devil!"

"That's the one that did for Clem Yeovil. He ought to be split in two for that."

"He's got a heart in him big as your fist!"

They were holding him tight. He tried every way to get free and find his cutlass. It was somewhere about on the deck. But it was no go. They had him.

They had Johnry, too, and they were bandaging up his arm for him. And there was Jim Doughty over there with his big legs spread out wide as he sat up rubbing the back of his head. There was East Toothaker and several others beginning to stir and sit up on the deck, groaning. There were a lot of friends left. They were all herded together, and there was a ring of British sailors walling them in. Somebody pushed him from behind into the midst of his friends.

John Dawn suddenly remembered. He fetched a great yell and leapt at the wall of Britishers. But he could not get over that wall of men.

A tall man who had gold lace at his sleeves reached out and took hold of him by the arms.

"There! my lad. Don't you know when you're beaten? You are a brave 'un, but don't you go and be a fool."

"My Pappy! my Pappy!—on the deck over there!"

"There's no deck there now."

John Dawn looked. It was so. Where his father's ship had been was only a high column of flame now. They were cutting the boom which bound the British ship to that flaming tower. The axes were going. As he watched, the boom gave, and the tower of fire floated off by itself on the sea. Above it, on a frail piece of wood right at the top of the flames, a bit of cloth fluttered. It was the stars and stripes flying at the mizzen still. It took fire, ravelled into nothing, and was gone.

Johndy let his arms fall. It was the kind of farewell his father would have chosen for himself, if he had had the choosing to do. The farewell in a thousand. The boy stood and watched the flame which stood up bright on the sea, without a tear in his eyes.

As he stood there, he felt something at his left side. He wondered what it was. After a little while, he remembered about the pewter cup his father had given him for his son in the years to come. It was safe.

XIII

"Any man who'd put cane sugar into a Dundee pudding where molasses ought to be would suck his grandmother's last egg."

"You may be a good gunner, East Toothaker, but as a cook you are small potatoes and few in a hill."

"I want to know, Jim Doughty, I want to know! I can cook vittles to put the whiskers on the bottom of your feet or anybody else's feet. And I'm not going to take any backwash from the likes of you. When I've got my arms up to my elbows in a Dundee pudding, I just soar! My Polly'll tell you so."

"You ain't going to have no Dundee pudding to put your elbows into for a good long time. I guess it will be when the robins wear boots before you'll get a sight of any more Maine cornmeal."

It was coming on sunset time. The blue shadows of the mountains on the port were reaching out toward them. The light was powdered blue on their faces and their hands as they lay in the lee of the forward hatch. Ten Merrymeeting men powdered blue on their faces by mountains far away from home, mountains unreal as something they might have dreamed about long years ago and were dreaming about again.

"It may be years before we see Merrymeeting Head

again, and you'll be a-snuffing a lot of ashes by that time, Easter Toothaker."

"Maybe so, Jim."

The sun was gone down past the unbelievable mountains. Long rays came up like reaching arms. The light thickened on the waves, and the ship heaved on into a tremendous lonesomeness. A single seagull was going home across the darkened waves. Far away on the edge of the land, a small white lighthouse looked a thousand times lonelier than they were. Forgotten on the shore of a dead land of lost mountains.

"Do you suppose we'll ever get back home?"

"Of course, we will. We'll be exchanged, or the war will end. We'll be home before you know it."

"You can talk, John Dawn. You are a young-one. You have all your years before you. Full of hopes. But me and East Toothaker here, we have our age on us, and we are married men, old married men."

"Cat's hind foot!—You are only twenty-eight years old, Jim Doughty, and East here is only twenty-nine!"

"But we have been through the mill, Johndy. Been married going on nine years. We've taken a lot of bumps, we have. And I have got a lump the size of a goose egg still on my knob. Thirty-eight days, and it hain't gone down one bit. I guess it'll always be there. Guess I'm marked for life. Peggy may not fancy me any more with a lump on my head like this."

"That's nothing, Jim Doughty. Look at me and my condition! You ain't the only one that got a crack on the head. I did, too. When it's a hot day, I can feel that saw-toothed break in my skull open and shut as plain as plain. You can stick half of your fingers right into my skull!"

"You are two old women. I'm ashamed of you. Whining over a few sore spots instead of getting up on your hind legs and doing something!"

"What on earth could we do, young Pantaloons?"

"We could take this ship if we wanted to and had guts enough. Take her right away from these Limejuicers, turn her around, and go back home all a-fluking!"

"You'd better stop up that leak in your head, boy, or some fine day your brains will run out."

"Honest, I mean it, East. This tub is lots the worse for wear. They are short-handed, and they got the gimp knocked out of them by the shaking up we gave them."

"Ten hands to thirty-two!"

"Oh, no!—You're forgetting that seven of the crew used to be Yankee fishermen before they were impressed into the British navy. I've talked with them. I know."

"By God! that's an idee, Jim! That's an idee!"

"Hist!—Shut your face to, East. Or the Limeys will hear you bellow."

"All right. Mumble it is. Let's have what you've got on your mind, Johndy."

All the men crept closer around the boy.

John Dawn's eyes were like candles lit ahead of the night coming on around them. He threw one of his arms over East's shoulders and the other over Jim's. He talked in a whisper:

"I've dreamt of it every night. The time is when we are all in the bunkhouse and the sailor brings in our biscuit and gruel. When it is not quite dark enough to make his lantern much good. In the thick light. One man for his knees and another for his arms, and then we can get the keys. Then the belaying pins outside, and we take the rest as they come. Get their cutlasses away from them, get their pistols."

"It's plain craziness!"

"It's Captain Jamie's kind of craziness, Jim. It is the old one speaking through the boy! His dead voice from the deep, Jim!"

"Tonight's our last chance. They are so near home they won't expect anything like it. It's our last chance. Once we are in Cardiff, the chance for our hornpipe is over."

"Cardiff?—How do you know it's Cardiff, young Dawn?"

"Because I've gone to school, Jim, and read maps. This is the Bristol Channel. That rock over there is Lundy, and the hills where the lights are beginning to twinkle is North Devon. It is now or never. The wind's right and ready to carry us back down past Lundy."

"We'd never be able to sail her, short-handed."

"There'd be the prisoners, Jim. We could keep some of the Britishers when we sent the rest ashore, and we could make them go into the yards at the point of a pistol."

"By the Great Horn Spoon! Johnny Dawn, I'm with

you! Jim Doughty, you can set there on your bottom till you grow bunions on it. I'm with Johndy. By God, but I am!"

"Wait a bit, East Toothaker. Don't you go to putting bunions on my bottom! Who's saying I'm not with Johndy to the last fathom? I am. And by God!—Johndy's going to be our captain!"

All the men took fire from Jim and Easter. They drew in their breaths and let them out again in a fierce whisper of applause. It took the quick mind of Johndy Dawn to fetch them up with a round turn in time.

"Move apart, men," John Dawn said in a matter-of-fact tone. "Move apart. Every yard-arm has eyes. We mustn't be seen setting on our eggs, or our eggs won't pip. Walk around."

It came on the round-eyed John O'Reilly that his brother was ordering grown men around as if he had done it all his life. He glowed red all through with pride.

"When I slap my left thigh, that will be the time to leap the man and get his pistol. You hog-tie him, Jim. He's an old friend of yours. You heard him say how he was the one that put the knob on your head for Peggy to admire. Every man of you jump when I slap my thigh. We'll have the ship in three shakes of a lamb's tail!"

John was speaking as if he was saying that the evening was a cool one.

The sun's glow was deep as burning embers behind the Welsh mountains. A chill had fallen on the world. A whistle blew. The men and the two boys fell into line along the forward hatch. A very shining and fine Britisher came down the line, looking them over.

"All right. Prisoners of war, to quarters!"

They poured down the knotted rope into the gloom below deck. The cover of the hatch was clamped down. They got settled. After a while, they heard the footsteps coming along the deck above them. All their hearts were knocking like hammers against their ribs. Johnny O'Reilly's mouth was dry as a cork leg. The hatchway opened, and the man with the lantern looked down. Once his lantern was let down into the place, they could see the stars out behind him. Then he put the lid down and locked it. They waited till his feet thumped the floor.

It worked like clockwork. Jim Doughty put both arms around the man. John Dawn caught the lantern lightly from his hand. The man opened his mouth, but Jim's big hand closed over it. In the lantern's light, Johndy could see the man's face and eyes working behind the clutch of Jim's vast paw. Easter Toothaker fished the key out of one pocket and the pistol out of the other.

"Easy, Jim!" whispered John.

But Jim Doughty wasn't being any too easy. He tied his dirty handkerchief so deep across the prisoner's mouth that John could see it only under the man's ears. He knotted the ends and tourniquetted the Englishman into a mighty silence. He hit him back of the knee with his knee, and sat down gravely on him as he fell. Once there, Jim felt over the man's eye lovingly. Then he drew back his right elbow and hit the eye with all the power he had in him. He got up.

"Take that eye," said Jim, "home to your wife, to keep the lump you put on my head company."

"Wait here," whispered John Dawn, "all of you. I am going aloft by myself to fetch down our Yankee fishermen friends."

"God!—Are you moonstruck?—You shan't go alone, Johndy!"

"Captain Dawn, you mean, Doughty, I guess. And I'm not moonstruck. I'll be back smartly."

The boy went up the rope like a young bobcat, unlocked the lid, and was lost among the stars.

After a while, sure as his word, John Dawn came back. Four shadows came down behind him and turned into men in the dim light of the lantern.

"Here we are," said the boy. "The other three didn't have enough gimp in their spines to come. But they've promised not to stand in our way, and they'll join us if we make a go of it. Sorry I was so long. But I had to interview one man and then send him on to talk over the others. And he had to take it easy because the Limejuicers were all over the place. See, men!—Our friend Mr. Wells here made a pretty collection of the trinkets the sailors had left around up there."

John Dawn gave out five pistols and three cutlasses. He had his pockets stuffed with handspikes, too.

"I collected these while I was waiting for Mr. Wells."

Everybody had some kind of weapon. Some of the men had two.

"All right. Now's the time!"

There wasn't any question about the order of their going. John Dawn went up first. John O'Reilly leaped ahead of Jim Doughty and was next up among the stars. The rest followed after.

They dogged the boy-leader. They all crouched by the starboard foremast shrouds.

The first Britisher went down like a sack of meal. They had his pistol while he was still falling. Then there were others that came along, and sudden voices in the dark. Spurts of fire made horizontal lines across the deck here and there. Somebody began to shriek and to call on God to help him.

John Dawn and his men worked aft. There was one spot where a great many of the spurts of fire started. John Dawn worked toward that. The tall British captain there suddenly felt a State of Maine bobcat strike him on his shoulders. This was an unusual experience for a British captain at home in his own Bristol Channel. He went down hard. The other two officers leaned over in the dark to make an end of the wiry bobcat so far from home. But one got an equally wiry specimen of the same make on his back as he did so. John O'Reilly went to the deck with him. Easter and Jim divided the other between them.

It was all over. Two dozen British seamen, with their blue coats mauled and torn, stood fuming and cursing low in the light of the lantern. The ship was hove to, her dark sails flapping. She was not going to reach Cardiff that night.

The Merrymeeting men hustled the British into one of the ship's boats. They saved out five likely-looking ones as men who might enjoy a trip back across the Atlantic and a chance to trim sail in Yankee fashion and have a vacation in Maine. Easter Toothaker was very particular about what one of them was chosen first. He picked out the man who had admitted he threw the oak block that had opened the seam in his skull.

"Don't you want to take your man along, Jim?"

"No," said Jim Doughty, "I want his wife to see his black eye before the bloom of it is rubbed off."

John Dawn stood with his pistol in his folded arms to see the boat loaded. When the British were all in, the new commander of a British frigate leaned over the rail and spoke to the man he had superseded:

"You will row away from us smartly, Sir. If you so much as ease up for an instant on the oars, I will make kindling of your boat with one of our guns. I've half a mind to, anyway, for my father's sake. But get along to hell with you. Good night, Sir, and goodbye."

The British tars leaned to the oars. The boat went rapidly off into the night.

"Well, Sir," said Easter Toothaker, addressing the new commander, "asking your pardon, but I'm as proud of your breeches as though I had spanked them into shape myself and you was my own young-one!"

"Amen," said Jim Doughty, "that goes for me, too."

"And now I'll get my elbows into that Dundee pudding after all, Jim Doughty!"

All the men cheered.

John Dawn opened his mouth to give his orders. But Easter Toothaker broke right in on him.

"We've got to have the installation first, Captain Johndy. Here you, Thaddeus Stephenson, go below and get what grog the Limejuicers have left."

So, in the light of the stars of British seas and a smoky lantern, the men of Merrymeeting stood up and drank stiffly, wiping their mouths as the bucket came around, happiness and long life to a boy of fourteen, just put in command of the first of his ships. They were three thousand miles from home. They did not know how in the Old Nick they were going to get home, with a ship shorthanded and out of everything including water. They knew that, if they didn't get out of the Bristol Channel before many hours, they would be shot down for what they had done. But they drank as heartily as if they were raising Merrymeeting Head and entering Merrymeeting Bay.

" 'Tain't the first ship you've commanded, Johndy. Remember the *Marjorie!*"

It was John O'Reilly who said it. He drank last, and he put his hand out to his brother. John Dawn threw his arm, in an uncaptain-like gesture, over John O'Reilly's shoulder.

"And here is my first mate," said he.

They held a council of war in the captain's cabin—the two Johnnies, Jim Doughty, and Easter Toothaker. Jim and East had both been made second mates. Jim was all for heading west as fast as wind and tide would let them, and taking a chance on making a wild part of Ireland before their water gave out completely. Easter said for Jim not to be a fool *all* his life, even if his education in maps had been neglected. They'd all die with their tongues hanging out big before they ever could get water in Ireland. He chose the coast of France as the better prospect. The sooner they got out of sight of the English coast the less likely they'd dance the hornpipe on nothing. He didn't want any Bristol cravat made of hemp, not for his. No, Siree! He allowed it might look well on Jim. He was for France. The French had no use for the Lime-juicers. The first mate said it was for the captain to decide. John Dawn said all right, he'd ship supplies and water in North Devon.

"Well, I'll be hornswoggled!" said Easter.

"You can kick me where my butts meet!" added James Doughty.

"Very good," said John Dawn. And he did so, albeit affectionately, as became a Yankee sea captain and as his father before him would have done it. "And now look alive, men. Tell off all hands. Fix the watches, and let's get under way."

XIV

It was coming on midnight when they cast anchor inside of Lundy. John Dawn had made a bee line for the only part of the coast of North Devon where a man could get a toe hold. He knew his map like a book. The place was only a small rift in the cliffs that went up high against the southern stars. They could hear running water, and smell the good smell of earth and cabbages and sheep. John Dawn, Jim, and East, and five other men, manned the boat. John O'Reilly was left in charge of the hands on the frigate.

They got the water first. That was easy. They grounded on a shelf of shingle some distance below the spit with the lighthouse, where they heard the stream coming down. In a quarter of an hour's time the casks were all filled and shipped in.

It was the meat that took them longest. They took a long time finding a place to get up the cliffs. They had to leave two men with pistols at the boat, to keep an eye on the lighthouse over the way, in case somebody got inquisitive there. Ready to shoot and warn the foragers to return, in case of have to. To shoot the coast guard, if it came to that.

John Dawn led the way on all fours. The others followed his white scut in the dark. He had not had time to try on any of his predecessor's trousers yet. He still wore his prison wear. It was lucky, for East and Jim and the rest found it easier to follow him. And he went fast. They barked their shins on unfamiliar rocks. It seemed as though they would never reach the top. Strange brambles they had never run afoul of tore their clothes. Jim got both big hands stung with something bad as a nest of Maine hornets. He swore fervently all the time. Softly, though, so as not to waken anybody's dog up. There were houses along to their starboard. They could make them out by a few lights here and there. They gave them a wide berth. How houses could hang on to such a devil-damned hill was more than Jim Doughty knew.

They got to the top of the place at last. It was the top of the whole earth, it seemed. They suddenly broke out on a spot curving up wide and vast, near the stars. A breeze lapped their hot faces. Even in the dimness, they could see for miles and miles. A dog was barking far away. They saw something like buildings, and began to walk toward them. It had been so long since they had trod on earth, they went very gingerly, with toes turned out and knees slightly sprung. And there was something that kept catching at their clothes and lined their trousers with pins and needles. Not honest Maine beggar-lice or burdocks, but something English and worse. East and Jim cursed every step they took, low and earnest.

The top of the night was wearing thin. A rooster struck up somewhere under the earth that seemed all so level. There must be valleys somewhere. Another rooster crew. It was coming close to morning. And morning was as good as death to all of them there. Everything had flattened out. They could not tell what way they had come. They had a vague feeling it was in a circle. John thought of the stars. The Dipper was over there. He'd keep it so. Under the Dipper somewhere was the *Warspite*, late frigate of the line and now a Yankee prize manned by a handful of Merrymeeting men, in the heart of Britannia's waves. On their port side it looked as though a vast city was burning somewhere. The fire was spreading. The breeze had a new coldness to it. It was coming dawn.

The men stumbled on. John Dawn had been taking the dim gray things that dotted the dark earth around them for ledges. They would have been ledges in Maine. But when he tried to set his foot on one of the near ones, it moved away with a husky groan. The boy put his hand to his belt and got his clasp knife. He threw himself on the next ledge and cut it under its smaller end. He held it stoutly till it stopped kicking.

"Sheep!" he called huskily. "Sheep! Get one, every son of a seacook of you! Quick!"

The men went for the gray patches. But the alarm had spread, and all the things were on the move. They huddled together and flowed into a point, and vanished, all but five or six. The men took after those. A bedlam of baas burst out. East threw himself upon his victim, felled him, and tossed him over his shoulder still kicking. Jim picked out another, but the gray thing started dwindling into a handkerchief, and when Jim reached to seize that, he ran his hands into something like a bobcat's mouth, only with longer teeth. His hands were pincushioned with unfamiliar thorns. He stepped back, got a start, and went through a whole world of thorns and tumbled free into a field full of the dim sheep again. The men still lacking a sheep came through the thorn hedge, too. They ran every which way. The sheep bleated like lost souls. The dawn fire was spreading and putting out the stars. The twigs in the hedgerows ran silver fire. A dust of soft light was powdering all their faces. There were hedges and hedges. Walls and more walls to climb. Low stone outhouses.

They each had a sheep now. The dead gray things dangled over their shoulders, and their blood dabbled down the men's coats in streams. They looked fearful to each other in the growing light. They looked like a troop of buccaneers, red-handed in crime. They had lost their bearings again, chasing the sheep. They did not know where to turn. The walls were closing them in quickly now. And high gables began to loom above their heads.

Young Captain Dawn led them the best way he knew. They came out on a broad road. A vast house with light at some of its panes stared them in the face. They were in a place where cows were moving, and men sprang up everywhere. The men yelled with surprise. The cows upped tails at the sight of them and stampeded. John chose a tack and set sail on it, the others at his seat. They came on a man bent over two great pails. He turned and saw them. His late tippling had brought him to this! A sorry end! He let out a yell and sprang. He tripped over his pails and went to earth in a billow of white milk.

They got out of the barnyard and out of men's sight. But the alarm had spread to the house. People were running about. The hunt was up. They heard a musket go. They heard long and quavering she-shouts of murder! murder! They ran into a new enclosure among cabbages. And there was a fourteen-foot wall staring them in the face at all but the one way they had come. Through a hedge, and it was flowerbeds now, but still that terrible wall around them. There was no getting over. They were trapped.

John ran to an arbor that might have a gate behind it. A girl came out of it and met him face to face. She might have been twelve years old. She had a white nightgown on, with little ruffles all over it. Her toes were bare, and they showed all pink in the light of dawn. It was almost the first thing John noticed, how pink her toes were.

The girl's eyes widened out as she looked at the blood-dabbled boy. But she did not scream or run.

"Who are you?" she asked in a small, steady voice.

"I'm the captain of a frigate," said John Dawn.

"Oh!" Her solemn blue eyes began to have a dancing light in them.

"Please, little girl, show us the way out of here." John spoke as fast and as calm as he could. "We have been stealing sheep. But we had to. We were starving for want of meat. We haven't had any meat since we left America."

"Oh, you are Americans!" The girl's voice was clear as a small silver bell. "Do all Americans look—look like you? And act the way you do? I suppose you have been killing my father's dairymen as well as his sheep."

Her eyes were the color of forget-me-nots, but forget-me-nots with the bright sun on them.

"No, we only upset one of them into a milk pail. But that was his fault. See here, we want to get out of this. We—we were prisoners of war, and we've escaped. We're desperate men!"

"I don't believe you are much older than I am."

John was taken aback.

"Why, I'm almost fifteen years old, and I command a man-of-war. I've been in two sea fights. And I captured a British frigate, and that's the ship I command."

"And now you've been captured by a British girl." Her eyes had gone cool, and they were brimming over with laughter. "What will you give me, young Commander, if I show you the gate?"

"I'll give you anything! I'll—I'll marry you even!"

The girl clapped her hands together, and laughed aloud. Then she turned and ran in her nightgown. Her nightgown billowed out like a big sail behind her. John ran after her. The shouts of men sounded somewhere close behind them.

The girl turned a hedge, threw open a little door half smothered in vines, and leaped through it. John and his men came out on a high shoulder of the earth. The land was bare as a tablecloth before them. It curved down in a mighty hill with bushes flaring with yellow blossoms all over its sides. Curled down like a seagull's windy wing to the sea. There was the whole Bristol Channel at the tips of their toes, light blue with the morning. And there was their boat, a dark pinpoint on the edge of it. A toy town with a toy lighthouse were close by it. The *Warspite* rode prettily a mile out on the blue.

The men bent low and legged it down the hill like rabbits. John Dawn turned to the girl.

"Thank you. That was a close shave. We'll be all right now. There's my ship. Thanks. Goodbye."

He held out his hand.

But the girl wouldn't take it. She danced three steps away on her bare toes. She looked up at him sidewise.

"Well, what about your promise?"

John's face went red as a beet.

"I'll do it," he said. "I promised, and I'll do it. We Dawns always keep our word."

The girl burst into laughter again. It was like a thin, beautiful little flute trilling there on the top of the hill, and it filled the whole bright morning. Then the laugher sprang back through the door. There was only the high blank wall.

John Dawn stood still as a young Merrymeeting oak tree for a whole moment. Then he came back to life. He turned and ran down the hill to the wide sea.

They got the boat off and rowed for dear life. A boat was making ready by the lighthouse. They were on the ship before it had gotten far under way. The men on board had the sails shaken out. John swung her into the morning breeze. They went away fast. John steered for the big cliff that stood up from the sea like a piece of onyx in the midst of the blue morning. There must be shelter there and a cove where they could hide out till twilight.

There was. When John had put the island between him and the lighthouse boat, he discovered a high-walled and lovely harbor. Not a sail there anywhere around Lundy. They put in close to the cliffs and hove to.

The day went by. There was no sign of pursuit. They stowed the water and salted down the meat. When it was twilight, and the stars were beginning to burn through the blue overhead, they worked their ship out to the harbor's mouth. A brisk breeze was blowing. They swung around Lundy and headed for home. A big ship built herself up astern on their port, and headed their way in the dusk. She had been patrolling the waters around Lundy and looking for them. They could see a white strip along her sides with chequerboard markings. A man-of-war.

They had the bone in their mouth, though. And every sail was bellied out full of wind—royal, gallant, upper-topsail, topsail, mizzensail, royal, gallant, upper-topsail, topsail, mainsail, royal, gallant, upper-topsail, topsail, foresail. The wind came merry behind them. The free Atlantic tumbled ahead of them. With starlit foam upon it. They made good way under the clustered stars. They had mutton and water. And freedom and the best part of their lives lay before them.

In the morning, the pursuing frigate was only a small square of a royal behind them, set like a handkerchief on the crinkled edge of the sea.

Next day, even that was gone.

John Dawn stood with legs apart at the wheel. He had his first deck for his very own under his young feet. He was headed for Merrymeeting. He looked ahead to dozens of other ships he would handle in his time. His father had gone to his rest under the Atlantic, the grave he would always have chosen for himself. It was cold down where he was. But he would never be cold while his son had the breath in his body.

John pointed his prow toward Maine. His mind was full of a girl with toes like apple blossoms under the hem of her British nightgown.

XV

At eighteen, John Dawn was handsomer than his father before him. In his stocking feet, he could look right over the heads of all the Merrymeeting men. He had the Dawn blondness and the Dawn blueness of eye. He was as good to look at as a Maine May morning.

He had got the long and narrow bones out of the Trefethen family, and their easy way of moving. But the iron in him, and the way he had of going at things as if he were the first person who had ever thought of being a man, he got from the Dawns. He was all Dawn when he got among the ribs of a ship that was making in the Merrymeeting yards. There wasn't a blacksmith who could swing a sledge as he could, or lay as many planks in a morning. It was a Dawn body he stripped to the waist and made sleek with sweat and sludge. He was up when the morning stars were still shining, and he worked till the evening ones were tangled into his hair.

He had never gone back to school after he got home from Devon. It didn't seem right to him that a commander of a man-of-war should sit at books with boys. He had made the frigate over into a cargo boat. For the war was over when he sailed into Merrymeeting, and no more prizes were to be had for the picking off the Banks. He put the cannon on the lawn in front of the Trefethen house. They made the old place look more like home.

Ever since the day of John's coming back, with the new guns on Merrymeeting Head booming and frightening the deer in the forest, all the free female hearts under Merrymeeting 'tires had been in a constant twitter. The Dawns mated young. Many a girl just put into her first regular shoes and stockings, and her hair put up, looked up at the gray cupola of the Trefethen mansion and wondered if she would have the task of making the rooms under it spick and span once more. The clapboards needed paint. The rooms needed turning out and dusting the worst kind. The rats and mice had carried on their housekeeping there a long time. After his wife had died, James Dawn had not paid much attention to anything but his whaling and his ships. He had lived in two rooms. The Trefethen place needed a woman there. All the mothers of young daughters said as much.

When the Rev. Ephraim Snodgrass, the minister settled on the community, gave his reluctant consent, in middle March, to a maple sugaring in the basement of the Merrymeeting Congregational Church, there was such starching of ruffles and primping of hair as Merrymeeting had not seen since before the War of 1812. Mothers herded their marriageable daughters to the place in droves.

That was the trouble with Ephraim Snodgrass. He was *too* settled, people said. He had grown into a round-bottomed man, and he had forgotten what it was to be young. It wasn't piousness. It was laziness, with him.

High time there was a social again and a chance for the young people to get to know each other better.

The ruffles gathered thickest around young John Dawn. He was a handsome sight in his tailed blue coat with silver buttons. The Trefethen in him, folks said, bigger than a woodchuck, when he was dressed up. The tails he wore were something to click a fan at. England was to blame for those. Tchk! tchk! Foreign ideas! Those tails weren't any more use in covering a man's back parts than two apron strings. Not real coat tails like the old-fashioned kind at all. Their fathers kept the weather out behind. The sons just hung these things on for looks. Vanity!

Hot maple sugar was poured over pans of new snow. It hardened into strings of amber that people could take up in their hands and bite into. Each man there was given a pan of snow of his own. Then the lady who filled his pan from her pitcher was his partner and sat down with him to enjoy the feast. Like as not, she had to be fed every mouthful by her supper companion.

Polly Toothaker was madder than a wet hen when Peggy Doughty picked out her husband and took him to a corner and was so helpless that she had to be fed the maple brittle the whole time. Peggy Doughty was too fond of sitting in corners with other men besides her own. Polly poured half a pint of red-hot sap out of her pitcher over Jim Doughty's knees. His hands were down there, and they got properly scalded. She felt bad for him, and she went and sat down by his side to make up for what she had done. Jim swore, for all it was in church. Not at her, but at his singed hands. Polly made him sit down where she could keep a weather eye on her husband. She had to bandage up one of Jim's hands in her own handkerchief. She did a fine job at it. Jim liked her doing it. He wondered if she hadn't better do the other one.

A dozen girls all tried to sugar John Dawn's pan at the same time. Little Susan Snow, who had such impossible carrot-colored red hair and *almost* a cross in her eyes, won the honor. She was that small, she got in under the arms of the others. As if a Snow could ever do for a big house like the Trefethen! The Snows couldn't keep ten rooms picked up, let alone thirty. All the mothers except Mrs. Snow were sharp as hornets all through the sugar eating.

They breathed easier again when it was time for the games. For John chose six different partners for six different ones. He went to Jerusalem with Jane Linscott, and spun the platter with Martha Giveen. He and his partner won every time.

Susan Snow never got John in her clutches again. That was some comfort to the other mothers. John O'Reilly got her in Going to Jerusalem, and he kept her all through until the bean-bag race. Of course, John O'Reilly was the next best thing to being a Dawn. People did say . . . ! And Captain James as good as said so, the way he had fathered that boy all the time he was young and growing up. But a back door wasn't the same as the front, the interested mothers all agreed behind their fans.

When the time for breaking up came, the mothers were in a high fever. It seemed like Hannah Chace. She had been bean-bagging with John. But it wasn't. It wasn't anybody. Of all the surprises! John Dawn didn't see any girl home. He took John O'Reilly by the arm, and he marched off up the hill with him and left the floor of the Congregational Church basement strewn with riven hearts. Still, it was better than his going home with a Snow!

The pussywillows by West Brook gave place to rhodora. The rhodora made way for fireweed. And the fireweed burned out, and goldenrod took its place. But John Dawn did not hang his hat in any Merrymeeting hall. He seemed to think ships were all a young man had to make. He was laying the longest keel ever seen in Merrymeeting. November saw it grow into a mighty hull. The masts and all up. And the ship was riding the bay, just before Christmas.

The snow came and buried the coast to the points of its firs. The snow melted down to mayflowers under the arrows of the geese. The brief Maine Summer came back, and all the hills smelled of sweetfern and bayberry. The maples caught fire one night, and the flames ran up all the hills. The geese came back in wedges that pointed south. The sky was spitting new snow, and the bay froze over.

But John Dawn, who had left Merrymeeting in his new tall ship with the breaking up of last Winter's ice, did not come home. The Winter wore out, and the geese came back high and hoarse, and John was still among the missing. Probably John was going the way so many Maine young captains had gone recently and would bring home a Newburyport young woman with him. And Newburyport girls were toplofty creatures. Several of the Merrymeeting girls took their eyes off the Trefethen cupola and got married. The Summer burned down to the embers of the goldenrod. The Winter came and went.

Then John Dawn came home with the first swallows from the bottom side of the earth, round the Horn, and by way of Boston. There were lights in the windows of the house on the hill, and talk of the big things John had done, in every house. He had brought home enough tea and teak and pepper to the houses on Beacon Hill to feather his nest for life. He was in clover. He could buy and sell all Merrymeeting. He could have any girl he whistled to. He could settle down and raise a family.

But John Dawn did not settle down at all. He stayed only long enough to overhaul his ship, and put in new sails. Then off he went, without a sign of a cargo, riding high as a year-old seagull and his new sails white as Sunday. He had never looked Susan Snow's way, anybody's way. He had boots to his feet that were bright and shiny as blueberries, and linen on him like Queen Anne's lace on an August morning. And he went off with Johnry O'Reilly and Jim and East and the rest of his crew as if women were nothing but the Spring grass under his feet.

Polly Toothaker was glad that at least she wouldn't have to keep her eye on Peggy Doughty any more nights.

If her man was gone, he was gone to a safe place. Heathen women, she thought, did not count.

It wasn't like the Dawns, the Merrymeeting women said, to turn their backs on the place where they had been born and raised. Perhaps it was the Trefethen coming out in John. The Trefethens had always been footloose. They had always been as much at home in Boston as in Merrymeeting. Perhaps John was going to settle down in Boston or Newburyport, or some other fancy place, and become a big-wig. It wasn't like a Dawn. Maine had always been good enough for them. And Maine women-folks. In the good old times.

That was the trouble, the Merrymeeting women said to one another, with this new business in China and Java and other outlandish places. Good plain Yankee men got toplofty notions and became too big for their trousers. Once they got to going to China, they couldn't get away from Maine soon enough. Wait and see, they said. John Dawn would make a bee line back round the Horn for China.

But John Dawn did not. When he had crossed the latitude that tips Nova Scotia, he swung his prow east. He took his men by surprise. But they got over it after a bit. They had sailed long enough with a Dawn to be ready to bring up among the seals of Baffin Land when they had started out after molasses of the Barbadoes. They put the change in direction down as part of their all having new duck trousers that shone in the sun and whistled when they walked in them. And were too stiff to sit down in easy. Every day, John O'Reilly, the mate of the *Merrymeeting II*, made all hands get down on their marrowbones and scrub the deck till you could eat a meal of victuals off it. Something was up. They did not know what it was. John O'Reilly did, but they might as well try to get blood out of a turnip as to get a word about it out of him.

There was something odd about Johnny O'Reilly this trip, too. He went around by himself all the time. All the fun was gone out of the man. Jim Doughty saw him standing at the rail, when he thought nobody was nigh, looking at nothing for hours. Especially around star-lighting time. Jim spoke his mind to Easter Toothaker about it:

"I don't like the look of it, nohow. 'Tain't natural for a man to look at nothing but the empty ocean like that. Something has got him down. He's low in his mind. Makes me think of the time I was sparking my Peggy. I was wobblecropped and off my feed for going on nigh unto a year. But Lord! She was worth it!"

"She was so, Jim!" said Easter Toothaker.

"Eh?—What do you know about it?"

"I was just expressing an opinion, *Mr.* Doughty."

"You keep your opinions till they're called for, East Toothaker."

They were so high in the water, from having no cargo aboard, that even the old hands like Jim and East were sick to their foot soles. There was a right pretty parcel of gales loose on the Atlantic that April in the year 1819.

They had their port or starboard rail wet most of the time. They carried a good deal of sail. Nobody like a Dawn to crowd on sail. John outdid all the Dawns before him. He wasn't happy unless every mast had sail, top, upper-top, gallant, and royal on, and all of them with a big bellyful of wind. There was wind enough and to spare, and mostly from astern. They fair flew over the Atlantic. Wherever they were bound, they were soon going to be there. The gulls could not keep up with them, and the Mother Carey chicks had to get out of their way.

One fine spanking day in late April, when the waves were running pure silver-gilt and melted copper in the sun, the watch in the crow's nest bellowed out, "Land ho!" The men poured up on deck. A high, square land was coming up ahead. In two hours more, they were between two high arms of land, and a fine bit of it was cutting up through the water dead ahead. It looked like a slab of honeycomb in the sun.

"That island looks like something you and me've seen before, Jim."

"Yes, by Gemini!—we have, sure's you're born! It's Lundy!"

"Well, blast me!"

"Oho!" said Jim Doughty, "and yon's the bit of coast where the pretty girl came down in her nightie and set us to rights and put us on our way that morning. Why, I'll be hauled through a knothole!"

Easter Toothaker smote himself a terrific blow on his wide rump.

"Ho! ho!—That's the way the wind lies! I might have know'd it, the captain being so spunky and sassy all Spring!—Well, bless her blue eyes! I forgive John making me wear pants that have pretty near made two of me. I forgive him the creases he has cut in my old keel!"

The word spread like a grass fire on Mast Meadow in March. Soon every man-jack on board had a grin on to the ears. Captain John did not mind. He was walking the rear deck like a rooster and eyeing the high cliffs south of Lundy to spy the dip in them.

The only face on the *Merrymeeting II* that did not have a smile on it was John O'Reilly's. It was sober and quiet, as it had been all across the Atlantic.

They swept to the south of golden Lundy and drew a big circle and tacked in under the high Devon coast. The breeze began to fail. The sails slackened. The white bone melted from their mouth. There was the white staircase of a town strung along the hill they had run down with the sheep carcasses on their backs. There was the lighthouse on the spit.

"Let go with the anchor! Stand by to go ashore with the boat!"

The anchor chain rattled down, the boat was lowered, and the men took their places at the oars.

"Down you go, Mr. O'Reilly."

"No, Sir. I'll stay with the ship."

John O'Reilly's voice was very quiet.

"I need you, Johnry. Come."

John Dawn's voice was very quiet, too.

"No. Three's a crowd in this business I'll stay here. Good luck."

"All right, Johnry. Sorry you won't come." John Dawn's words were said very low. "This won't make any difference between you and me. You know that. I've said so all along."

"Maybe. Goodbye. And best of luck."

Johnry seemed insistent on his having good luck. As if a Dawn ever had any other kind!—The young captain slid down the rope to the long-boat's stern.

Somehow or other, though, half of the heat seemed suddenly to have gone out of the bright day. For the life of him, John Dawn could not have said why. But the smile was gone from his face.

His eyes were as bright and shining as ever, though, as the keel grated on the pebbles of Clovelly Harbor. He took only East and Jim along. He left the others to look after the boat, fill the casks with water, and see to it that the boat should be ready instantly when he should want it.

Once the three old friends were alone together, John Dawn spoke out. He was as cool as though he were telling them about hoisting a sail.

"I've come over here after a wife. You remember the girl who let us out of the garden somewhere around here? She's the one. I've come for her. I don't know where her house is or what her name is. But I am going to get her."

Jim and East did not bat an eyelash. It was just what they knew he would say. It was just what his father would have said before him. It was just like a Dawn.

They went up the hill, through the gorse. The afternoon had ebbed as they had come over from the ship. Now the air was filled with a golden and silvery light. The hills had grown immense, and the twilight was coming down the deep valleys in them. Flowers they did not know the names for, yellow as pats of new Maine butter, stood out clean and clear in the fading light. There were violets here, just like those at home, a month earlier than Merrymeeting's. The sun was going down below tremendous mountains of lovely clouds. The sunbeams came level into the men's faces and powdered them bright so their eyes gleamed bluer. Some strange small birds had apparently gone crazy and were flying higher and higher into the high evening, and the song they were singing was falling down around them like showers of beads.

"Pretty evening," said Easter Toothaker.

"Yes, pretty as a paper of pins."

The younger man did not say anything.

They went silently through an evening air that was like honey poured out. Milder than anything in Maine. The sun had gone under the sea, and a star was standing out clear over the glowing west, when they came up to the place. They would have known that wall among a thousand. There was the door they had come out through. John Dawn did not hesitate a second. He put his shoulder against it.

It was locked.

"All right. I shall have to go up over. You wait here. I won't be long."

Five years meant nothing to him, or a fourteen-foot wall with broken glass set into the top.

The young man took hold of the skeletons of old ivy vines and went up over the crumbling stones as quick as a squirrel.

John Dawn stood alone among a smell of roses that filled the whole narrow evening between the garden walls. The roses were out in thousands, big with the evening, single-petalled, touched with dim gold at their ivory hearts. Their petals showered his sea boots as he stood among the bushes. The roses loomed all about him.

It might have been five minutes. It might have been an hour. But she came, as he knew she would come. She had on white again, but her feet were not bare any longer. She was taller. But for all the dusk, he would have known her anywhere.

She knew him as he went to meet her. He was sure. He put his long arms around her and kissed her. He kissed her for a long time.

"Was it long, waiting?"

"No," she said. "It doesn't seem so, now."

She was without surprise. John Dawn knew by these few words that she was the one in all the earth for him.

"You knew I would come back?"

"You said so."

He kissed her for a long time again. She was a strange and beautiful part of a world foreign to him. Softer and warmer than anything ever in Maine. Unless it was the wild strawberries in the salt marsh grasses of Merrymeeting. Wild strawberries he had tasted as a boy. She was the strange soft thing he needed as a man. She had been made for him. Under three thousand miles of deep and cold sea the strange life thread had run. It had brought them together now.

"Are you ready to go with me now?"

"So soon as this?—You do not even know my name."

"I know it isn't lovely enough for you."

"You do not know who I am."

"You are the one who is going to be my wife."

"Yes, I know. And my name is Ruth. And it's time you told me yours!"

"John. John Dawn. Of the ship *Merrymeeting*, of Merrymeeting Bay."

"What splendid names!—To live with, I mean."

The girl had not asked what he did in the world or who his family was. She had taken him at once for what he was, for good and all, for life.

They did not say anything more for some minutes. They began to walk down the path between the rose-bushes. It seemed the most natural thing in the world to them to step off so, side by side. Over them, the pale English sky deepened to violet, a night-jar zoomed, and the stars blossomed down the deep valleys of space until thousands of them were there. Homebound sheep bleated, meek and far away. The smell of sea-coal and Devon butter came up the hill and over the dark wall. Snug and safe and sweet English things the girl loved like life were close around her. But she was ready to go away to a new twilight and wild things she had never seen, beyond the hill of the ocean. She might never come home here again, but she knew she would be with a man who would be home and all to her, to the end.

"Are we sailing so soon?—John?" The girl asked at last, when they reached the end of the walk.

"Yes. Tonight. My boat is waiting near the lighthouse down there."

"Can't you wait to ask my father?"

"He might object?"

"Yes. Mightily. You see, I am his only child. And my mother is dead."

"Then we had better not ask him. You can leave a letter for him and tell him what you have done."

"But oughtn't we to be—be married? Before we sail?"

"That doesn't matter now. That can wait."

The young American captain said it as though he was laying down a law of life.

"But we will—will live together on your ship."

"Of course. On our ship."

It was settled. They were silent again for a while.

"Mayn't I take something with me?"

"Yes, you could pack up a few things. I can wait for that."

"It will be hard leaving these roses here."

"I will take up a slip of them," said John Dawn, "while you are getting your things together. You shall have your roses by your own door. Go now, darling. I'll see to the roses."

The English girl left his arms and walked straight to the door which led into the high house.

John took off his coat and folded it carefully. Then he got down on his knees and grubbed around a small shoot of the rosebush with his long fingers. In a few minutes he had the roots of it up and wrapped in a piece of canvas the gardener had left near the bush. He made a neat parcel, put on his coat, tucked the rose slip under his arm, and waited.

A silvery church bell began to chime far below, under the hill.

She had a good name, and she had a good courage. She was the one for him. To the end.

After a time, the church spoke up again. It told off the last of the English girl's moments at home, with slow strokes.

Then Ruth came. She was muffled in a cloak. She had a bag in her hand. John took it from her, and hove it aloft on his shoulder. He leaned down to her and took her arm. It was hard now to see her eyes, in the shadow of her hood. But John knew she was crying. It was to be expected. He did not say anything as he led her down through the falling roses. The petals showered their feet.

Just as they came to the doorway in the wall, the girl spoke:

"It is forever."

"Yes, forever."

It was hard to manage with the bag on his shoulder. But John found her face in the dark, and tasted her tears.

"I have your rosebush safe. Have you still got the key?" John couldn't keep the merriment out of his voice.

"Yes."

He heard the key turn in the wards of the lock. The door swung, and John saw the starlit sea through the square space.

Two shadows leaped up beside them as they went through. The girl started back.

"Meet my friends, Ruth. This is Easter Toothaker and Jim Doughty. Here, East!"

He tossed Ruth's bag to the man. But he did not give up the rosebush.

"Well, I'll be hornswoggled!" East Toothaker whispered to Jim. It was all he trusted himself to say.

They went down the hill quickly. They found the boat waiting. They all got in, and rowed quietly away in the darkness. They showed no light.

"Anybody bother you?" John asked of the rowers.

"The man at the lighthouse sent over to ask for our papers."

"What'd you give him?"

"I sent him over an American flag."

"Good!"

They located the lighted ports of the *Merrymeeting II* at last. They made fast. John handed Ruth up the rope ladder. Easter Toothaker followed with the bag.

"Where'll I stow this dunnage, Captain John?"

"In my cabin, of course."

East waited till he was out of earshot of John and he and Jim were in the captain's lighted cabin.

"Hell's bells!—That's what you'd call working fast, Jim! Phew!"

"Yes. It's the old Pappy in him.—God Almighty!"

"What is it, Jim?"

"Look!—Will you look at that!" James Doughty said. He was pointing his finger at the bag East was carrying. East looked at the bag. It had white capital letters on it. And they spelled out LADY GREVILLE-PYNE.

"Well, I'll be knocked flat with a feather!—John certainly picks 'em high!"

The captain had taken Ruth forward on deck, looking for John O'Reilly. He was nowhere to be seen. Nobody knew where he had gone. Somebody suggested he might have turned in below.

John thought that unlikely. When John O'Reilly was left in charge of a ship, he wasn't the man to lie down. Not for an instant. But John would go see. He told Ruth to wait on deck for him. He would have to make certain arrangements. In the cabin bunks. Now he had brought a bride aboard. Johnry would have to make up his bed somewhere else.

That would seem strange, at first. The two Johns had not slept a night apart since the time John Dawn could remember. It would be hard. It would be as hard a thing as John had had to face in his life.

John O'Reilly wasn't in the cabin. John ushered Ruth

into her quarters. He went back to hunt up his brother. He set all the men to search. They turned the ship inside out. Johnry was nowhere to be found.

John Dawn began to feel a strange something pressing into him and tearing him apart. He paced up and down with clenched hands and a queer coldness settling upon him in the night. It was time they were hoisting sail, if they wanted to be clear of Devon and trouble in the morning. But he could not go without his brother. A fear—such a fear as he had not known in all his life—began to creep upon him. What if?—he dared not let his mind go to the edge of that precipice. He began to remember how odd Johnry had been all the way across the Atlantic. What was it about their parting by the ship's rail this afternoon?—*Good luck. Good luck. Goodbye.*

Cold water commenced to well out of nowhere and flow down John's spine. If his getting a wife had led to anything so black as—! It was not to be thought of.

It was hours later, and the cocks over in Devon were crowing against the coming of the morning, when John Dawn in his pacing found himself back in his own cabin. Ruth was huddled in a corner of the place. He had well nigh forgotten her. Her eyes were deep with weeping. She looked up at him, knowing something was the matter. John looked down at her and couldn't say anything. Then he happened to look at the bedding at her feet. There were Johnry's clothes, folded neatly in a bundle.

John Dawn came out with a great sob. He threw himself upon his brother's clothes. There was some writing pinned to them. He read the words in the lantern's flicker:

Goodbye, Johndy. It would not be the same ever again with us now. I am leaving the clothes—which have always been your clothes. I am going my way. You go yours. I can make the shore easy, with no clothes on to bother me. God keep you. Johnry.

It was the first time since he could remember that John Dawn had wept. He stood there and sobbed before his bride-to-be. His body shook for a long time, and fierce tears scalded his cheeks. The woman could not stand it, at last. She got up and put her arms over his shoulders.

"There! there!—John!—Is it somebody you loved very much?"

"My brother," said John.

The girl spoke very gently:

"I have lost a father, and you have lost a brother, John. We will make it up to each other, somehow. I will make it up to you for the brother you have lost."

Ruth put her arms around the man and drew him down upon her breast. It was strange and quieting lying there so. After a long time, the man's tears did not flow. His heart came back to him. Lovely life surged through his body, and the rhythm of it rose and fell. John felt his life swell in him. He felt the woman's life beneath him. His rhythm began to be her rhythm. They gave in to the life in them tenderly and completely. And when the morning stars had begun to shine over Devon and bring day over upon the sea, John and Ruth became man and wife. It was the moment they would remember as the peak of all that they had ever known or done. A high, golden hill they would never quite reach the crest of again. And the hill would be lovelier always to them both in their looking back, because they had come to its top with their mouths full of the bitter taste of tears.

XVI

It wasn't until they were half way down across the Bay of Biscay that John discovered he was a husband to a real English lady. He didn't notice the lettering on Ruth's bag. He had wondered for some time what had come over East and Jim. They stood awfully stiff whenever Ruth was around, and they both kept putting their fingers to the tips of their hats in a funny sort of way when she spoke to them. John stumbled on the secret one morning when the *Merrymeeting II* was showing her keel to the porpoises and he trying to shave himself in their cabin. The room gave a lee lurch, and he went sprawling over Ruth's pigskin case. He looked at it hard, and then he whistled. He looked at the woman on his bed with wonder in his eyes.

"Land of glory! Do you mean to tell me you are Lady —what is it?—Greville-Pyne?"

"Yes, John."

"Why on earth didn't you tell me?"

"Why didn't you ask, you beautiful stupid. You never cared enough about me to ask my name." Ruth made believe she was pouting.

"I did, too. I asked. And you said it was Ruth."

"Well, I had to be Ruth *Something*, didn't I?" She broke out of her pout into a smile. "Would you have taken me just the same if you had known what kind of a tail I had on me?"

"Yes, of course, I would. But I might have been lots meeker."

Ruth burst out laughing.

"You meek!—Why, John Dawn, I've lived with you four whole days, and I know you haven't a meek bone in your body!"

"What have you got *two* names for?"

"It's a long story, John. Two families, very proud of their old Devon names. They came together, a hundred years ago. But the wife was a Greville, and she had the Armada in her family tree—and goodness knows what else—and she couldn't forget about it. She was bound you should know about it some day. So she stuck it on in front of her son's name. And so here I am!"

"Was that the Spanish Armada?"

"Oh, yes. We have the Spanish Armada in our family cupboard. Along with a lot of skeletons. You aren't the only man who's sailed ships, John. My ancestors sailed the seas when they were cutting their teeth. They sailed all over the Atlantic. Some of them are laying right here under us now, maybe. You didn't call at the front door of my house, or you would have seen six perfectly beautiful Armada cannon, all inlaid with silver, stuck down along the drive. A souvenir of the Dons. But it's just as well you didn't call at the front door, for it's likely you would have stolen the cannon. You stole about everything you saw. Our sheep. And me. Oh, yes, John. We've been great sailors in our time!"

"Well, I'll be hung up by the thumbs!—But I thought from the first time I ever laid eyes on you, there was something nice about you, like the sea!"

"Five hundred years of it. And we've got a Saracen, too."

"A Saracen?"

"Yes, the head of one—and quite a big one. It's dried and cured and still right in the helmet where it was when an ancestor sliced it off on one of the Crusades."

"You are jesting!"

"No. Cross my heart and hope to die! And we've got a ghost, too."

"No!"

"Yes, we have. Another man from Horns' Cross never got back alive from his foreign wars. But his wife grieved and took on so, he used to come back every year, at Christmas time, to spend the night with her. Farmers around saw him going across the snow from Horns' Cross, all gray in the light of Christmas morning. Their dogs would howl. They looked, but they could see no tracks in the snow next day. There's an old song someone made up about it:

'Who is it goes there in the morning,
When infant Jesu is a-borning?

'Who is it crosses on the snow?
The lover of the long ago!

'Tie the dog, and turn the key,
Cover the eyes lest they may see.

'God will not suffer the lady grieve
Under the moon on Christ his eve.'

That's the Horns' Cross carol."

"Horns' Cross?—what is that?" asked John.

"Why, our house, stupid! That's the name of it."

"And is your father a lord or something?"

"Only a baronet. Sir Robert Greville-Pyne. And I can tell you, he'll never forgive you for running off with me this way. He will shoot you on sight, most likely."

John Dawn may have had no meekness in him, as Ruth said, but he did act shy toward her all the rest of that day on Biscay. When night time came, she had to take things into her hands.

"Now, John, you needn't be afraid to come to bed with a lady. She isn't a lady any more, anyway, now she has married a commoner and a rebel. A Yankee rebel, too!"

Ruth asked about John's people, after that.

"Oh, they weren't any big pumpkins, like yours," John said. "They just made ships. And I'm aiming to go on doing the same. I built this one. For our honeymoon."

"You built it for our honeymoon?"

"Yes, that's why I took so long coming back after you. You see, it had to be a fine one. It took time. I had to make the money, first, to put into it. I'd have been back two years ago, but I wanted money enough for a first-class ship."

"John, you darling!—You are going to build a lot more ships, aren't you?"

"Oh, yes, and lots bigger ones. You'll see."

For the life of them, Jim Doughty and Easter Toothaker couldn't make out why John was going so far south before heading west for home, in a month like May. There was no call to fear storms now. When the capes of Portugal began to show up on their port rail, they wondered all the more. They rolled out of their hammocks one bright day, and saw a white city like a flight of alabaster stairs going up the blue hills.

"If that ain't Cadiz over there," said Easter Toothaker, "I'll eat both my boots."

"You needn't. 'Cause it is. Them boots of yours are safe, East. That *is* Cadiz."

"I'll be damned!—We are going home all round Robin Hood's barn!"

"There's no telling what a man will do when he's in love," Jim Doughty said, as they rounded Spain and headed east where the indigo of the Mediterranean spread out fanwise before them. "Look at me and Peggy. Look at us. We lived on nothing but flapjacks until the first baby came along and we needed something more rugged."

They were for the Mediterranean, sure enough. In a few hours, the legs of Hercules were astride them—Gibraltar tipped up perilously out of the sea, and Ceuta, a vast, single rock, upended from the deep, towering so high that the clouds swept around it half way down. It was the captain's whim to hug the shore of Africa here. They went in with their high sails under mountains in a dream, mountains made of precious stones, onyx and jasper and chalcedony. A painted land, like the evil tail of a peacock. Stark and quiet, not a tree, and not a breath of human life anywhere.

Except on one forlorn beach that ran for miles abreast of them under the mighty mountains. There was a solitary figure there. They could make it out without the spy-glass. Head buried in a burnous, long gray robe flying behind him like a single wing. The figure was running without a stop, keeping abreast of them. Bent on some evil purpose, maybe, rushing on with fierce power through that dead world. Like an evil angel with a broken wing.

"Sailormen say as how there's a road under us here," said Jim Doughty. "Right smack in under the barnacles on our keel, and monkeys come out of Africa and go over into Spain along it."

"And I'll bet my bottom dollar them varmints in the mountains over yonder know about that road, too. I shouldn't wonder if that one running along there now was looking for the hole!"

"Yes. I shouldn't wonder. There's bad ones enough in Spain," said Jim. "There was one woman in Cadiz in my Pap's day. He met up with her, somehow. You know how it is when married men are away from home. Well, he had a scar on his arm like a gorilla's teeth had set into him there. He said it was lucky he didn't have a piece of him gone somewhere else he could spare less. My Pap used to roll up his sleeves and show me that place. 'Jim,' he would say, 'Let that be a warning to you to give women a wide berth. That's what women will do for you!'"

They sailed for two days along past the Sierra Nevadas. Walls of turquoise and gold, lovelier than time, with only now and then a single lighthouse making a little star on the water's edge, as the night came on, suddener than in Maine, and covered over the whole high sky with stars that came out all at once.

"You'll always take me with you everywhere you go, won't you, John?"

"Yes, Ruth, we'll keep on as we have started." And John put his arm around the slender woman who was looking at the Spanish mountains with him. "It is forever."

"Forever."

They skirted the Balearic Isles, the peaks of some lost and sunken land, burning like tall bonfires in the sun.

"They say those are Circe's islands, over there," said John.

"I don't wonder," answered Ruth. "They look like pieces of the sun."

They put in at Marseilles. John fell in with an old friend, Captain Jeremiah Bailey, a Merrymeeting man, and sent home orders by him to have the Trefethen house put into shape.

"Why, are you thinking of setting up housekeeping, John?"

"Yes. Here's my housekeeper, Lady Greville-Pyne-Dawn."

"Well tar my sides!—Pleased to meet any housekeeper of yours, John!"

The Lady Greville-Pyne-Dawn met a Britisher at dinner one night.

"Don't you want to write home?" John asked. "Here's your chance to send a letter."

"No. I said goodbye in the letter I left. It is forever. I haven't any home now but you."

The American sea captain shocked the Englishman by kissing his wife right there in the midst of company.

They ran over to Italy, skirted the coast down through the straits and up along the Adriatic. Ruth had never seen Venice. She had said so one day in Marseilles.

"We'll go see it," said John.

John bought their china there. He had it made to order. They lived in a drafty palace that had seen better days, while the dinner set was a-making. Ruth caught a cold, and John had to nurse her for days. Easter Toothaker went home with a flower seller, and some complications followed. John had to go down and pay good money to her or somebody else's husband to get his right-hand man back. Jim Doughty went to some gallery of paintings or other, and he came home thanking his lucky stars his wife Peggy was not along looking at the pictures with him. It was no place for a Christian woman, and he hoped he'd not be called on to look at so many naked women again at one time.

Ruth and John went shopping in a little street that had all its windows shining with precious stones, and Ruth saw a necklace of topazes she thought were beautiful, and John went up and bought it on the spot. It took the English girl's breath away, when he did it.

"But, John, do all American men buy everything their wives want?"

"They do if they know which side their bread's buttered on. And if they have the dollars to do it with."

"But this is extravagance!"

"Not for Lady Greville-Pyne-Dawn."

"Then I'll have to be careful how I like things after this."

John paid no attention to Ruth. He asked the jewel merchant to let him see some rings, too. There was an ancient gold one with a stone like a star on an October night. John bought that.

When they were out among the pigeons of St. Mark's, John brought out the ring. He made Ruth put out her hand. He slipped the ring on her slender finger.

"There, now! you can prove we are betrothed, anyway," he said. He thought it was a great jest.

But Ruth fell very quiet of a sudden. She did not say anything for a long while. They had fed a hundred pigeons, and they had looked at the winged lions till their eyes were tired from looking up so much at the sky. The shadows had lengthened around them. They were in a golden dusk.

"John?"

"Yes, darling."

"Don't you suppose it might be best if we—if— This ring, you know. Aren't there Protestant clergymen in Venice?"

"No," said John Dawn firmly. "The place for us to be married is at home. We must wait till we get there. Maine is the only place for it."

"Then hadn't we better not go too far?"

"I have planned to have a good honeymoon, and we are going to have it."

"Where are you going after this?"

"Around the world," said John.

Somehow, it seemed to call for another kiss. And John did it right in the square of St. Mark's, with winged lions and pigeons and Italians looking on. Ruth had learned by this time not to mind. All the Venetians who were loitering there smiled all over their faces.

"The Yankees—they do not think twice. They are babes, those. Bambinos!"

"Eh, well?—but if the women are so pretty!"

John took Ruth out in a gondola. He hired two musicians. They quarrelled eventually, and fought. One of the mandolins was broken. The gondolier had to disembark one of the musicians. He said bad words. But the two lovers paid no attention to anything but the blue velvet sky and the nails of golden stars that held it up over Venice. The nails were so close that the two of them were all the time confusing them with the lamps on the quays. It was a beautiful night. Alien life sang and shouted and quarrelled around them, but they floated along lost in the tide of each other's love.

The china was ready at last. It had the Greville-Pyne coat of arms on it, all the sixteen quarterings. It took Ruth by surprise. John had ferretted out the thing somewhere without letting her know.

"Why, I thought you rebel Americans despised such things, John!—And what is that ship above the shield?"

"That's me," answered John. "That's us! Now and forever!"

And that also called for their going into each other's arms and staying there a long time.

When Ruth was packing the china away, John fetched in a battered old pewter cup and asked Ruth to pack that with the rest.

"Whatever for?—What is it, John?"

"The mug all the Dawn male babies cut their teeth on. Luck of the Dawns, you see."

"And why do you want it to go in here with the dishes?"

"For him."

"For whom?"

"Our son. He'll be with us, maybe, by the time we unpack."

The *Merrymeeting II* sailed back through the Mediterranean. She ran into the Mistral, and for three days she drove along with only the hurricane sails, and the next, with bare poles. Ruth was terribly seasick. John was, too, and that took the curse off it.

"I didn't know captains got seasick!"

"All the best ones do, darling."

They went back between the legs of Hercules. They put in at Tangier, and John bought Ruth a kashmir shawl covered all over with blossoms of the East.

"John, you mustn't."

"When you have a lady aboard, you have to dress her up like a lady."

The Bey's harem impressed East Toothaker immensely. He thought it might be worth having any number of wives if a man had such a robin's-egg-blue place to put them all in. Jim said East ought to be ashamed of thinking such thoughts. Jim bought Peggy a leather folder to put her receipts in.

After Tangier, they had nothing but the gray Atlantic for days and days. Easter and Jim could not believe their eyes when they saw they were not sailing west but south.

"By God!" said East, "John's made this a regular wedding trip. He's going to take his wife right around the old ball!"

John made all hands come on deck to see him jump across the Line with Ruth in his arms. Later on, nothing would do but they must touch at St. Helena. John took them all up to have a look at the Emperor. They did not get nigh enough to hail him, though East wanted to. There were too many walls to climb. But they had a good look at him. He was standing in his flat-fronted hat with the tricolor on it, right on a rock in a bed of geraniums, and he was gazing off into the empty sea.

"A great man," said Jim Doughty solemnly, "ruined by women."

Ruth was very quiet all through their climb up the rocky way and down again. John asked her if she hadn't enjoyed it.

"My only brother was killed at Waterloo," she said —"Robert."

"Bless me, darling, I didn't know. I'm sorry."

John made it up to her by being especially tender to her all that evening.

Their ship rounded Table Rock and plowed up into the Indian Ocean. Weeks of opalescent and level days went by. The lovers lived in a void, colored like a moonstone. There was no up and no down, no east, no west. Then a great storm gathered up at the north, or where the north should be. They rocked two days in a yellow and raving twilight. After that, more quiet days. Then unbearable heat, till the tar cooked and bubbled along every seam in the planking.

One day, Ruth came up on deck and saw the fairyland of her childhood picture books lying to their starboard. A blue, painted land going up into a row of flowers that were mountains capped with everlasting snow. Iridescent flying fish went along with them, and rainbows of sunlit spray. They landed in the heart of a rainbow.

Men and women like gorgeous dolls ran through cities made like flowers. The Javanese night came down on them sudden, like black silk dropped quickly. And were those fireflies, or wandering planets, drifting over the forests? Ruth heard thin and unreal music from the other side of the moon. Birds like splinters of the sun and flakes of the moon, singing songs like fountains running and bottles filling up with water. One day, Ruth and John walked into the country a long way from Batavia, and they saw thousands of the brown dolls, with the stringy moustaches of dolls on their lips and little straw houses on their heads, bending along ribbons of silvery silk among heads of grain looking like resplendent pearls. Showers kept coming over from the mountains, and they strung the sunbeams with glistening silver and green and blue and golden beads. Ruth saw a white bird fly over, and he had a little bonfire burning on his breast. The woods were like the woods made out of feather dusters at home in Devon. But she loved the kingfishers and the humming-birds best. The kingfishers were no bigger than a thimble, and they threw themselves like little live pebbles into the streams. The humming-birds were bobbins, flying fast and standing still on nothing, winding up the honey threads out of flowers that could swallow up a dozen of them. Little pieces of fire with diamond eyes. They were more wonderful than the paper birds, big as seagulls almost, which John solemnly told her were butterflies, not pieces of the sky and not blue tissue paper.

It was on their own deck, with the Javanese night around them and Batavia and the fireflies twinkling under their prow, that Ruth told John that their baby was on its way. John did nothing but hold her tightly to him for what seemed hours and hours. He said something at last. It was something low. It sounded as if he said, "If only Johnry could know."

They sailed from Java and on past Borneo.

Jim took his courage and his hat in his hand one day and went up to John on deck.

"John, could I have a word with you?"

"Of course, Jim."

"Well, it's like this. Me and East, we got to thinking the other night, and we says to each other, it would sure be a thing we could never live down if we was to put into Merrymeeting with not a bale or a box or a tierce or hogshead in our hold. We'd never live it down, John—not if we was to live a thousand years. Couldn't we just pick up something to take home?"

John Dawn laughed heartily and hit Jim a great blow on his back.

"I'll think about it, Jim. I'll think about it."

They put in at the Ladrones, and John filled the hold up with coconuts. Jim and Easter heaved a big sigh after the hairy things were all hatched down.

It was the open Pacific after that. Days and weeks went by until Ruth lost count of them. Some days they flew, some days they bucked the wind. But all the days were alike to Ruth and John. They stood or sat together and listened to each other's breathing and did not often feel the need of talking at all. Sun and rain and night and day, they swam through an everlasting Summer. They lived in such a holiday as they both knew they would never have again while they lived.

California's tail at last, and then the iced cakes of Mexican mountains. They coasted down Peru, down Chile. The heat let up. The skies clouded over. They ran into doldrums and stayed almost motionless for days. At last, they raised the bleak peaks of Patagonia, cold as New England charity, as Jim would say, bare and sinister, the brooding place of wicked gales. One night their masts dripped evil blue light from globes that appeared upon them. The next day, every rope shrieked with warning. A gale struck them. John had to be lashed to the wheel. The sea curved up into mountains. Hideous ranges ran alongside them. The ship rode poised over terrible abysses. The foremast went, and the forward hatch was stove in. The hens in the hen-coop there went off cackling their weak and warm little sounds into the immense waste of cold and ruinous waters.

And one of the men of Merrymeeting went over the rail, too, never to be seen again. John went about in the great hell of waters and tacked till black night came down on the chaos, in the hope of finding him. Then he gave up and fought on. Mountains of brine came down on the ship. And Ruth sat quiet in her reeling room, her eyes wide open and staring into the dark, and her ears straining to hear the men's voices between the roars of the storm. Her fingers locked and unlocked themselves. Now and then, she tried to pray. But she could only think of a childhood prayer. A slender and weak little thing sent out among the codas played by the organs of the storm. But she said it over and over:

> *"Four angels round my head,*
> *One to watch and one to pray*
> *And two to bear my soul away."*

It made her feel better. When the dawn came, it came with a clear sun. Ruth saw it rising through her cabin window, between great Andes of the maddened ocean. It shed a red light on their bursting sides. After the sun came, John came. His face was ten years older. Hollows scooped under his cheek bones, hollows under his eyes. He told her about the man who went overboard. Ruth put him to bed and smoothed him on the hair till he was sound asleep. She never moved her arm from under his neck until the sun had gone up over the masts and come down again and was shining between the waves once more through the small cabin window, but on the other side of the ship.

They got around the Horn at last.

An albatross followed them north for days and days. It hung over them on the wind and flexed no feather of its wings for hour after hour, riding like peace and salvation above their heads.

They put into a harbor that was like a harbor painted

on the backdrop of a stage. A dozen mountains coming up through the sea, a city like a white dawn, and a harbor deep blue under the shadow of the lovely, high earth. Rio.

John bought Ruth silks enough there to make her the gowns of three lifetimes.

They rounded Brazil, and cut through water yellowed by the great river a hundred miles out of sight of land. They sailed on through a sea that was green as the land with stuff like the grass on an English lawn. Over the Line, and John leaped back again with Ruth in his arms, heavier now, but still laughing.

One morning Easter Toothaker hailed Jim Doughty:

"I know one thing, Jim, and that ain't two. If Johndy don't get to Maine pretty soon, there's going to be a wedding and a christening right together!"

"East," said Jim, severely, "don't let me hear you talking this coarse again, or God damn me, I'll kick you in the sit-down and spoil your duck pants!"

They began to sail into a growing cold. Ruth remembered then. They were going into Winter right out of the Summer of the southern half of the world, into the midst of it. The waves became leaden. The days shortened in and in. The air grew bitter and bitterer. One morning, Ruth saw ice shining on the ropes around her on deck. It all seemed like a cloud closing over a golden day. It made her think how near they were to coming out of their dream. Strange people ahead. A strange, wintry place. Foreign faces. A strange new baby of her own. The holiday was nearly done. The loveliness was all gone. Nothing could come out of these dull skies and gray, chill waves and the hail that hissed sullenly into them.

She was in for a surprise. For when she came out on deck one morning, the sky was clear as crystal. The air ran silver, and the cold world rang like a bell. And there under the boom at their bow a shore was coming up out of the sea. It was all marble and dazzling pearl. It was quilted with snow, but it was fringed with trees cut out of green and gold lace, all powdered with the splinters of diamonds. Trees conical and even, every dazzling shade of green. Wall on wall of green trees till they faded into azure and gray and mauve. Green turned to azure, and the azure to silver again. Trees cut out of lace. Taller trees of a feathery green which turned to molten silver where the wind ran through their everlasting leaves, then to golden needles sunnier than the sun itself when the wind dropped. Tall trees like plumes, too lovely to be seen outside of sleep, etched on a lighter haze of forests beyond forests. High cliffs were lifting their shimmering heads as they drew in toward land. Where the snow left off, the rocks themselves shone white with granite. At their foot, in the tides' way, dead salt grass spread like a golden frieze. Gulls were flying like pieces blown off from the snow. Light and dark, dark and light. The sky was like a transparent enamel too bright to look at long. And every last thing there, rock and sedge and tree and hill, seemed to throw out a nimbus and bathed itself from its own brightness in a glory like that of the pebbles at the bottom of a clear stream of water.

Now square pieces of rock candy began to stand out among the evergreens. And there was one with a steeple —like those in England, only ten times whiter and more fragile than stone could be! A largest square of rock candy of all, at the top of a hill. Why, those squares must be houses! They had windows. People lived in such sharp and lovely things. People walked every day through such splinters of rainbows.

"John! John!"

John Dawn was smiling at Ruth's elbow.

"What is this lovely place?"

"Home!—Maine!—Merrymeeting! Do you like it?"

"Like it!—Oh, darling, I do. I do! Now I know why you are like what you are. Oh, John, it looks like *you!*"

XVII

ALL Merrymeeting was at the wharf that December day.

Peggy Doughty was in the midst of her mince meat, but she was there ahead of Polly Toothaker, who was all through her mince meat and half through her hulled corn. Peggy told the canary Easter Toothaker had brought her from the West Injies that you could never tell what monkeyshines a man who'd been so long at sea might be up to the first time he saw a woman.

All the mothers were there. They had to see with their own eyes before they'd believe John Dawn had gone farther and done better than he could have in Merrymeeting. They were all in a great twitter. They expected the strange woman would be dressed in some kind of outlandish gown and not take any notice of them. They were afraid she would be what they called "head up and tail over the dashboard." Hadn't somebody brought home word she was a duke's daughter?—Yes, Cap'n Jerry Bailey, he was the one. She might wear a what-do-you-call-it. Peggy didn't know the name. But Polly Toothaker did. A tiara. Cap'n Jerry hadn't mentioned it. But then, men never noticed such things. Peggy Doughty wasn't sure it was a tiara at all. Tiara!—cat's hind foot!—That was a foreign word for earth, the land. *Tiara firma.*

The *Merrymeeting* drew in on the flooding tide. Her

sails were whiter than the frost of the clear December morning. Seagulls swept down and circled around her square sails like a sudden snow squall. Capstans creaked. The anchor went down in a plume of spray. The sails began to crumple up into nothing. Husbands and fathers no bigger than dolls inched about on nothing high up above the people's heads. The wives held their breaths. The mothers and daughters lifted up their chins in pride.

Polly Toothaker slipped and fell overboard.

No one knew how. But she did. There she was. Her Sunday-go-to-meeting bonnet still tied primly under her chin, her lace still starched and dry. She was spouting water. She must have swallowed some, though her bonnet had not gone under water. Somebody threw a loose rope. Somebody else climbed down the legs of the wharf and gave her a hand up.

Peggy Doughty would always believe Polly did it on purpose. To make herself big in her husband's eyes, and make him coddle her. But she came out on the little end of the horn. For neighbors hustled her right away home for fear she would get her death a-cold.

A boat was lowered from the gleaming side of the *Merrymeeting II*. The captain was in it. And she was, too. The captain had his silver-gilt buttons all shined up. She had a dress on as wide as a sail.

Being Merrymeeting people, they all moved back as the boat came up to the pier. Only the small boys stayed at the edge looking down. They bent over so that all their elders could see were their narrow bottoms, tight in their long trousers. Nothing more of them but trousers. Some mothers gave little warning cries and half moved to snatch the boys back. But they didn't go the whole way. They were too much Merrymeeting mothers to do that.

She came up first. Captain John handed her up over the timbers. All the women caught their breath. Why, Cap'n Jerry hadn't told them that John had married a belle, a beauty, as well as a title!

But it was the whispered opinion of most of the women there that she was too much like an apple blossom to stand many Maine Winters. Such color in cheeks they had never seen this side of the May apple blossoms. They said as how people said the English women had good color because they lived outdoors all the time, their houses being so cold. It wouldn't do here. Not in Maine. People had to have a house over their heads in Winter.

They all stood back, silent. John Dawn came clambering up and stood beside the apple blossom of a woman.

"Hello, neighbors! We're back by the way of the Horn, and I'm glad to see you all. You are a sight for sore eyes! This is Ruth."

He patted his wife on her small shoulder.

There was a commotion in the crowd, and a shy breeze of a man came slowly forward, propelled from the rear. He had a paper in his hand. He unrolled it, adjusted his spectacles, gasped and swallowed his adam's apple once or twice, and began to read in a sing-song voice and as fast as he could go:

"Welcome home, O thou who hast
Done business in great waters far,
Home to Merrymeeting's shore
'Neath the chilly Polar Star!
O welcome, welcome home!

"Thy neighbors greet thee on this day,
Thou wanderer from a foreign strand,
And the tears bedim their eye
To see the native son touch land.
O welcome, welcome home!

"Thou hast gained a beauteous bride,
Fairer than—than the—the——"

The voice of Edward Stover, the Merrymeeting bard, gave out completely. His adam's apple wedged down hard and stayed. He managed to get out a husky close:

"O welcome, welcome home!"

He retired in some confusion.

Some of the older men went forward and shook hands with John very warmly and gravely. The English woman looked up and down along the wharf and smiled and bowed this way and that to everybody.

"She hasn't any what-do-you-call-it on her head at all!" whispered Peggy Doughty.

Peggy ran forward looking for her husband, and ran right into Easter Toothaker. He had to put out his arms to keep her from going overboard.

"Why, Peggy!—I'm tickled pink to see you! And here's one to last till you get one from your good-for-nothing Jim."

And Easter smacked Peggy before the whole crowd.

Jim came up, looking black as thunder.

"You ought to save your sweetness for your own old woman, Easter Toothaker. She can stomach it better. 'Tain't every woman that is strong enough to stomach——"

"Where *is* my old woman, Peggy?"

"She fell in and had to go home and dry off."

"Well, I'll be hung up by the thumbs! If that ain't just like my Polly!"

Peggy was everywhere among the men as they came ashore. But she was the one who first noticed it, for all that.

"There's going to be a little Dawn before two moons!"

"No!"

"Then don't trust me as have had my seven children. Look for yourselves!"

It was so. The word ran around among all the women without there being hardly a discernible whisper passed. All the women nodded their heads to one another. The men, too, became aware of it somehow. They showed it in their eyes. There were twinkles in them, and the small wrinkles puckered up at the corners of their eyes. So there was one more Dawn under way! Well, the Dawns were fast breeders. Fast workers. Look at James Dawn, before this one! Married less than ten months. Well, that was the way. Only trouble was, they never had many. That was the trouble. Their women didn't last. And the men were left with all their eggs in one basket. This John would be wise if he stayed right at home and laid the keel for a second heir. To ward off the Dawn bad luck. Died young, the Dawns did. Jacob, James, John. All J's—all hard luck. The Dawns died young.

Captain John marched home with his lady on his arm. All the Merrymeeting people followed after. Even the small boys did not run so far ahead as to get in front of the tallest man in Merrymeeting. John led Ruth up the high hill.

"Why, John!—Are we going to live here? in this lovely house?"

"Yes, darling. It's ours."

The old house on the hill was a shade brighter than the snow. Painters and carpenters had been at work on it. The broken panes were all filled now. Even the cupola gleamed with new glass. And the people of Merrymeeting had been on hand there. When John threw open his door with the American eagle shining on its square lock, every door in the house was open, every room was aired, and a fire was blazing in every hearth. Sprays of pine and wintergreen were hung everywhere. Ground pine curved up the mahogany rail of the staircase. The dressers gleamed with pewter scrubbed white with sand. Not a speck of dust, not a cobweb. The place shone like a Christmas tree. Every crystal on the great chandelier in the west parlor had been scoured with soap and water, and rinsed in two warm waters afterwards, and polished until it was a hardened little rainbow.

"Oh, John, this is lovely! I didn't know you had a big house, too! I didn't know there were such things in America. People might have lived here for a hundred years. I never dreamed——"

"Thought we lived in tepees and snuffed ashes, did you?"

John pinched Ruth on the lobe of her small ear. It was his favorite place.

"Thought your husband camped out in a bull-spruce, did you?—Confess, now!—This isn't Horns' Cross, but it's a house that's just as good. Even if it hasn't got a wall with a door in it to let sheep-stealers out!"

"And a key to the door."

"Have you got it still?"

"See! Here it is."

"Well, I've got the rosebush. I shall have it put into a big pot tomorrow. And in the Spring we'll set it out by the front doorstep. And you will have a bit of Devon to look at all your life long."

"Oh, John, you were so good to bother with it."

"You were so good to look down and smile on me, Lady Greville-Pyne-Dawn!"

"Dawn?—Darling, now we are home, we must see to it that—that I *am* a Dawn soon."

"You shall be, this week."

"But very quietly. Nobody but Jim and Easter."

"Not by a jugful, Lady Greville-Pyne-Dawn!—

We'll be married in the Congregational Church and invite all the town!"

"John, you mustn't!"

"Please, Ruth, please?—You are the captain here. This is your house, and what you say is law. Please let's have the town there!"

"All right, darling. It's no use trying to civilize you."

She went into his wide arms and hid her face on his shoulder.

"Isn't it good to be home, dear?"

"Yes, John—it's lovely."

They remained fast embraced a long, long time. Two young householders in the great, quiet, clean and shining house on the hill.

Down on the village street, Peggy Doughty was running in a bee line for the nearest neighbor's. It happened to be Polly Toothaker's house. She burst through the kitchen door, and nearly upset the tub of hot mustard water Polly Toothaker was soaking her feet in.

"Polly Toothaker!—She isn't married yet! And she going to have a baby and all! I wormed it out of my Jim. He was dumb-gutted about it, and didn't want to let the cat out of the bag. But I found out. Oh, isn't it scandalous! Such a thing hasn't happened in Merrymeeting since—since Betsy O'Reilly had her wood's colt and the tracks led to the Dawn house on the hill. Tchk! tchk! —Such goings-on!

"And did you hear?—Johnry—John O'Reilly has disappeared. Hopped right off overboard from the ship the minute John Dawn went to fetch this woman! Never hide nor hair seen of him since. My Jim thinks he's drownded. He says John Dawn was cut up terrible over it, it being his own brother, though left-handed, as you might say. John O'Reilly's gone for good."

"Oh, *what* will his poor mother say?"

"Mrs. Dan Holbrook?—Oh, she's got her heart and hands full. Her house is swarming with brats. She'll never miss one, more or less. One won't make any difference to her.

"Another wood's colt!—Oh, Lord, isn't it a scandal! Another back-door baby! Tchk! tchk!—And another Dawn one, too!"

XVIII

The wind had come up with the dawn of the late January day. It was a gale now, and all the world of Merrymeeting shook with it. The trees sang like strings upon a harp spread from the east to the west. Vast chords went past the house on the hill. It was bright weather, for all the gale and its flying clouds. The clouds were blowing out to sea, ten thousand of them, tall as ships and keeled over at their bottoms, racing all together down the sky but keeping clear of the sun. The snow was coming up the hill like dust of diamonds. The wind flowed sparks of fire. Out on the unfrozen bay, the waves ran like mountains peaked with snow as they, too, hurried out to sea and disappeared over the horizon. The sky and land and sea were one morning splendor.

A person could not stand at the window and look at the bright day for long. Betsy Holbrook turned away and rubbed at her sleepy eyes with the corner of her apron.

"Lord! just another such a morning!—and I was bringing the baby that made this baby into the world. I remember it just as well as if it was yesterday. And me that flustered, and the captain standing and shouting below and calling me trollop and everything he could lay his tongue to. The way men are when they're wanting a boy! Lord!"

"Do you think it will be a boy, Betsy?"

"Sure to be, Polly Toothaker. The Dawns run to boys. Never was a girl among the lot of them. Some men run to male. Nobody on the face of the earth was more he-folks than the Dawns. Johndy, his Daddy, has his name all picked out for him. He's that sure!"

"What is it?"

"Joel."

"Another J!—Do you think it will be a handsome boy, Betsy?"

"Bound to. Captain Dawn, he's handsome as the day is long, and Mrs. John's not short on looks whatever. And you know the ones made out of wedlock are always handsomer than the others. More gimp to them. Saucier. Arrah! they come into the world without as much as a by-your-leave, the love children!"

"But this one will be born in wedlock."

" 'Tain't so as he was started in it. Wedlock, is it?—Arrah! Locking the barn when the horse is gone, that's what I call it! Going to church with the cradle, that's all it is whatever! But by the same token, the lad will be the lusty sannup his father was before him. Spunky as tunket. Just as my own Johnry was. Oh, Johnry was the spit and image of his Daddy.—Oh, my poor Johnry! my Johnry!—The best boy I ever birthed. Dan, he could try for years and never do as well. My Johnry!—and he thrown away on the waters of the world, on the other side of the earth!"

Mrs. Holbrook burst into tears, using her apron to soak them up.

"You mustn't! you mustn't! Betsy! You mustn't take on so. What if the captain heard you and got upset, too! —You've done nothing for weeks but carry on over that boy. It won't do him no good. And you'll be down sick."

"I can't help it, Polly darling. I think of him out there on the waves of the world, in the dead of night, and he naked as the night he came into the world! Oh! he had the loveliest body! No baby ever had such a body as his whatever. Like silk it was, and strawberries and cream. Oh, dear me! dear me!"

She buried her big round face again.

"I should think Dan would get up on his ear. You taking on so over Johnry this way. A boy as ain't his own son!"

"Johnry isn't no business of his, Polly Toothaker. Johnry was before his time. It's no cause for worry I've given him since the day I married him. But what's before's before. You can't have all the grists that's run through a mill."

"Why I am shocked at you, Betsy Holbrook. I am! a married woman talking so!"

"It's the Gospel's truth. And it's no skin off your bottom, either!—It's never a string I've had on your pork, Polly Toothaker. I've never run after your man, as some women I could name. I've never gone night after night to Mast Meadow, in the Spring of the year, with——"

A trampling of feet sounded suddenly overhead.

"He's a-coming! he's a-coming!—Up with you, Polly!—Upstairs! Look alive!"

Mrs. Holbrook seized Mrs. Toothaker by the arm and ran upstairs two steps at once.

When John Dawn came down the stairs, he had a bundle in his arms. He went over to the southern windows and stood there with it. He took a deep breath and held it hard, and then he leaned over and uncovered one corner of the coverlet. He still held in his breath.

Betsy was coming down with an armful of baby things.

"Oh, Johndy, you mustn't let the light strike its eyes. You will ruin its eyes whatever! 'Twill be blind as a bat all its born days!"

"Betsy, Betsy!—Are you sure it's a boy?" The man's voice was not much more than a whisper.

"As sure, Sir, as I am of you! And I was the first in the world to see you before ever your clothes were on!"

The young sea captain held the cloth up and let the sun fall on what he held. A small pucker of a face, like a last year's greening in the apple loft. But the head that had it went up high over the ears and was as finely sculptured as John's own. The fine hair on it caught the sunlight on its curls, and each spear of hair was like a little curving rainbow. John had the hollow of his arm full of small rainbows. He did not dare to breathe naturally for a long spell.

"Yes," John Dawn said at last, to the day outside the panes and to all the world beyond, "it is a boy, as I said it should be. My son!"

The two small fists came up into the sunshine. The father's big hand closed over them and held them tight. The old clock in the hall beyond was ticking off the seconds of the new life John held. The golden pendulum of it passed back and forth at the opening. It caught the sun each time and sent a tongue of flame across the ceiling of the room beyond over the new father's head. Outside, the whole of Merrymeeting was filled with mighty radiances, and the moving towers of sifted snow built themselves up under the unspeakably white clouds.

"Isn't he handsome, Betsy!"

"He'll be blind as a bat, Johndy—that's what he'll be. Arrah! and then a lot of good his handsomeness will do him!"

"Isn't he a fine one, though!"

"Oh, he is, Johndy, he is! It's after you the lad takes. Like my poor boy I shall never see again. Oh!—" Betsy's voice choked with the rising up of tears. "My son! my son! My Johnry!" She collapsed into an armchair and put her head down into the new baby's coverlets and wet them with salt tears. She was too busy weeping to see what John Dawn was doing.

John Dawn was standing there as though he had been hit a tremendous blow. He was not looking at his son any more. His eyes were blurred, and he was looking away toward the line of sharp blue which was the beginning of the Atlantic. After a time, a drop trickled down along his brown cheek, hesitated, grew in size beside the man's nose. Then it dropped down like a single diamond falling through the sunlight and struck on the face of the sleeping child. The child twisted up its small face and began to cry in the middle of the bright morning there in the big house on the hill.

XIX

POLLY TOOTHAKER'S huckleberry pies hadn't turned out right. She had been so flustered over the noise of the pounding going on in the Dawn shipyard, while she was making them, that she had forgotten all about the sugar that should have gone into them, this Summer of 1830 being so pindling a one, what with a frost in June and another in mid-August, and the huckleberries not having had sun enough and heat to ripen in well and so needing extra sugar. No Summer so cold in the memory of living Merrymeetingites.

And Polly had had to fall back on her custard pies, and the sounds in the shipyard so loud all the time now, the custard hadn't got mixed enough, and so it curdled in the oven. She could have cried. She did not have time to. Peggy Doughty would be there with her tarts—her crab-apple ones—and flaky enough to fall apart in people's fingers when they so much as touched them.

The September sun beat into the kitchen and showed up the smudges of flour on Polly's cheeks and chin. Of course, now the frost had killed everything, the sun would be hot enough to roast a person. The clock ticked on, and the hands swept on toward twelve. Polly's best Paisley and her lavender crêpe bonnet were hung on the doorknob of the kitchen, ready for her to jump into them. The hammers were going like a hundred woodpeckers now. And people were cheering. The plop-plop of hundreds of horses' hooves going down the road with new merrymakers behind them got into her head. Voices came up to her through the heat. The heat from the brick oven was blinding. Polly's head was going round. She pushed the pies into the basket still smoking. She ran down the cellar stairs and fetched the raspberry shrub. *That* she could vouch for, she had been able to make that right. She'd strained it yesterday and set it down in the cool cellarway to clear. She gathered up a crock of her molasses cookies on her way up, to take the edge off the soggy pies.

Down on the shore of the bay, a half dozen men were bringing quahaugs and clams and emptying them upon rockweed heaped green on the glowing coals. Boys were up to their elbows and knees and dredging up new armfuls of rockweed. The men were piling that on top of the hissing clams. Already a fragrant smell of roasting shellfish was spreading along the shore.

People were descending the hill in carryalls, buggies, wagons, and carts. Whole families, from white-headed grandparents to creeping babies, were pouring out on the cropped grass. The fence along the meadow was lined with horses stamping at greenhead horseflies, and oxen were there, too, in their polished yokes, turning their great lapis-lazuli eyes on the crowds in innocent wonder. New vehicles were coming. The road for a mile was smoking with them.

Crowds of older boys had run wild and free of all

authority, and were swooping down on the tables and the baskets beside them. Women were crying out and shooing them away from the cider jugs and the baskets of gingerbread.

And over all, high up above the oak trees of the shore, the white ship that was the reason for all this gathering and all these heaps of food towered with sheer sides in the sun. Men on its decks. Men under it. Crowds of men with sledges and hammers and axes were cutting at the skeleton in which it had taken shape, smashing away blocks, knocking down timbers, and sending white splinters flying. Yoke on yoke of oxen strained and swayed in unison up the trampled bank with drags heaped with timbers behind them. Such *whoa-haishes* and *gee-haws* as one would not hear in a whole dozen of years together. Cries of men and curses and gruntings and commands. There were many men stripped to the waist and velvety with their sweat, swinging sledges over their heads and bringing them down on iron and wood. The thousand tons of honest Maine pine and oak stood above them, still as the ancient rocks. But it was waiting only for the tide of the year to come high, to make the first motion that would take it many times around the world.

Joel Dawn was very proud of his new velvet trousers. They were tight, and they cut him along under the keel and nearly made two of him. But he would have died before he would have said so. They had straps under his boots like his father's. And his coat had the same kind of silver-gilt buttons as his father's had. It was dark blue and had a collar which had started out white that morning but was getting to be gray now. The boy did not say a word to anyone, but he walked about where the men were the thickest and cursing the hardest with their hair over their eyes. He listened to them and curved up his lips and said what they said to himself. He walked the way they did. He was one of them. He looked up at the high prow over his head. It had a great cluster of golden oak leaves around it, and out of their midst rose a woman with eyes as sharp and bright as a fish-hawk's. She thrust her two breasts out against all the winds of the world there should blow. The ship's name was on her. The *Ruth of Devon*. In gold. That was his mother. It was the family's finest ship. Biggest ever launched at Merrymeeting. A ship Joel would sail himself some day.

Down on the beach, the men were dragging the smoking rockweed from the clams in clouds of steam. The chowder kettles were boiling over. The clamshell spoons were ready. The men waved their arms. Up near the cookhouse, a trumpet blew.

All the hammers stopped as by magic. The crowds moved shoreward from the meadow. The workmen poured along the beach from the ship. They came together, and came on together and closed in around the fragrant steam of the clams.

John Dawn had slipped his coat on. But his sweating neck showed bare above it. He raised his long arm, and all the talking and laughing ceased.

"The Rev. Snodgrass will ask the blessing."

The Rev. Ephraim Snodgrass, grown portly beyond all the soul-shepherds Merrymeeting had ever seen, raised his two arms as high as he could get them, locked his hands together, lowered his eyes, and rocked backward and forward in the flow of his emotion:

"O God who art the giver of every good gift, thou who holdest the sea in the hollow of thine hand, descend on these thy people gathered here today to glorify thee. Temper and refine their appetites, lift their minds above the corruptions of the belly, which are spread out here as a snare to the spirit——"

Polly Toothaker sniffed audibly.

"Turn their minds to the heavenly manna that never faileth. Fill them with the food of a contrite heart, salt and season their lives with wholesome tribulation and——"

"Make it short, Mr. Snodgrass, make it short." John Dawn leaned over and whispered loudly, "We want to fall to. The clams are getting cold!"

The minister made an end somehow. A roar swept through the crowd. Everybody pitched into the piping hot shellfish. Delicate mothers of model children seized the hot clams, tore off the top shell, scalded their fingers with the juice, lifted out the tidbit, raised it aloft smoking in their fingers, and dropped it into their mouths. And rapture flowed over their faces after. Men snatched up quahaugs, tossed them from hand to hand, wrenched the meat out, and threw the creamy shells with purple edges to the right and left, hoed into the coals and rockweed for more. Children burned their fingers and howled and danced for the pain. No one noticed them. Rev. Snodgrass had the biggest mound of shells around him. Easter Toothaker tossed a choice clam now and then across the embers to Peggy Doughty. He winked at her openly. The only person who was not eating much was Jim Doughty. He sat on his haunches apart, and every time East Toothaker winked at his Peggy, he ground his teeth and grew thundery in his faded blue eyes.

Everybody was in the clams to the elbows. Two or three women went about with pitchers of cool cider, and the eaters would stop and drink the burn out of their mouths.

After the clambake was a shellheap, the ears of green corn were pulled from the rockweed of other fires and downed. The cobs joined the litter of the clamshells. Then the kettles of chowder were taken off their fires. Clamshell spoons were doled out. Everybody fell to eating. Shouts from the boys announced the finding of the lucky bones from the cods' heads. People ate the stuff red-hot, bones and soaked crackers and all. The cider made the rounds again, and the people poured the amber coolness down their hot throats. The feast ended with doughnuts. The servers went about with the doughnuts strung on herring sticks, and slid them off two or three at a time into the eaters' laps.

The people rose at last and went back to the afternoon's business. The women and visiting folks to the long tables in the orchard, the working men to the ship. The hammers began again all at once. The steady lilt of iron on seasoned wood sounded over the meadows and the sea. There was almost the tingle of bells in the resonance of the tough timbers under the rain of blows. Men's voices between the blows, deep and vibrant as chords from cellos.

There was other music, too. Under the trees, on a raised platform, a dozen good men sat with fiddles and flutes and played as if their hearts would break with all the sounds of jollity under the bright afternoon sky. The gulls were frightened away and cut their circles higher and higher up in the blue, and they had to come at the debris of the clamshells at long tangents.

The day was drawing in. Joel had so much to see that his eyes were getting rounder and rounder as the light ebbed and the evening came on. Joel wanted to be with the men, and he wanted to hear the fiddles, too. He tried to divide himself between them. The lady with great breasts, who certainly did not look much like his mother, rode all golden in the light of the setting sun, high on the ship's prow.

Peggy Doughty had finished her work at the supper tables, and she had come close to the tall hull and stood in the shadow there to see the men work. Easter was there under her eyes. The woman's eyes gleamed in the shadow of the ship to see him swing his sledge hammer as if it were a jackstraw in his hands. Her husband was there working, too, but all the fire seemed to have gone out of his shoulders and arms. He rested his sledge on the ground often, and gazed straight ahead at nothing.

"I have told you for the last time, East Toothaker," he hissed the words out in a whisper, "I've told you to be careful how you plague a man. Talking of such things as horns and all. You can drive a man too far. You can drive me."

For answer Easter Toothaker brought his sledge down on a timber and made every fibre of it ring.

In the meadow, in the thickening light under the apple trees, the long tables were being set. A score of women were bustling about there. Stones held the white cloths from being blown away. Caraway cookies, angel cake and devil cake, pies, and doughnuts were being placed along. Platters of boned turkey, calves'-head cheese, pats of butter printed with homemade American eagles and clover leaves, cold roasted chicken, cider in jugs, spruce beer in earthen jugs whose corks were held in by bows of twine, lobster meat piled high on two-foot platters—red and white meat in the center, ringed with the green tomalley. Mashed potatoes, mashed squash, mashed turnip. Sliced beef, cold roast pork. Apples, green and blue grapes, pears and plums in baskets. Slabs of honey in the comb about which puzzled and belated bees lingered, drowsy with gorging themselves. Pitchers of molasses, and yellow-jackets on their lips. Women were shooing them away with their aprons. Slim girls were running to and fro with billowing skirts, bringing down from the house on the hill new burdens of dainties and substantials for the tables. Boys were bringing water in buckets and filling the glasses at each place. And the young men and the girls were drifting together and apart like some dim music of life.

The trumpet blew again, all silvery with the dew and the evening. Again the music of the hammers stopped in the middle of chords. The working men swarmed into the meadows, under the apples that gleamed golden on the boughs with the light of the setting September sun. The people in their holiday clothes came, the men in tall hats and with white lace at their throats and the women like the Queen Anne's lace through which they walked. They all took their places by the white-spread tables. John Dawn, the tallest and best man of them there, stood at the head of the longest table, in the center, and his golden-haired Ruth stood up beside him, Joel on his left hand.

A hush fell on all the laughter and talk. Ephraim Snodgrass asked the blessing again. His voice was alone in the midst of the millions of crickets saying their grace in the grass. As the preacher was speaking, the vast and fiery and flattened sun slipped into the spruce woods beyond Merrymeeting's waters. And as he came to his close in the flow of the deepening after-sunshine, the great full moon began to slide up from the spruces on the other side of the bay. It came like a globed lamp of the evening and began to fill the east with a light softer than light. The people stood there hushed at the tables between the two radiances, the eastern and the western, their hair and their faces were full of the day and the night. They remained quiet for a moment, and there was nothing but the crickets. Then a violin scraped a single chord. All the voices of all the men, women, and children suddenly rose and poured out a hymn between the sun and the moon:

> *"The years roll on, but there is not*
> *Shadow of change in thee,*
> *Great God, whose right hand holds the hills*
> *And left hand holds the sea.*
>
> *"The sun, the moon, the stars of night*
> *Bow down before thy plan,*
> *Who upon thy chain hast hung*
> *The jewel which is man.*
>
> *"Men build great ships, beget tall sons,*
> *And sons and ships decay,*
> *But ages hence thy sons will shine*
> *As now and yesterday."*

The hymn ended and went out over the sea between the day and the night.

Laughter burst out and took its place. All the grave ranks of men and women and children bent and broke as they took their seats at the tables. The dishes began to clatter and forks and knives to rattle. Shouts and jests filled all the twilight up. The people fell upon the food to the music of flutes and fiddles. The crickets were heard no more.

By the time the supper was drawing to a close, it was full evening, and torchlights were beginning to flicker and smoke under the trees. The launching men rose, drew in their belts, and marched back to their hammers and the greatest ship that had ever been built in Merry-meeting. It was the latest of the ten that had borne the mark of John Dawn, and it was the best. The men closed in around it, and went on with knocking away the last of the timbers that held it to the land. They loomed unreal and larger than life in the flare of the torches and the softer light of the rising moon.

Jim Doughty was standing beside Easter Toothaker, as he had stood through most of his life. He put down his sledge and walked away from his friend directly under a huge beam that was leaning already as it toppled over from the ship's side. It could not have been timed better. The vast thing came over slowly, but it caught Jim across the shoulders at the last and crushed him into the mire many feet had made. His body surged up once, and then crumpled flatter than life.

It was Easter who got to him first. The beam had slipped clear of the bare and broken upper part of his friend. East lifted the man up as he might have lifted a child.

It was John Dawn who got there next. He came out of the dark and took hold on Jim's feet, sharing the burden with East. They said nothing to each other, but they carried Jim away from the ship. The crowd parted and let them through. Even most of the people close at hand were still singing and talking. The two men went slowly toward the cook-house. Behind them, the hammers had not let up at all but went steadily on in the night.

They put him down on the floor of the cook-house. East put his coat in under his head to hold it up. The doctor was sent for and came. He looked at the man, while John Dawn held the torchlight down. East had both his arms under Jim's neck. The doctor did not take long. He got up and shook his head.

John Dawn got down on his knees beside his workman and spoke his name in his ear. Jim opened his eyes and smiled feebly at his captain. And then he moved his head side to side on East's arms just as the doctor had done. He knew.

John Dawn could not bear to see more. He put his chin down on his breast and went out after the doctor into the evening. But Easter Toothaker stayed there with both his arms locked about his friend's neck. He put his face down until his mouth touched on Jim's hair.

Jim Doughty was saying something in the dark. East leaned his head lower, and he could hear what it was.

"They are not worth it . . . women. . . . Not worth it. Breaking up friends."

"No, Jim, no!"

It was all East Toothaker could trust himself to say.

Outside, the work went on. Only a few people had heard. Peggy did not know. East's Polly did not know. John could not tell them, yet. It was best so. They had no right in what was going on in the dark in there, in the cook-house. Only a handful of the men knew, and they went around with tight lips. They picked up their tools and went back to work on the ship.

But Ruth knew. She came and put her arms around her husband in the hazy light of the mounting moon.

"Bad?—John?"

"Very bad. Can't last through the night."

"How did it happen?"

John told her in a breaking voice. East had whispered it all to him up in the cook-house when they first put Jim in there. John's own voice was nothing but a whisper at the end.

"You feel very badly about it, don't you, darling?"

"They were the best men I had. Always have been all for me, heart and hands. No one else quite like them. Somehow, they have meant my going ahead. Going ahead and up."

"But East is left."

"One without the other won't mean the same thing. They belonged together. Always, they were there together. When my father died. When you came. Now it may not be the same with me. They were—were—like a part of me."

But the tide was flooding and full of rising silver under the big moon. The tide could not wait. Men had to take it when it suited. John left his wife and went back to the last blows of the sledges. The hammers quickened as a man's pulse in a fever. As the moon climbed, they beat faster and louder.

The moon was at the top of its circle at last. A sudden dead calm fell. Men moved away from the high, gleaming thing that stood huge yet slim there, independent now, done with men with hammers, free of the last supports it would ever have except the ocean waves themselves. Slim and narrow because it was so high and fine. The crickets could be heard again in all their quiet yet feverish millions of night-long prayers. Men's work was done, but theirs went on.

The crowd closed in under the high prow. John took Ruth's arm, and they and the minister and the chosen few climbed the ladder that went up to the deck. James Doughty was not there. John's heart was heavy within him. His face was pale in the moon. The principals took their places. Ruth gripped the bottle of wine in her two hands. The minister raised his hand.

Down on the ground, right under the prow and the gilded lady on it, Joel Dawn was sobbing as if his heart would break. Nothing Polly Toothaker or Peggy Doughty could do or say could quiet him. He wanted to be up there beside his father. Up there against the great moon. He wanted to slide off with them on the beginning of the ship's ride to the ends of the world. His body shook with sobs, the tears stained his face in floods.

The minister's hand ran silver. His voice was small and lost up there high beside the moon. Then something flashed in Joel's mother's hand. There came a quick tingle of breaking glass. Joel stopped crying.

"I christen thee *Ruth of Devon.* And may God ever

guide and keep thee on thy way, through storm, through shine!"

A single, last sledge struck a clean blow.

Then the prow was not so near as it had been. The moon seemed to be rising up above it, slowly, but higher and higher. The earth underfoot began to tremble. All the people caught their breath. They gave a shout as one.

Up in the dark in the cook-house, Jim Doughty spoke his thin words quickly and clearly:

"Hold me up, East. I want to see. Hold me up!—Quick!"

Easter Toothaker raised the man till his eyes were level with the single window. There was light enough. White in the moon—unearthly white—the ship slid down in loveliness and struck the sea. Two long hills of pure silver curled away from it each side. Jim's eyes were full of that silver as he closed them for good and all.

A DREARIER day John Dawn had never seen. It was his ninth voyage in the *Ruth of Devon.* They had been beating down the Pacific toward the Horn since the year had turned and 1840 had come in. Three weeks of it, in a sea the color of lead, and head winds that came at them with the same insane clouds, day after day after day. They had given the Horn a wide berth, they had made the turn and gone up many miles to the north of it. They had seen none of the evil mountains which marked the end of all the land that led across two continents to home. But they had seen evil clouds. Clouds like faces full of threat bending down over them until they worked themselves into all the men's minds. Gray, dead gray. Nothing else in the world but gray.

They saw no living thing but the great albatrosses that came on wide wings, wider than any man was tall, came out of nowhere and hovered over them so close they could see their innocent, blank, big eyes like meaningless beads. They had shot the albatrosses one after one, as they came. They wanted to see how big they could get to be. It got to be a senseless game. There was nothing else to do. Nothing else to see. The birds still came out of nowhere, and they killed them, and measured them from wing tip to wing tip. Twelve feet, nine-foot-four, eleven feet, twelve-foot-ten. A kind of game.

It was cold. So cold that even walking on the lines and holding to the yards stirred no heat in a man's body. They had been forever on the yards, day in, day out. The winds veered and grew and abated, without reason and without aim. They had to be always on the alert. There was no trusting any wind for more than an hour or two. All the sails on all three masts, then only a hurricane canvas. Day by day the same. It had been days now they had been in the Atlantic. But the Atlantic was like the Pacific. The same tumbling mountains of dull lead. The same senseless albatrosses coming to be killed. More coming to be killed. And in all these weeks now, no sign of the sun. Not even the dull disk of it behind the clouds that rolled over them. It had got on their nerves.

It had got on John Dawn's especially. He showed it in his shortness with the officers and men. The captain's wife being the way she was, and never on deck, was a part of it. In his nine years as mate on the *Ruth of Devon* Easter Toothaker had never felt so low in body and mind.

The captain was part of it, too. He was always walking the deck and staring into the sea and the clouds. He was silent hour after hour.

Every bone in East's body warned him to look out for something to happen. It might have been different with young Joel along. But he had his own ship under him now. He was walking his own deck, just half the world away, on the Indian Ocean.

This particular day had been the worst of all. It had

been the coldest and dreariest. As it came on dark, the queer fires which sailing men cannot explain, and which always leave a mark on their minds, had begun to gather at their mastheads. Like sickly candles. Corpse-candles like those in the marshes of Merrymeeting, up over the shoulder of the world, another quarter of the world away.

East was taking his turn at the wheel when he heard it. At first, he told himself he did not hear it. But it was no use. He did. It was almost as if it was under his feet. He strained his ears. He could hear it through the doleful moaning that the rigging made. The moaning that had gone on for weeks till it had eaten into East's mind like a rat's teeth.

A cry of a person. Somebody in agony. There was no one nigh East. He felt his spine running cold water in the lonesome evening.

Then East heard John's voice at his elbow.

"It's Ruth, East. She's taken bad. She is in the beginning of childbirth."

East's bones felt a chill to their marrow. He might have known this would have to happen.

"I've got to have help, East. You've got to stand by me. You've got to come and give me a hand."

"Of course I will, John," Easter said. "Send Fred Davis up here and let him take the wheel."

When Davis had come, East went to the cabin.

Ruth was whiter than wax in the lantern's light. She was holding the blankets in great handfuls. Her forehead was beaded. The pains were coming close together now. Hardly a minute in between them.

East had never been within a mile of such a thing. Every time Polly had been taken so, he had put as much distance between himself and the house as his heels would let him. He couldn't abide hearing a woman in such a plight. But he gritted his teeth now and stayed. He hung the lantern lower. He got towels and water. John Dawn was more helpless than he was. John was all trembling thumbs. John's helplessness gave East the courage to go on. The bravest and clearest-minded one there was Ruth herself. She told her husband and the mate how they should do. Their big hands were trembling like leaves. They turned down the covers and exposed the woman's white body to the terrible chill of the close cabin. John Dawn worked with his eyes turned half away. East wanted to, too, but he did not dare to trust his hands. He felt deathly sick at his stomach. He had to keep his eyes on what no man ought ever to look at.

It was a miracle how they did it. One man with his eyes somewhere else and trembling like a leaf. One man seeing it all and trembling like a leaf, too. East had been present when his cow Brindle had had a calf one night back in Merrymeeting. That helped. Probably it was the woman herself who fought her mind clear of pain who pulled them through. East always said so.

There was another member of the crew of the *Ruth of Devon* at last. Another human being out there in the gray waste of waters. It was over. The newcomer was red as could be and yelled like a good one. It was gifted with good lungs. East was astonished what sounds could come out of so small a thing. The baby was lean and hard and long. A ship's baby, not fattened and blowzy with the high living of the land. And it, East proudly noted, was a he. East said afterwards that he could not have stood it if it had been a female after all they had been through to get it out into the world.

His name was Robert. Ruth had said so just before she had given up at last and gone down into the deep water of unconsciousness after the thing was finished. Robert, for her father, in Devon. And the brother under the shallow clay of Waterloo.

East could not help speaking out what was on his mind.

"Well, John, the curse of the Dawns is knocked galley-west at last!"

"The curse of the Dawns?—What on earth do you mean?"

"Why, you know!—The Dawns have always had just one son, and then they have got their going-home-a-crying, some way or other, before they could lay the keel for another one. Now you've got two sons. A Dawn has his eggs in more than one basket, at last!"

Easter Toothaker went up on deck into another bleak and sunless day. But the sun was out bright in his mind.

XXI

The sun was out in all its glory on John Dawn's forty-fifth year, stronger than it had ever been in all the sunlit days of his life.

He stood at his wheel piloting the *Ruth of Devon* toward the sweeping green hills of South Devon, with Plymouth Ho coming up out of the jewelled water to meet him. The Channel was blue past believing, and every last wave had a nightcap on. Ruth was beside John with her eyes shining under her wide, ruffled bonnet, and her sprigged muslin skirt was making her look like an angel in the breeze, and it was winding itself around John's long trouser legs. John had fifteen good ships knocking at the ports of the wide world this year of our Lord 1845. His son Joel sailed the best of them, one that put even the *Ruth of Devon* into the shade. He was at this moment taking on tea and a new fortune for himself under the snowy mountains of Java, directly under Ruth's feet and his own. His boy Robert was standing on John's other side in the first pair of trousers he had worn without skirts above them, slim in the legs, looking like a man. His curls under his cap were the only thing left of his babyhood.

A Yankee family, a Maine family, and a good-looking one! Rulers of the sea sailing into the port of the nation that had once boasted that the sea was her own! Columbia standing up to Britannia, a head and shoulders above her! Masts without a flaw in them and taller than any England could grow. Maine pines, bent forward with American sails!

Every man-jack on this ship—on all John's ships—native Americans. Natives of Maine. Many of them Merrymeeting men. You could tell the bottom of a Merrymeeting man in any port of the world. John Dawn could. It had a swing to it as it went along. You couldn't mistake it. You could spot one in most of the ports on the globe. British ships had riff-raff in their hulls—men of the Mediterranean, dark sons of Asia and India, sawed-off Cockneys not born to the sea, underbred men the mate and bosuns had to use belaying pins on. But the Dawn ships were full of free men. Every man-jack as good as the captain was and willing to prove it in fair, hard ways. Every man a captain or a mate tomorrow. Even the cabin boys. Independent, as Maine folks put it, as a hog on the ice. Taking no man's backwash, ready to sail in and prove his right to wear trousers with his fists as well as his mind. Every tub on its own bottom. Down to the smallest. Thrifty as they made them. Even the cabin boys had a share in the Dawn ships. John was no commander of slaves. He was one of his own crew. He was able to take off his jacket and do a day's work with the rest. He was ready and able to go into the yards with the best man that ever warmed his trousers with his work a hundred and twenty feet above water in a gale of wind. He did not save himself in any weather. He went where the knocks were the hardest. And he throve on them.

John had money enough. He had not touched one penny his father had put by. He had multiplied that sum by ten. He was the richest man between the Saco and the Bay of Fundy. He could buy and sell the Merrymans of Damariscotta and the Sewalls of Bath. He would double his fortune before he was through. He could quit sailing tomorrow, and live like a nabob to the end of his days. He would as soon have thought of walking to the stern of his ship this day and stepping off into an ocean grave.

He had land. The whole shore of Merrymeeting Bay was his now, and most of both capes that bounded it east and west. His yards covered the whole village front. He had the forests behind, to keep his yards busy. A thousand acres of virgin pine, untouched first growth, sleeping masts, waiting his word of command to march from their forest home and circle the globe wearing sails. He had a hundred men who worked for him on the land. Thrice that number on the sea.

He had the best house in Merrymeeting. He had added a wing to the house on the hill, and had done most of the original rooms over. He liked big rooms, where a man could breathe. He had torn down partitions. He liked a room big enough so a man had to shout to make himself heard on the other side of it. Ship's carpenters had carved him out mantels like those he had seen in fine London town houses, only better ones. A Yankee had a better eye for the lines of Greek columns and dentils and cornices than any Britisher going. He had had his staircase decorated with Greek waves flowing upwards to bed and love-making and sleep. Every room of his house was different in its woodwork. Shallow flutings graduated to suit doorcase or window frame, like those on Greek columns, key borders, egg-and-dart. The finest designs. His rugs had been woven for him in Antwerp and Bruges. His door-guards had been made from his own designs in gilt and blue in Rotterdam. He had gathered the best furniture from England and the Continent. He had English oaken chairs and carved dressers, French mirrors with laurels and eagles of pure gold, candlesticks of old Sheffield, vases of Carrara marble. His house shone with enamel and porcelain, silver, and Waterford glass. He had fine chandeliers like the eaves of a Maine house after a January thaw and a freeze. He liked things that caught the light of fireplace and sun, twinkling things that sent scimitars of light along the ceiling, that were reflected deep in the polished vistas of dark wood. Fourteen fireplaces, and all of them going full blast in Winter. The light of their flames dancing on the woodwork and in Ruth's eyes.

He must not forget Ruth's rosebush, either. That was a part of the house now. The rosebush he had brought from Devon had run like wildfire all across the front of the house and covered the high front lawn. He went home from the yards through walls of roses in June and July, blossoms that were a part of Ruth.

He had the ships. The best ships between Salem and Bristol. Better than most of those that came out of the Merrimac and Newburyport. Longer, wider in the beam, faster. He held the record from the Horn to Boston, from Liverpool to Ceylon. No dishonest work in wood or iron had ever gone into them. Only two wrecks to his name, and both of them no fault of Merrymeeting workmanship or Merrymeeting men. A China-Sea typhoon and a Mistral in the Gulf of the Lion. No ship of his had ever gone out of commission. Some of them had ports of England as their hailing ports, but they stood up high and proud among the best of the British ships.

His cargoes were the best. No common lumber or salt or coal. He did not soil his hands in coal, so popular now with many traders. It was sugar or Porto Rican molasses, pepper and spices of Borneo, tea and teak and mahogany, chinaware and coffee or wheat. He let the small fry dirty their hands with the cargoes that soiled ships and men. That smelled bad. Some of them were even carrying guano now, from the western shelf of the Andes, around the Horn, to Europe and America. Dirty stuff no Dawn would stoop to, for all the money there was in it.

There was the new academy on the hill next to the one John's house stood on. The Dawn Free Academy. He had given it to the town. His portrait was hanging in it. Dawn was a name known in the world now, around the whole globe. His father had said it should be, and John had made it come true. John wished his father could have known.

John had the sons. One sea captain already at home on all seven of the seas, and another one coming along. This slim lad by his side.

He had the wife. Ruth! Her cheeks as much like the apple blossoms as the day she first came into his bed. A wife who could still make a man feel like a man. A beauty and a sailor, too. Had been on all his voyages but one. She had kept house around the globe twelve times.

"John, isn't it about time to ease up and think about anchoring?"

"Bold water here, darling. Can sail right up into the Limejuicers' laps."

They were well into Plymouth Harbor. The roofs of the town, with a thousand honey-colored chimney pots, spread to the port and starboard. The *Ruth of Devon* was passing English craft within twenty fathoms, still at full speed, her sails big with the breeze.

John swung the wheel and set the trumpet to his lips at last. The men swarmed into the yards, the sails fluttered loose, slatted with cracks like pistol shots, and were clewed up. The ship's headway took her swiftly within a cable's length of one tall Britisher. They could see the color of the Britishers' eyes. A man with gilt on his cap bellowed at John:

"Stand off there! Do you want to sink me?"

"Not worth the bother," John bellowed back, "the rats and Toledo worms will tend to that."

"God damn you!" said the Britisher.

"Go to hell!" replied John.

He gave order for them to let the anchor go. The chain rattled out through the hawse.

Easter Toothaker came lurching up. He had his coat off, for the day was warm. His linen was not the cleanest, for he had been tarring some rope and had gotten pretty well plastered with it. He had some on the port side of his nose. And his seat was not what it had been this morning. His collar was open, and his adam's apple showed in all its glory.

"Ain't we at rather close hail, John?"

"Close enough. We can see what the Limeys are having for dinner, I guess," his captain answered.

A harbor lighter had come out from behind the Limejuicer. It had the ensign of the Royal Navy flying at its stern. It drew alongside the *Ruth*. An officer all shining boots and buttons and white ducks came up smartly on the ladder which had been let down at his whistle. John was talking to his wife and pointing out the spire of a church to her. East was slouched at the starboard rail, not paying much attention to the craft boarding him.

The resplendent officer, glittering like the rainbow, clicked the heels of his polished boots.

"Who's in command here, my man?"

"Well, I sort of guess I be," said East. He had not moved from the rail. It was lazy weather. "You see, I'm the mate."

"That's no way to address an officer. Stand up and salute, you Yankee lubber, or I'll have you taken before the port officer for contempt! Your clothes are dirtier than—"

The sentence was never finished. In the midst of it, John Dawn, who had come up quietly, took a huge handful of the Britisher's trousers' seat, lifted him aloft, and threw him bodily into Plymouth Harbor.

"Why, John darling!" cried Ruth.

The officer did not come back aboard. He went away in the lighter.

Within an hour's time, John was haled before the port officer. The man was a full-fledged rear-admiral, and he looked it and dressed the part, and he said so, too.

"I want you to apologize, Sir, to my lieutenant for your outrageous conduct this afternoon."

"And I want to tell you, Sir, that I'll be damned if I, my mate, or any other Yankee on my ship will apologize to any God-damned Limejuicer alive!"

"Are you aware that I can put you in irons for what you have said to me here in a British port?"

"Are you aware, you and your upstart lieutenant, that the deck of my ship is part of the United States of America, and that I and my men will do as we please on it? And we will not be insulted by any Britisher there. We will throw any man who speaks to us as your lieutenant did into the sea every time. I'll not apologize to you or anybody else, not even your King himself, for throwing any son of a —— overboard who dares to criticize my men or my ways on my own ship!"

The admiral was a rather stout man inclined towards the apoplectic type. He very nearly strangled in his rage. He got purple in the face and could not utter a word.

John Dawn saluted.

"Good day, Sir. And damn the lot of you!"

He turned on his heel, went out of the building, and down over the cobblestones to his waiting boat. Nobody laid hands on him.

"Well, how'd you make out with the admiral, John?" was the first thing East Toothaker asked.

"Fine," said Captain Dawn. "I cussed him up into a little peak, and then cussed the peak off."

When they got back to the ship, the big Britisher that was so close to them had upped anchor and gone.

"She's going to give you a wide berth, John. She's gone and put the Channel between her and you!"

There was a shining dinner that night, at the Blue Boar in Ship Street. Ten Yankee captains—and all Maine men—who happened to be in port that Spring day sat down in the candlelight to the pewter-covered platters. The other nine captains were full of John's adventure with Sir Montagu Rodney, the British admiral. Word had got around. It was all over the streets of Plymouth. The Yankee ships in the roads had pealed with laughter all the afternoon long. The captains drank Ruth's health, and the healths of the three other wives present, in sixty-year-old port. They ate the best of three muttons, five pullets, twenty pounds of sausage, and a whole Cheddar cheese. They talked about nothing but Maine and the broiled-live lobsters there, the venison, baked beans, Indian pudding, and blueberry pies there. And they talked about Maine ships that could outsail, outgale, and outcarry anything any Britisher ever could make.

"My wife was a benighted Britisher," said John Dawn, "but she saw her mistake in time and married me."

They all roared and drank another health to Ruth. They said goodbye, a good run home, and promised to see one another soon on God's side of the sea.

"John darling?" Ruth whispered in bed that night.

John came out of the beginning of a lovely dream of a field of Maine daisies blowing in a June wind.

"I know what it is you want, darling. Now we're so close to what was your home once, you are wondering if we couldn't go up and see the place. Well, we will. I've arranged it all. I've even written to Sir Robert. The coach I've engaged will be at the quay at seven o'clock tomorrow morning."

Ruth went to sleep with her eyes full of tears. And she dreamt of nothing but a field of Devon bluebells looking like smoke under the trees.

John was as good as his word. The coach was there waiting when they landed in the morning. It was a coach to dream about, too. It had a sun painted on it. It had made John think of the Luck of the Dawns now down under the globe in Joel's sea chest under the Line. That was why John had picked it out. The coach was upholstered in gray velvet, to match the gray gown he knew Ruth would be wearing. There were postillions, too, and one had a silver horn as long as himself. The coachman had a pheasant's feather in his tall beaver and a face like a raw beefsteak. He handled the leather ribbons like strings on a violin. He was, as John put it, a daisy. When Ruth wondered about all the splendor of the equipage, John confessed he had had to have the coachman and the postillions ordered specially from Exeter, and he had sent specifications weeks ahead of their leaving Merrymeeting! He had set his heart on light blue coats and pearl-colored breeches, and white pearl buttons, for the men on the coach. They had had to have the breeches made up to his order in Exeter. There was nothing so gorgeous in Plymouth. And wouldn't it cost them a fearful lot, Ruth wondered? Cost be damned, said John, nothing was too good for the prodigal daughter returning to eat husks at her father's! And, anyway, it was their second honeymoon. It was the best coach in southwest England. He had insisted on its being that. They were going to Horns' Cross in style.

John himself had on his very best bib and tucker. The shaggy blue coat with the double row of gold buttons and a cravat that was like a pear tree full-blossomed in the moonlight. Young Robert was dressed for the occasion, too, in gray velvet trousers, and he even had a diminutive beaver John had gotten at the best haberdasher's in Plymouth. Where the admiral of the port, Sir Montagu

Rodney, always bought his, John added with a twinkle in both eyes.

They had breakfast at an inn two miles out of town. It had been ordered the day before. It was kidneys and kippered haddock, marmalade, and Devon strawberries and clotted cream. Then they took the highroad up the hills and away. The postillion with the horn played Irish jigs by the hundreds till the high woods by the way and the sleepy combes of Devon echoed with them. Farmers' boys came running out and followed the coach for a mile at a time, their fat British buttocks straining their flannel breeches and their cheeks like the sunny side of a Sheldon pear. Robert crowed with joy and waved to them. And John threw them big English pennies every so often to keep them coming. He had thought to get a pocketful for the occasion. He threw them out some with the American eagle on them, too. And they whooped at that and ran an extra mile in the hopes to get a tomahawk or something. Plowmen dropped their plow handles and came running to the road to see them go by. They plucked their damp forelocks to John and his lady. Just as if John were a duke, John said. Robert's eyes were like saucers, and he danced up and down in the coach most of the way. He was half out of the window a dozen times, and his father had to take him by the full of his seat to save him from going out altogether.

There was a change of horses in the forenoon, and another in the afternoon. Everything was ready for them everywhere. John had seen to that.

They came out at last on the long backbone of the whole world and saw the shining Bristol Channel between them and the westering sun. There was Lundy like an emerald some giant had carelessly dropped on the blue floor of the sea. The hill swept down. There were the elms with rooks in them. The square church tower with the spire on top. There were the red chimneys of Horns' Cross. Ruth leaned hard on John's shoulder and wept like a child.

The Horns' Cross hostlers took charge of the coach and horses. It was evident that they were expected. All the outdoor servants were gathered by the walk. Ruth ran from old friend to old friend, and there were pluckings of forelocks without end. John looked for the dairyman he had upset into the milk, but did not spy him. Inside, John shook hands with the butler and slapped him on the back, half mistaking him, maybe, in the confusion, of being Sir Robert himself. The butler blushed for the second time in his life—the first having been on his wedding night. They were ushered, not into a downstairs room, but into an upstairs one.

As they went into the great room, John saw between the tall mullioned windows a huge bed, and on the bed was a man who looked like an oil painting—a very old and fine one. His face was pale as a waxwork. But his eyes were full of a deep fire. They never moved off John's from the instant John entered the room. They followed him as he crossed it.

Ruth went to her knees beside the bed with a low cry.

She seized the waxen hands and kissed and kissed them. Sir Robert's eyes were still on John. When he was near enough, John tipped his head and said, "How do you do, Sir." And he reached out his big brown paw over his wife's hair. The man on the bed did not raise his hand. He did not make any reply for a long and deep minute. Then, at last, he spoke. His voice was faint yet deep as if a strong man were speaking through a wall:

"So this is the Black Republican who stole away my daughter."

No more for another moment, and then:

"But it is a handsome one. Lud!—a handsome one!"

He lowered his sharp eyes at last and let them rest on John's hands.

"Yes, a gentleman who works with his hands. So I've been told, Sir. Let me see your hands!"

John held out both vast hands, palms up, with a widening smile.

"Yes, they were right. The Yankee captains have hands like a ditcher's."

There was still nothing warm in Sir Robert's voice. And he had made no move to shake his son-in-law's hand.

But the spell broke. For young Robert Dawn came boldly up to the bedside with a smile and stood there with one arm around his father's thigh to give him confidence. He stretched out his hand to his grandfather, and said, "How do you do, Grandpa!"

The figure sitting up in bed stiffened, the eyes dilated,

his lips parted in astonishment, and delight rushed into Sir Robert's face. He put out a hand like a withered leaf trembling in a gale of wind. He drew it back again. He tried to speak, tried again, in a broken voice:

"My son!—my—Robert! Robert!—The image—the very image of him!"

"Yes, Father," said Ruth very quietly, wiping the tears from the corner of her eyes with her handkerchief, "I meant him to look like Robert. That's why I gave him my brother's name before ever he was born."

The old man put both thin hands on the small boy's head. He held them there in silence for a long while. In perfect silence.

"I give you my blessing, Robert," he said.

Then his hand moved slowly to John Dawn's, and John Dawn took it in his own hand and found it warm with amazing life.

"I forgive you, Black Republican—Yankee!" he whispered.

They left their son there with his grandfather when they went out to look at the garden and the door in the wall. The roses were just the same. The petals of them drifted down and showered their feet with shells of fragile ivory as they walked between the bushes. At the door in the wall, John gathered Ruth into his arms, and he kissed her as a man kisses before he marries.

"The roses do not grow any older, John," Ruth said. "We are the ones that grow old. They will be here for the ones who come after us just the same as now. The same a hundred years from now." And then, in a lighter voice: "See!—I still have the key!"

When they came back into the bedchamber, the slow English twilight had come into the room. Dim loveliness was everywhere there. The sky through the windows was full of late larks. They were dropping down beads of bright sound that seemed to be turning into the earliest stars. It was very quiet there in the bedchamber. Sir Robert was fast asleep. Young Robert was, too. He had got up on the bed and had gone to sleep there like a lamb after his long day. And in sleep, the old man's arm had gone around the young body and his hand rested under the small boy's cheek.

XXII

It was a bitter Pacific. Winter had once more come down on it, down as far south even as the mid-Californian coast. And it was a bitter errand John Dawn had come on, in this January of 1850.

His sea-captain son, Joel, was somewhere among the dreary gray hills that stood out cold in the evening ahead of the bowsprit of the *Ruth of Devon.* On hills where no sailor had any business to be. He had left his ship to foul up and be wormed in the Bay of San Francisco. His mate had written home to tell John. He alone had stayed on board. All the other men had gone. The whole lot of them, after their captain had abandoned ship and gone on his fool's errand, seeking gold.

A Dawn to come to this!—Joel had no need to seek a fortune on land. His father had fortune enough for ten Joels. It must have been the adventure of the thing. The mate had written home as if it had been a disease. A fever. That was the word he had used. Joel had caught the fever. He had gone off into the California mountains for fool's gold.

But his father had come to fetch him home. He had come all the way round the Horn to do it. And he would do it. He had come alone. Ruth had begged to come. But for the second time in their life together, John had shaken his head. There was a heaviness upon him such as he had never felt in all his life before. He might be in for a hard time, making a young man give up an adventure like this. He remembered how it had been with himself, when he was very young. But that was before he was married. And Joel was older. Old enough to have married two wives by this and seen to it that they had babies as women should have. It had been a great disappointment to John, Joel's not thinking about marrying. A man could not do it too early. To give him balance. Now there was this to prove it.

After he had gotten half way down the Atlantic, John had repented not bringing his wife along. She was a wonderful woman. She might know how to go about bringing Joel to his senses better than he did. Sorry he hadn't brought her.

It had been a bad, hard trip. Storms on the way down. Doldrums on the way up. Days they had drifted with slack sails and seen the hours go by. Day after day. And John had gotten to thinking on how much this delay and that delay might mean when he got to California. He had got to dreaming bad dreams at night. And then the cold weather off California. A hard trip. But it was nearly done now. In an hour, John would put his anchor down in San Francisco Bay.

"She seems to be coming a bit too much our way, John."

The captain did not know that Easter Toothaker was anywhere near him on deck.

"What's coming our way, East?"

"Why, that old ship there," and East pointed to their starboard.

"My God!"

The knuckles on Captain Dawn's hands went white in the twilight. He swayed forward and nearly fell. The wheel saved him. But his jaw was like water. He straightened up slowly. He did not look the ship's way again. He kept his eyes straight ahead on the dim Californian mountains. He did not glance to starboard. He had no need to. He knew every shroud and yard-arm and patched gray sail on the ship bearing down upon them. He did not need to look again and see that there was not a soul in the yards, not a living soul on the deck, not even at the wheel.

What John Dawn had to think about was what he would find ahead of him in those strange, bare hills they were heading for. How it would be. Not by water or storm. But he knew he would find his first-born, Joel, dead.

"By God!—She's gone!" cried East. "Well, blast my innerds! It wan't no ship at all! It was one of them damned mirages. Not a sign of a ship!—By God! that makes me think of something I heard tell of once. About a ship—some kind of a queer thing about a ship. What was it, now?—Something queer. Off the coast home."

He had no need to try to think of it. Captain John Dawn knew what it was. He even knew what the name on the ship was, though he had not read it this time. It was the *Harpswell*. John said nothing to his mate. The

Winter lay the whole length of the marrow of his spine. And there was something about this Winter, he knew, that would never lift.

It was a bad dream, San Francisco. John left the ship in East's hands. With orders to shoot any man that tried to desert it. What he had to do, he would do alone. A bad dream in a dirty overnight town of shacks. Laughter late in the night. The people did not sleep. That was a bad sign. There were bad women at dark street corners. Washings hung out in front of front doors of the cabins. That was a bad sign, too. Litter of boxes and barrel staves along the muddy streets. John's clean Merrymeeting soul revolted at all the filth and slackness. And behind all his loathing was that weight of death in his mind. He knew he would not be in time. He had come too late. If the doldrums had not slowed them down, it might have been a different story.

He picked up the trail at last. A Yankee sea captain like Joel could not be lost for good even in such a place of drifters. The trail was cold. But it led out of the ramshackle town, out of the nightmare into the hills. It led at last to a valley. Joel came into it on a cold evening. The sky did not seem like any sky he had seen before in his life. Clear and cold green, and yet heavy as lead. In the packing-box postoffice, John found out about the last of the trail he would have to go. He knew what was at the end of it.

It led high into a ravine, already full of evil night. It ended in a place that grew lonesomer and lonesomer.

There were a few shacks, but all deserted now. John knew which one to go to of the three that jutted up jagged on the last glow of the west. He went into it. It was close and foul. He struck a light and lifted his lantern. Nothing in the room. He felt a strange warmth beginning to creep into him. But then he noticed the other door. The warmth died away. He waited a long time till the tremble was out of his body before he opened the door. Then he swung it and went in.

Joel was lying on a bed made of cheap boxes, his hands out stiff toward his father. John Dawn turned his son over. There was a sheath knife still in him. He had been dead for some days.

John never remembered much of the rest of that night. But he recalled afterwards how in his goings and comings his foot struck something metallic. He bent down and felt it over. It was the old pewter mug, with the sun on it and the letters J. DAWN. It was dented and crushed. Whoever had left it there had kicked it aside as a thing worth nothing. John remembered picking it up and straightening it out with his fingers. It took a long time. And he put it into his pocket. John Dawn remembered one terrible thing more very clearly. How hard it had been to pull out the knife, blunt and big and clumsy, from between the cold ribs of his son.

It was the next day that John fell in with the man from Joel's ship. He was a woebegone derelict of a man. He had been drinking for days and was sour with stale whisky. He was half out of his head. But he told John about the three men who had robbed and killed his son. He had been in the fight. He had a wound himself. He had run away after he got it. Run away and left Joel. The three men were all bigger than he was. One of them had a scar from the corner of his eye to his chin. The man told John he would know that one and the others in a thousand.

John waited a day and fed the man and brought him round. Then they set off together into the hills beyond the hill where the body lay, sewn into canvas by John's own hands and left with a man paid to guard it against the coyotes. They went into hills beyond those hills. And into ones beyond. Their way led them through a week more of nightmare. They got the scent now and then and went on. Men answering to the description had been seen here and seen again there. The captain and the sailor followed them on. The sailor was not afraid, now John Dawn was with him. The trail led them into a desert valley full of scrub growth at last.

John caught up with the quarry one evening at sunset time. He and Joel's man lay in the sagebrush and watched the three men they were dogging go past near enough to touch and on down into a cabin they had there in an arroyo, under a dune of sand. Then the man with him had been afraid.

But John did not ask his guide to go with him. He went away by himself, after the big and unfamiliar stars had come out. All he had with him to do with was the blunt knife he had taken from Joel's body. It was all he wanted. His companion begged him to take his pistol. John would not touch it.

The captain was gone for an hour. When he came back to the trembling fellow in the sagebrush, he said they could start back home at once. He had three jagged pieces of something that looked like leather but had hair on it. In his boyhood days, he told his companion, he had heard his father tell how the old Indians used to go about scalping a man. He took nothing else from the shack. There was some gold there, he said, quite a lot of it. But he did not touch it. He had killed all three of the ruffians with their own knife.

They got back to the body after some days. John bought a cart, and he and the other Merrymeeting man took Joel's body to San Francisco. They put it on the ship. East had kept the crew together. They were able to start almost at once.

An hour after they had hoisted sail and slipped out of Frisco Bay, a tall man came down to the water front where John Dawn's ship had been. He inquired of sailors there about the Merrymeeting captain. The sailors told him all they knew. He seemed upset over missing the Maine man. He finally went away, though. One thing stuck in the mind of one sailor there who had had a chance to size up the captain of the *Ruth of Devon*. It was odd. But he had looked a great deal like the tall stranger who had come inquiring for him.

John waited till they were around the Horn and in the Atlantic. The Atlantic would be more like home, he said.

Then he buried his son at sea, where sailing men should be buried. And he threw the three pieces of hairy leather in, too.

None of the men of Merrymeeting could shake the heaviness of that voyage off, even after that. It was like a kind of dream all the way up to Maine. It was East Toothaker who took the whole business the hardest. Harder than the captain, even, it seemed. He had never spoken a word with the captain about that night at the Golden Gate. But it had weighed like a ton on his mind. He wasn't a dreaming man, but he had taken to dreaming now. And he did not like it. He hadn't wanted to, but he had kept thinking and trying to remember about that ship, that was queer in some way. He remembered it at last. It was at that time the dreaming began. It was all confused. Everything. When he was awake and walking the deck, even. Somehow the whole business was mixed up with Jim Doughty and that night of the launching of the *Ruth of Devon.* He felt, somehow, that everything might have turned out different, if he had only kept that queer ship he had seen coming down on them there at the Golden Gate to himself and had not breathed a word about it to John Dawn. He might have known there was something funny about it, with no men to be seen on the deck and all. If he had only kept quiet a minute more, the captain might not have noticed a thing. The ship would have gone away into thin air. John Dawn might have sailed into Frisco a different man. And Joel might not be lying two miles down in the Atlantic. Joel might not have gotten that knife blade in him at all, but might have been alive and kicking and on this deck at this very minute. East felt he was to blame for it all. The feeling grew on him, the nearer they got to home and Maine. His not sleeping at night made it worse. He did not want to dream, and so he did not dare to go to sleep much. He grew quieter and quieter. He never had a thing to say to anybody much. Not even John. When he did happen to fall asleep, he kept seeing Jim Doughty's face, with the moon on it, the way it looked in the light of the full moon, that night East lifted him up in his arms to see his last launching. That night he lifted Jim up to see this ship East was on now take the high tide in Merrymeeting Bay. It was that full moon that bothered East most.

Bad business all around. East got up one night, because he did not dare to sleep, and walked the forward deck. There was a full moon now, just the same as that night of the launching. That was bad. East looked ahead. And there it came, rushing down on him with all twelve sails set and its yards empty of men, and all its decks. He told himself it was a dream. Like the face of Jim Doughty. He had fallen asleep on his feet, walking the deck. But it was not a dream. It was there! He could see the bone in her mouth as she came flying. He could see her shadow on the water. He wanted to scream. But he bit his tongue and did not make a sound. John Dawn might hear him, if he did, and come on deck, and see it for a second time this trip. East was not going to have two nights like that on his mind.

The ship would not be there at all in another minute, East knew. When he looked up, it would be gone for good. As long as he gritted his teeth and stayed still and did not scream, it would go out in the air. East looked again. It was there! It was still there! There!—God! —there! He'd——

He rushed to the rail, put a leg up, pulled the other after it, and went down into the sea.

The man at the wheel saw it happen. He fetched a yell. He told Captain Dawn the mate was overboard. John had the ship hove to in no time. They put out a boat. They luffed there in the bright light of the full moon all the hours of the night, while John sat in the ship's boat and watched the long Atlantic swells come up around him, break over, and turn into cloth of silver under the moon. They stayed till the day came, and for an hour after. Then they gave up and sailed on. And John Dawn had another weight on his years to come. Another weight to carry home to Merrymeeting.

The captain was very particular in questioning the man who had been at the wheel. Had he seen anything strange just before East leaped over? No, he could see for miles every direction. There had been nothing. Easter Toothaker had come on deck and had stared hard at nothing at all. Then he had gone and jumped over.

The evening after, they made Merrymeeting. John

had the wheel, as he always had when they were entering his home bay. John could see the lights of the village at last. Then, suddenly, he knew it was coming again. Knew it long before he turned his eyes and saw her coming down on them, high against the rising moon. All sails set, not a mother's son of a sailor on her. Rushing on and towering over them, her bowsprit almost at their mizzen shrouds. John looked ahead at the lights of Merrymeeting, calmly. He did not even watch it melt away. The cold sweat stood on him. But he looked straight at home. He knew, though, what thing it would be.

When John landed, they brought him word that Ruth had died the night before of pneumonia.

XXIII

Polly Toothaker went through the potato parings again, to see if there were any portions of good potato she could save from the waste and boil up with the rest. She didn't really need to do that. But she had been brought up saving, and she couldn't stop at this late day.

And it might be a good thing for this house if there was someone in it who did save the thicker parts of potato parings. Times had changed, and if things went on the way they had been going for the last nine years in Merrymeeting and the world, John Dawn and his might thank a body for saving them all a body could.

Ever since her Easter had been lost, and he almost on his own doorstep, and Mrs. Dawn had been taken, things on the hill had been going from bad to worse. The two of them, East and Mrs. Dawn, going so together as you might say, had sort of started it. After Mrs. Dawn went, there hadn't been many days in this old house that you could stand up and crow about.

Of course, Polly had done all *she* could. She'd had her heart and hands full. The minute Captain Dawn had hinted that they belonged together, being as how both of them had lost a half of themselves, kind of, she had packed right up and come up here to the Dawn house and taken charge. She saw her duty, and she'd done it. The captain, of course, had lost two halves of himself. His son going like that in California, and his wife on top of that. Losing a son was worse than losing a wife, when all was said and done. Sons were the future. A wife was only the present. And the past. Mrs. Dawn really had never been long for this world. Polly'd said so, always, from the minute she'd first laid eyes on her. Those English women didn't wear. She'd said so the first thing. Peggy Doughty had, too. After a son or two had come out of them, their bloom did not last. And Mrs. Dawn had been too good for this world. She had too soft a heart. She was better than a body should be. You couldn't say such a thing about most women. Peggy Doughty, for instance. Well, bygones should be bygones. But Polly would always say to her dying hour that Peggy Doughty was as much to blame for East's going as though she had stood behind him and pushed him right over the rail. She got her going-home-a-crying, though. She wasn't satisfied with two men, and she had lost them both. You couldn't sing your song and eat your cheese at the same time. But there! Let the dead rest.

Some people were lucky. They went in time, before they had come down in the world, and had to pull in their horns and eat Job's turkey. Peggy Doughty and her Jim. And Polly's own Easter. If Mrs. Dawn had lived, she would have had to moderate her style of living and make two loaves go in place of five. Make gingham go where silks and satin had been. For the Dawns were coming out on the little end of the horn. East's going had had a lot to do with the change, Polly liked to think. He was the best first mate the Dawns had ever had. Men like East didn't grow on every gooseberry bush. He was a man all over, and that was more than Polly could say for some husbands. No wonder he was run after by other men's wives. They knew which side their bread was buttered on. They knew a man when they saw one. East had a level head, too, and you couldn't always say as much for the Dawns. He knew his breastbone from his backside. The Dawns often lived as if every day was Sunday. Easter knew enough to look at both ends of a horse. Captain John was too much up in the clouds most of the time. He didn't reckon on having to pay the fiddler. People had to. It was ups and downs, as Polly saw it. Mostly downs. Life was funny, like that. A feast or a famine.

Famine enough now, the good Lord knew. What with banks closing their doors, and widows and orphans crying in the streets for a crust of bread. The Dawns weren't the only ones the shoe pinched. Thousands more. If they had many more years like 1857, they'd all be in the poorhouse, together.

Captain John had caught it where the wool was short. He had buried too many bones in one hole. Boston had burned everybody's fingers. Of course, Captain John had more to lose than the rest. The tall trees caught the lightning first. Of course two ships would have to go and burn up just when the fire insurance companies had been dragged under by the banks. And of course there would have to come a year of great blows and hurricanes all round the world this year, on top of the panic year of '57. It never rained but it poured. Fine tall ships cast away up and down the coast. Right in people's laps, almost. Four of the Dawns'—more than they had lost before in all the years they'd been going.

Bad news never came single. One day, along came word that one of their ships was ashore and breaking up on Hatteras. Next day, a letter saying, "We beg to inform you that our bank has gone bust." And as if that wasn't enough to ruin a man and make his dinner set crooked on his crop, a friend of the family ran in next day and told a man how another ship had gone down in the Bay of Biscay. The Old Boy let loose, and putting his finger into every pie cooking. Your ship was wrecked on Tuesday, your ship was burned on Wednesday, and Thursday it would be the bank and another ship. And Lord knew what on Friday.

The loss of the *Ruth of Devon* had been the worst. They'd never have another ship like that. It would never have happened if Captain John had been sailing her. He'd been so broken up in that year after Joel's death that he let somebody else take her. And that was the end of that. Of course, the *Ruth of Devon* had been a hard luck ship from the first. There was Jim Doughty and then Joel and Mrs. Dawn and East. Some ships were like that. Marked. It had been Peggy, really, who did the marking. Polly couldn't blame East. A soft woman could do more harm than a hurricane. But, then, people shouldn't speak ill of the dead.

The captain had matter enough on his mind to go around looking as though he'd lost the last friend he had in the world. Trouble enough to make any man wobble-cropped and woebegone. Of course the main woodlot would have to catch afire and burn up a dozen ships that might have been, in the virgin pine there.

And it wasn't as if everything was apple pie and tea all turned out at home. It wasn't for Polly to poke her nose into other folks' business, and it wasn't for her to pass judgment. But young Robert wasn't making his father any too happy, between you and me and the bed-post. He with his nose in a book all the time and not caring about sailing before the mast at all. And his being bound to stay on at the Academy when he was filled out enough to marry and father children. Always scribbling, he was, too. Poems and such. O Lord, what would it be next!

Not that Robert wasn't lovable. He was. Lovable as the day was long. You couldn't ask for an easier boy to have around the house. But that was just it. He hung around the house. Hanging around a house was no business for a boy old enough to shave. Robert didn't shave, either. Not his upper lip. That bothered his father, too. Captain John didn't take to these newfangled moustaches all the young men were wearing. Couldn't stomach them. He'd never had one, or his father before him. Why should Robert? It didn't look right to him.

Mrs. Toothaker tried to imagine how Easter would have looked with a moustache on him. She couldn't picture it. It didn't seem right. It would have been like going to bed with a stranger!

Yes, Captain John had his heart and hands full. It wasn't as if things would blow over tomorrow, either. Shipping was in a bad way. In the doldrums. There weren't the cargoes there'd been once upon a time. What with newfangled trains carrying most of the goods to the West and South. Taking the bread out of honest people's mouths! Nasty, smoking things. Mrs. Toothaker had been up to Portland, and she'd seen one of those infernal bull-gine things. They couldn't get her to step one foot on one of those coaches that rolled along on iron rails. She'd just as lief trust her two hundred pounds to a balloon. Rather. Balloons were safer. At least a body could see what he was going to strike.

And now they were talking about putting those bull-gines right into ships and pushing ships right across the Atlantic against the wind, against the tide, against the Devil himself in the smell of onions! It wasn't natural. But they were doing it, too, already. More cargoes to kiss goodbye!

That wasn't the worst of it. There were worse things than lost cargoes and men having to carry gull manure where they'd carried tea and china dishes in their bottoms. There were the crews. They weren't the crews that used to sail the ocean. Scum of the earth people, they were now. Loafers. Loafers you had to run down in cities and hog-tie before you could get them to go aboard. Weak, pindling, knock-kneed men, not thick enough through the trousers to stay on the yards when a good wind piped up.

Polly slammed the potatoes on to boil, wiped the smudge of fir charcoal off her nose, and flounced over to begin work on a pie.

Foreigners, even! They'd fallen as low as that. Had to take foreigners where they could find them. Singapore and Ceylon monkey men. When it came to hiring foreigners for a crew, you might as well stop. It wasn't safe for a captain to take his wife along any more. Likely as not she'd be raped, if nothing more, the minute he turned his back. It was getting harder and harder to find Yankees who were willing to go to sea and take hard knocks. They had things too soft, now. Sat back and got fat and lazy. No guts, no gumption left. Or if they did have, they went traipsing off to Boston or New York or California to get rich quick and live off the fat of the land. If they kept on this way, they'd soon find it hard sledding to find even a mate that was a Yankee and had some pride in keeping his vessel shipshape and Bristol-fashion.

Times were bad, but men were worse. Petering out. It was a wonder they could still raise families or have anything but girls. The juice was so gone out of them. What women would do for husbands pretty soon was beyond Polly Toothaker.

Men like Captain John were done. They didn't come that way any more. Why, even Robert wasn't within three inches of his Daddy. Men were getting shorter and runtier. The end of the litter. Bred-out shoats. Why,

Polly's East could have broken most of the sailors in two who worked the Dawn ships now, in his two hands. Men with long moustaches, and rings in their ears, like as not, if you didn't watch out. East was lucky, going so soon as he did. His heart would be broken now.

John Dawn was the kind of man to make a woman want to have babies every year. Handsome as a basket of russet apples. Strong and quick, and smelled of rope and the sea. An outdoors man. Not one moping around a house and scribbling on paper. Smart as a cricket. Bright as a silver dollar. Full of salt, full of guts. The kind of a man you leave it to the sun and stars and the wind to raise.

It was the kind of man bad luck picked out to hit. The oak tree always got it in a thunder storm.

Such men did not change. Any more than the sea changed, or the stars. But the world changed. The tide ebbed out and left such men high and dry on the shore. People stopped wanting fine silk to wear and teak to sit on and minding their own business. They poked their noses into other people's. They wanted to set niggers free, that did not belong to them. They got into hot water. Could not let well enough alone. And so they talked about going to war, about states' rights, got riled up over a few niggers. They let ships rot away, for want of cargoes. Let men like John Dawn sit around in port with nothing to do.

Polly put the top crust on the mince pie. She snatched up the kitchen knife and slashed the top this way and that, so it looked like a flock of wild geese going over. She bounced the pie into her oven and slammed the door.

Well, she'd stand by the Dawns till she had no legs left to stand on.

She heard the voices in the big sitting room, two rooms away. She hadn't meant to eavesdrop or listen to other folks' business. She had always had plenty of her own. Each tub on its own bottom. But the doors were both open. She couldn't help hearing. The Dawns had full voices, good in a gale of wind.

"I've wanted to see you, Father, about this, for weeks," Robert was saying. "It's been on my mind. I know you like people to speak up in meeting and say what they think. There's no use beating about the bush. I don't want to sail on the *James Dawn II*. I want to go to Beaudoin College."

"You don't want to go out and make a man of yourself?"

"I'm man enough now, Father. You don't have to sail on a ship to be a man."

"The Dawns do."

"Maybe I'm not enough of a Dawn, then."

"That's it, I guess. I guess you're right. Too much old Sir Robert in you. You've always been willing to sit back and not dirty your lily hands, be a gentleman. Playing with pen and paper, like a girl. I wanted a he-man for a son. I had one, but I lost him. You haven't got the —the guts."

"I'm sorry, Father." Robert's voice had gone very

grave and low. "I'd like to do what you want me to do. I've tried to like the sea. I've tried hard. You can't say I haven't. I went on the voyage you wanted me to go on. I've tried to like sailing. But it's no go. I can't. Sailing seems a dull business to me."

"Did it ever occur to you that your grub may depend on your taking hold and helping me? Times are hard. You know what I've been through. Maybe you will wake up some fine morning and discover that you've got to take off your coat and hustle for a living."

"I know that. I don't expect you to give me my board and keep all my life."

"What are you planning to do, then?"

"Go to college, and then get a job."

"What kind of a job do you think you'll get, except loafing?"

"I might be a writer."

"And who's going to pay your way while you are at Beaudoin?"

"I can work my way through. Other men do. I can stay out every other year and teach school."

"Act the wet-nurse to children still damp behind the ears!—I never expected to hear of a Dawn's doing that."

"You are narrow-minded, Father. You think a man can't be a man unless he is working with his hands. A man can work with his head, too."

"Woman's business!—teaching school! It's what a half-bottomed man would pick out."

"I think my bottom is as whole a one as anybody's."

"All right. It's no use arguing with you. The *James Dawn II* will sail next week without you. You can stay home where you are safe, and go to Beaudoin College. You can study to be a school teacher or a minister, and welcome. I'll go on by myself, as I've had to do these last ten years. I know where I belong, and I know where men belong. And I know some men who aren't much different from women except they wear clothes that have an open space between the legs."

A door slammed to. John Dawn had gone outdoors.

Polly Toothaker hung the rolling pin up in its place, and wiped the flour off her hands.

It was the fine tall trees that caught it worst in a storm.

XXIV

It was raining still. It seemed to John Dawn that it had been raining ever since he had left Maine. People said heavy firing brought down rain. Maybe so. Maybe there was something in it. It wasn't like a Maine rain. Not clean and sharp. It had mud and stickiness in it, and steam. It made the red clay stick to a pair of boots till a man couldn't make much headway.

It didn't matter, though, whether he made any headway or not. Not now. Not since he had sailed from Merrymeeting Bay that September morning that seemed like two lifetimes ago, and saw the thing again. He had swung about and gone straight home, packed his valise, and made for the depot. He had been travelling ever since. It was something to be moving. It took his mind off things.

The guns had been going there, off to the south, ever since he had been in Maryland. Making rain, making trouble. For him, for everybody in the country, North and South.

A long time, sixty-two years. Enough to give any man a bellyful of living.

Funny. He had known it was coming before it had appeared suddenly there and cut off the sun from his face, that bright September morning. Not a cloud in the sky, and then this cool shadow on his face. None of the crew had seen it. But crews a sailing ship had now never would.

A man used to the sea had no business to be going over hills and through woods. It tuckered him out quick.

The other Robert—Sir Robert's Robert—had gone this way, too. At Waterloo. It had been raining for days. Ruth used to tell John how it had been. She had heard all about it from other men who had been there. The sun had been very bright on the wet plowland. The sun was lowering, but it picked out the puddles and made them shine like pieces of a vast mirror shattered over the land. The soldiers had wet feet. The rain trickled down their loins, too. Their high fur hats were all they had dry. They had kept them under their capes. Going on fifty years ago. The bones must be pretty well sweetened out now, by the soil and the rain. Robert's and the others'. John's wife had told him how she had heard tell that the men minded being wet in their trousers, around the loins, most of all. Uncomfortable, being wet there. It took the gimp out of a man. Made him think of babyhood, maybe, and his first pair of breeches and having waited too long and having had an accident. John's trousers were sopping now.

They had thought the whole thing was a false alarm, the English. Then, all at once, they saw the shining plowlands moving—a whole continent of them. And when they looked again, they were the French, the whole French army. They were coming across the fields toward them. They sopped up and put out all the pieces of looking glass that were really puddles. They seemed to be catching on fire here and there. Flames would shoot up. But it was the brass and buttons of the marching men. And things on the ends of their rifles. It began to thunder, though there were no clouds around the sun at all, and the moving plowlands began to heave up here and there, and white puffs of steam came out of them. But they kept on coming. They grew together again and slid on. The English could not help it, they cheered. It was like an enormous shadow from clouds not there overhead, from out of the east and away to the west. It moved like a cloud's shadow, too. Beautiful and slow, but steady.

When it reached the valley's bottom and started up the hill, it turned into a vast mass of muddy men, breathing hard like one big thing, and having white masks for faces. They must have smelled sweaty to each other and all kinds of ways dirty—so many lusty men packed together that way, stomachs to seats, seats to flies, several hundred deep. The faces grew to mouths first, and then eyes. By that time, the English could hear the grunting of the separate men and the sucking of thousands of feet in the mud. From the east to the west. The English could see the length of what was stuck on the muzzles of the rifles. The whole earth began to quake all through now, though, queerly enough, it had seemed awfully quiet all the time. It was the vibration that got into the Englishmen's minds. They were ordered to fire, and they did. But it made no difference to the continent creeping upon them. There seemed to be just as many mouths like holes burnt in a blanket, just as many bright splinters of sunlight on the rifles' ends. Just then the continent hit them and was alive and came over them. And it could cut and hack and trample, and it did. And Englishmen put their hands to their trouser fronts and tried to hold in what had tumbled out there and hung from them after bayonets had gone in. Some men were sick to the stomach on themselves and on others. Some turned and tried to run from what was going into them. Some stood stupidly with buttocks apart and only slowly went to their knees.

And Lieutenant Robert Greville-Pyne got one thing at his middle that went from there down through his trousers and left a gigantic beginning to a pain so that he did not mind the wetness to his trousers any more. And he got another thing, quicker moving, in his head just over his eyes, and that thing turned at once into a thing in place of brain and feeling and fear and sparkled and shone and sent out violet glints, wheeled around and poured off ineffable streamers, and remained for everlasting. He never knew anything at all about how the continent broke apart, was trampled back, and became a part of Belgium's soil again, and how a great number of English soldiers were still standing on their feet in a daze and yelling rather quietly and thinking in the same breath about the taste of English cabbages and about lifting a bare thigh to get into bed to wives they had not seen for a long time.

It was odd, it seemed to John Dawn. Here he was

thinking about an old battle fought half a hundred years ago that did not concern himself at all. Queer, and now that he thought of it, the sun was out bright on the steaming hills of Maryland, there were plowed fields, and they were full of puddles gleaming like broken window panes. There were men with shining things on the ends of their rifles down ahead in the next valley. And his own son Robert was somewhere ahead of him where the guns were pounding away.

That was what Beaudoin had led him to. It had led him into a war. It had marched him away as a lieutenant into two years of hell, in Virginia and Maryland.

It seemed very odd to John that he could not get an old battle out of his head, and mixed up another Robert with this one.

This one was his son, and he ought to keep his mind on him, seeing what was ahead of him this day.

A son was a strange thing. Made in a minute or two, when a man was feeling very good and not thinking about anybody but himself, not even his wife. And then the son came along, and a man was proud of him and made out to himself that he knew what he was about when he made him, and held him in his arms and worshipped him. But after a few years, the son could run around by himself, and he upset things and made noise and bother, and felt cold and foreign when a man took him up. He got into trouble. He worried his father with his sicknesses and littleness and weakness. A man took care of him for years. And then the son grew up and made his father feel shy toward him and unable to speak to him as he would to another man, was another man altogether, turned his back on his father, did just what he wanted to, went his own way, as though he did not belong to the father at all. As though he was anybody's son. A father was independent of him when he begot him, and the son was independent of his father when he got his manhood upon him. The same thing as among animals and birds. It was the law of life.

A pretty village, all whitewashed cottages and elm trees, stood over yonder. It had a steeple in the middle of it. It looked as if it was always Sunday there. But there was a dark strip this side of it, all along this side of it as far back as John could see. And the strip was horribly alive and moving like a blacksnake, with its head so far away and its tail so far that you could not see them. It was made of men. Thousands on thousands of men. It had sparks running along it. But those were buttons catching the sunlight. Enough men to beget sons to man all the ships of the Atlantic for years and years to come. All able to make son after son with no trouble at all, if they had the chance. Women were waiting for them all somewhere, waiting for the sons. And many of them would go down under the damp rot of roots without ever having been used, the parts of them so intricately made and full of life dropping away from them and wasted and defeated as blighted apple blossoms.

Over there across the valley was a little stone church all by its lonesome, on a road. There was no village there. And this side of it was a peach orchard as neat as a pin. But there were small tufts of cotton batting floating among the trees, and under the boughs the earth was alive and crawling with men. And the little church suddenly got all white at its windows. The roof tipped back into nothing, and flames came out of the whole building and stood up straight in the air higher than any of the trees. The sunny grass around it wasn't grass any more but men the color of the grass. They stood up out of somewhere, grew shadows, and came spreading down the valley's side like a queer kind of stain, toward the orchard where the white puffs floated above the whitewashed tree trunks. At that, all the length of that hill for miles began to move and slide down, too. The stonewalls along it disappeared, and the shadows of all the trees.

Down below the orchard ran a silver thread of a stream. But it was gone in a minute. For dark shadows like the markings on mackerel began to flow right over it. They moved up to meet the sliding hill. John Dawn thought of all the endless coils and scrollwork of the insides of men's bodies there must be in those mackerel markings, how many muscles laid on over one another like the wood fibres in a ship, how many precious pumps of red and firm tissue there were at work all by themselves with no hand working them, how many fine proofs of manhood, well protected by the structure of men's bodies, how many furrows of fat full of sparks of fire and making up thoughts out of themselves were moving along there and having dull spheres of lead cutting them to ribbons and smashing the sparkle and goodness and sweetness of life into excremental jellies and sickening rags. The blue shadows went up, and the brown shadows came down. They almost met. But just before they did, a new ribbon of white cotton came into being between them, as far as John could see each way, the white strip of cotton was there. Cotton full of glinting needles. Only it wasn't cotton at all, of course, it was smoke. Smoke from ten thousand rifles, and the Frenchmen and Englishmen were catching those needles of fire in the most precious parts of their bodies and getting holes that nothing could mend. No, not Frenchmen and Englishmen—Americans! All of them were Americans!

It was a battle, and a big one. John's son was somewhere there in the midst of it. A small bit of John. So small that it could not show up alone. It took a dozen such bits, a dozen Roberts, to show up at this distance. A dozen men old enough and able enough to be fathers. Robert had never been a father. A college made a man wait. Now he had waited too long. What might have made a father of him would be scattered and lost in the tangles of trampled grass over there.

John Dawn doubted if any man of all those armies with smoke between them knew what battle he was taking part in. They didn't know it was to be called Waterloo until they were marching toward France, next morning, in that old war. This battle had no name to it. Robert would never know one for it. The other Robert had never known.

The road John was walking had two other roads coming into it a hundred yards farther on. Both the other ones were crawling with dark men. The columns met and fused and spilled out into the fields. John's way was closed. He could not go along any farther. He might as well sit down here on the stonewall and wait.

The stones were dry, but John's trousers weren't. They were damp around the crotch with the rain he had been through. The Englishmen had spoken of that. It took the fire out of a man to be wet there.

It wasn't like a fight on the sea. Nothing like that time when the *James Dawn II* and the *Warspite* came together. No, the *James Dawn*, not the *James Dawn II*. That was the ship he had hoped Robert would go on. Robert's bunk was made up for him that time, and it had nobody in it all the voyage. Nobody in it any voyage up till the storm when John left it, like a piece of himself, hurricane sails still flying, doomed, in the Bay of Biscay.

No, fighting on the land wasn't the same as fighting on the water. On the water you had a chance to rest and keep your dander up till you had a chance to use it all at once. But here on the land, a man was all used up—he had so far to walk to get at the man he wanted to fight. He was tuckered out, and he hit only half as hard when he got up to the other man. And it wasn't so clean, either. A soldier had to eat his peck of dirt and fight at the same time. Fight on sore feet.

If he were younger, he might fight, too, down there. There was something about it you never found in anything else. A rage that wasn't a rage, something that took the whole of you, like love-making, only colder. But he was too short in the wind now. And it was miles to go to get there. Must be all of two miles to that ribbon of smoke.

Strange to think of Robert's being able to be in a battle! Why, a little time ago, his father had to help him unbutton his small trousers at the front! Strong, tall men coming at Robert with both hands on the butt of a rifle and a steel knife the length of a man's thigh on the other end of it.

It would be like stabbing Ruth. There was a lot of his mother in Robert. He was mostly mother. And he was partly that lieutenant waiting on the hill at Waterloo. His body had never felt to John the way Joel's body had felt, when he was young. All Ruth.

And suddenly John Dawn's errand became more of an errand that had to do with Ruth, the Ruth of Devon whose rosebush had spread all around the doorstep at Merrymeeting. It was not a son John had on his mind, but a wife. It was for her sake he was down here sitting and waiting on a wall.

John Dawn did not know what was the matter with his mind. Never in all his born days had it run on like this. Like a clock unwinding. He had never been a man to let his mind bother him. He planned things, he did things. He did them mostly with his hands. And then he rested all over. But he could not stop his mind now. It was jumping from one thing to another, this way and that.

Why should he, for no reason at all, be thinking this very minute of the way Maine pines turned into molten silver when the wind blew through their needles in the Winter? Think of that when a battle was going on?

Well, maybe it was trouble did that to a man.

The ribbon of smoke was still there, with men on both sides of it. But it was beginning to break now. Like a Maine fog over hot Summer land. It was spilling down the hill toward him. There was sound, John suddenly realized, going on all the time. Like popping corn. The fog washed its way down to the stream in one place. It ate up most of the peach orchard. But there was an island left surrounded by it far back near the burning church. All at once, John felt he must watch that island. He saw nothing else. It was so small, and the fog as even around it as a ring a man might make of a puff of smoke. And the ring was closing on itself. He marked the spot in his mind. It was more important to him than the rest of the battle, than all the rest of the earth. All around it, a terrible avalanche of grass-colored men was sliding into the creek, wiping it away. Thousands of little live things were crawling away from it like blue maggots. But the small island of blue maggots was there in the middle of the avalanche, like a rock the avalanche could not grind quite under. Why didn't the blue maggots crawling along all the roads below him hurry to save that island?

The sun was going down. Shadows of the western hills came out long toward the valley of the fog, touched it, covered it. They made the fog seem more substantial and showed up lovely early fireflies in it. Only they weren't fireflies. They were flashes of flame from rifles, and each one had a deadly pellet in it.

The maggots had held at the creek. They were beginning to eat their way back up through the terrible grass. They were in the orchard, and the fireflies danced like mad there. They were through the orchard. Fireflies twinkled around them as they crawled on. The church was nothing but a high tower of thin smoke on the sunset. But the island was still there. It was woefully small now. Almost not there. A terrible stab of something worse than pain went through John Dawn suddenly. That was it, he knew. It was over and done.

It was getting to be night. The creeping edge of the mass of dark crawlers touched the island. It was safe.

Safe?—John Dawn felt as safe as a man the solid earth had dropped away from, drifting alone among the hungry, patient, mindless stars. The stars were coming out thick over Maryland and over the world, over the far away coast of Maine. Another night had come. And another night, for many men over there on the hill of fireflies, that would last beyond the twinkle of the last dying star in the universe.

The Maine captain sat there on the wall and let the

night go over him. It was hours and hours. It was getting cold. He got down and started off on his way. His legs were stiff, and he went slowly. There were sounds of men on the road. He took to the dark fields. He could go to that place with his eyes blindfolded. He could go to it across a hundred miles of unknown land.

The whole night was very uneasy. There were walls and hedges to climb. And behind them all men seemed to be somewhere and talking and singing. There were lights now and then, but not many. There were more men standing or sitting in the dark. John could smell the smell of their unwashed bodies as he went roundabout to avoid them. He heard two men talking low about their bodies as though they were not men but bulls in a bull-pen nosing about bulling cows. He had often heard his own men talking that way, and he hadn't minded it a dight. He had sometimes thought that way, too, to himself—and talked that way, maybe, to a few close friends like East and Jim. But here it did not seem the right place to do it. It made him a bit sick to his stomach. He gave those two men a wide berth and went far out around them.

Someone was singing somewhere. A thin wistful song came wavering out of the distance in the midst of the night:

"The birds they were singing in the morning,
The ivy and the myrtle were in bloom,
And the sun on the eastern hill was dawning,
It was then they laid her in the tomb."

It made John feel sad, being there among so many strange, unseen men in the middle of the night. He walked on, alone with what he had in his mind and with his age.

He stepped on something that gave horribly in the dark. He stumbled and went to his knees and felt of it. It was a man's arm. He wanted terribly to feel up the cold arm and try to make out the man's face with his fingers. But he knew it was not time. He had not gone far enough. He stumbled to his feet and went on.

There were many more such things to step on before he reached the stream even. He got used to them by then. At the water's edge, there was nowhere else to place one's feet in the dark. He let himself down the bank. The water was only up to his groin in the deepest part. He climbed up at the other bank and went on. Everywhere around him there were lanterns now. Bobbing about and then coming to a long rest. There was a steady clicking sound in his ears. It came from the places where the lanterns had come to rest. John made a wide circle to keep away from the lights and the men who were bending over, larger than life, beside them and sending up shadows right against the stars. A sudden bad thought came to him. What if he got there too late? . . . He hurried faster.

John came over a wall, and found two men with clinking shovels working at a black hole in the earth right before him. There was one of the things lying this side of the hole. It had two parts of it up, and they were arms with clenched hands. The lantern's light silvered the face and made a golden fringe of the moustache on it. And then he saw another body on the other side, stripped, with parts that should not be seen naked to the light. The men rolled it over into the hole. It would not go in, at first, it was so rigid. Its nakedness loomed monstrous as they eased the edges of the hole away to let it down into the dark that would be for good. It was an oldish man. Maybe, a man with many sons. That would not be so bad.

John Dawn went past and up the hill. He was a little off his course. But when he came to a big hole full of light, he knew it for the church. He stood on the rim, and he felt the glow of the embers warming his face. It felt strange after all the dew and the damp. Somewhere, years ago, there had been another such a fire. He tried to think. He began to remember. Something about his father standing and looking down into embers where a building had been. Ah, yes—he had it now. He remembered years ago seeing the green and peaceful depression on the edge of Mast Meadow at Merrymeeting where his father as a young man had stood and gazed down at what was left of home.

He had his bearings now. He moved out into the night again. It would not be far from here. There weren't so many of the lanterns up this far. But there were people moving about like himself, in the dark. He heard a sudden low sound. A moaning began and went on and on and on in a monotone without a change or a break. It got upon his mind. Then it ended in a sharp thud. The silence which followed was worse than the moaning. John Dawn quickened his pace.

The things were so thick underfoot now that he had to go slowly. And it must be he was near the spot. It was fearful, there were so many of the things. Some of them still could move a little. John had to get down on his hands and knees. He began to feel them over in the night. His fingers went along the buttons of the tunics, and always worked up. They hesitated when the cloth came to an end. Then they went on. They felt over the clean chins, and they shivered each time as they moved higher and felt the ruff of hair over the mouth. They all had moustaches, seemingly. A moustache was no help to him. His eyes filled up with moisture, and he fumbled helplessly and hopelessly on in the dark.

"Halt! Who goes there?—Quick! shine your lantern, Bill! Here's another of them body lice!"

A light was suddenly shining all around John, and he got to his feet.

"Caught red-handed, going through the pockets of the dead. Stand back, Bill, I'll take this one! It's my turn. Shine your light on his face!"

"I am looking for my son."

"A new one!—Eyah!—Throw your light on his buttons, Bill, I'll try him through the guts. It's an old rooster."

The lantern fell full on Captain Dawn's face and

blinded his eyes. He put up his two hands to ward off the light.

"Well, I snum!—He's got buttons all right. But them ain't no army buttons. Let's have a look. Why it's an old grand-daddy, as I live! What are you doing out here so late at night, Grand-daddy? The night air is bad for your lungs.—Hello!—He's got anchors on his buttons. It's a sailor!—What in hell are you up to here?"

"I am looking for my son Robert, I told you. Robert Dawn. He is lying here somewhere. Dead."

John Dawn lowered his hands to his sides and stood there quiet.

An odd silence fell on the two gravediggers. They were standing there under the high lantern without a word to say. After a long while one of them spoke up:

"Good God, old man!—Your son? How do you know he is here?"

"He would be here. This is where the men were surrounded and held out so long. Let me take the lantern and find him."

"We'll come along and help you."

So the three men fell in side by side and walked along the mounds of the dead. Face after face stared up at them. The men on each side looked straight ahead. The old man between them looked down always as they went their slow way. Sometimes he would have to stoop over to see the face. Once he made a sound and went down. But it wasn't the right one.

A rooster was crowing far away. The morning stars would be coming up soon.

John Dawn knew him at once. Robert was lying on his side, his right arm up over his head. The breast of his jacket was a thing not to be looked at. But his face was calm in the lantern light. It was almost contented. The eyes were closed very lightly. And now a strange thing had been accomplished. For John Dawn, looking down into his son's face, saw that it was his own face, years ago. Not Ruth's face, but his own. Mysterious correspondences, unnoticed in life, had come out in the brow and chin and nose. Death had slipped a mask off, and it was young John Dawn lying there. Not a proud lieutenant of another race lying on the field of Waterloo, but an honest, plain man of Merrymeeting, a Yankee with Maine beauty hovering around his dead mouth and closed eyes.

Captain Dawn did not cry out. He did not say a word. He stood there straight and still, looking down. But his night companions knew their search was ended, and knew the father had found the son. Anyone could tell they looked alike. They set the lantern down. They were very quiet about it. They took up their spades and began to lay open the dark earth together. The light was too low to show the dead man's face. John Dawn bent down, raised it aloft, and held it there. He never took his eyes off the face.

They had it finished at last. They went and stood, one at the feet and the other at the head. Suddenly something occurred to one of the soldiers. He stooped over and ran his hand into the dead officer's pocket. He took out the thing that was making the bulge there. He passed it over to the father. John took it in his hands. It was the pewter mug, with the rising sun on it. The Luck of the Dawns. He had not known that Robert had taken it from home. He did not know that Robert knew or cared anything about it. John Dawn turned it round once in his hands. Then he gave it back to the soldier. The man knew what to do with it without a word's being said. He put it back into the pocket of the dead.

The two men took off their caps. John took off his. They stooped together and lowered the body into the earth. Then they took up their shovels. The man with the lantern lifted it higher and looked at the face till the first shovelful of earth covered it up. John held the light till the earth was all put back.

He never said goodbye to his helpers. But they shook hands with him, one by each hand. And the captain turned and went down the hill, under the two bright morning stars.

The starlight touched his gray hair and made it silver.

There was an end to having sons and having grieving and hoping to do.

XXV

It was to be an afternoon launching. The tide would suit at half-past four, but it was October, and that would mean they would have to look lively to get the *John O'Reilly* into the bay and clear of the shoals before the daylight failed. Some wag from New Merrymeeting said they would have to look lively to get the ship afloat by the time of the Exposition in Philadelphia, next year.

Nobody seemed to know who John O'Reilly was, or why a ship should be named after him. When ships were getting to be so scarce nowadays, people thought they ought to be named for more important folks.

Men in tall stovepipes had been arriving in buggies and shays ever since one o'clock. The editor of the *New Merrymeeting Record* had written a glowing editorial on the courage of Maine shipbuilders in building sailing vessels still in a day when the steamship was universally successful and acclaimed. Steam was faster, safer, more economical. But the editor's hat was off to the glory of the past. It would be a sad day when the wind-ships would no longer dot the ocean, as coal carriers at least. Of course, they were behind the times, but they were a relict of a noble day and as such should be revered. And they looked beautiful. There was nothing more beautiful to look at than a full-rigged ship under sail. The editor was no *laudator temporis acti*. He was a man who believed in the future. He could envisage a day when New Merrymeeting would have not one but two railroads coming into it, and the old docks on Merrymeeting Bay would have been replaced by uptodate piers and steamships would bring the fruits of the earth to New Merrymeeting doorsteps, when their town would have grown into a busy metropolis, humming with factories and manufacturing goods for half the world, when every point along the bay would be graced with edifices of trade. He saw New Merrymeeting rising from her sleep like Rip Van Winkle, shaking off her sloth, and spreading out till she became another Liverpool, rich with the spoils of ocean, proud in her brick and stone, sending up the incense of vast factories to the gods of commerce, rich, and happy, and busy, a true daughter of Columbia, brushing her head on the stars. Where the deer had once roamed, the steamcars would fly; where frogs had sung in the Mast Meadow swamp, a thousand spindles would sing; where the tall pines had stood, brownstone houses would shine in their beauty and usefulness. New Merrymeeting had by far the best air of any town in Maine. Show the editor a harbor better suited to the introduction of a steamship line. There were none on the Maine coast! But though he was no *laudator temporis acti*, the editor believed the citizens of New Merrymeeting owed a debt of gratitude to the men of Old Merrymeeting who had added so many illustrious pages to the glorious history of Maine's distinguished past. Captain John Dawn was an ornament to the community and deserved all the encomiums that were sure to be heaped upon him when his ship, the *John O'Brien*, "took the waves" tomorrow.

Many of the young men in plaid trousers with belled bottoms and yellow-kid gloves thought Captain John Dawn deserved to be prosecuted for having so many rotting piers along the bay that would not bear the weight of a man and his sweetheart when they wanted to be out of the crowd.

The Governor could not come. He sent his regrets. Judge Boody of Portland was there, though, and two members of the legislature.

The small boys who had come down to the launching expected to see the high hull keel over when it struck the water. They crowded close to the ways so as not to miss the splash that would follow.

The old men walked about in their dark, best suits with seats shiny from the family pews, smoked their pipes, and shook their heads. It wasn't going to be a launching to hold a candle to the old ones, before the war. The *John O'Reilly* was only six hundred tons. A mere shaving to the ships they had seen ride these ways, in their time. Ships did not come big as they used to. Men did not, either. The ones now couldn't raise the families they had raised. Their own sons couldn't. Didn't have the stuff in them. A man now thought he had done his duty when he had begot five children. Not the dozen every man used to have.

It was probably the last ship that would go off the ways in Merrymeeting Bay. Once Merrymeeting had been famous for its scores of vessels. The Dawn ships had been known the world around. But the Rebel raiders had accounted for lots of them. The *Alabama* had sunk four. Time had accounted for many of the others. A few were carrying guano and coal and lumber, and Kennebec ice to Norfolk and New York. But they didn't come back to Merrymeeting Bay, they hailed from ports farther south now, Philadelphia and Quincy and Newport News. The railroad had cut its way right along the whole coast, and it had sucked the life out of the Maine shipyards and had left them high and dry.

Percivale Robbins, the bard of New Merrymeeting, had written a long poem for the occasion. He had brought in almost all of the chaster Greek ladies he had encountered in his books at Beaudoin. He lamented the passing of the local Drakes and Raleighs. Captain John Dawn emerged as Sir Walter Raleigh, setting off for the Orinoco in the sunset of his days. Poseidon and the Tritons were awaiting him with open arms at the entrance of Merrymeeting Bay. Proteus was sitting on Merrymeeting Head blowing on a conch. They had made a soft bed of sea-moss-farine for the old sea-dog, under the blue waves. Sirens whom even Queen Victoria would approve of were calling:

"Thou art weary, now 'tis sunset,
Leave, O leave that darkening shore!
Seek the cradle of our bosoms,
Thy peregrinations now are o'er!"

The women of the New Merrymeeting Literary Circle thought the poem was the finest literary effusion that had yet come out of Maine, not excepting even *Uncle Tom's Cabin.* They had committed it to memory.

A great many plainer people of the town, though, thought it was too bad to bury old Captain Dawn before he was dead, even for the sake of a good poem.

Old Polly Toothaker was stumbling about the kitchen of the Dawn house with her old eyes misted over with fierce tears. She had seen the *New Merrymeeting Record* and the editorial, and she had stuffed the paper into the kitchen stove and ruined her fire for half an hour. But Captain John would not see the thing. Polly had other troubles, too. Since her eyesight had well nigh failed her, she had had to depend on other people for getting her caraway seeds for her best cookies. She had depended on that young scalliwag of a Tom Fuller, Peggy Doughty's grandson, for them this time. And he had failed her. She had made apple pies and mince turnovers and crab-apple tarts. But a launching was not a launching to Polly without her crinkly caraway cookies.

She had done her best. But folks nowadays did not appreciate the pains a body took for them. Like as not all the visitors would bring their own suppers with them to-day and not take the trouble to climb the hill and eat the good things Polly had set out for them in the dining room and the kitchen. They would fetch down their boughten cookies—baker's stuff. Polly sniffed. She had just as soon put so much sawdust into her mouth as baker's cookies. In the old times, all the hundreds of people at a launching had eaten the fine victuals of the Dawns. They had sat down at the Dawn tables horsed up in the meadows, three or four hundred strong. Or in the house, if the launching was late in the Fall. There used to be torchlights and prayers and speeches and fiddles. Today there wouldn't be so much as a single fiddle, and only a handful of the old Merrymeeting folks would come near the house.

She knew how it would be. She remembered the last launching, three years ago, in '72. They had had hard work to get even the Baptist minister to come down and say a few words before the last block was knocked away. And the Lord knew a Baptist minister was next to nothing.

People had changed. The country was filling up with riff-raff. The new town they had built, New Merrymeeting, wasn't even on the bay. It was on the railroad. And Polly had just as soon walk off Merrymeeting Head as trust herself to climb into one of those dirty herring boxes and be pulled along by a stinking iron horse. People on the bay had turned into herring-chokers and clam-diggers. She was glad her Easter had not lived to see such a come-down in the world.

You couldn't get white men to man your ships now. It was dagoes and square-heads, and the Lord knew what worse. The tall and handsome men were all gone. All but one.

Polly felt like crying. And she cried all she wanted to,

too, as she blundered about the kitchen in the afternoon sunlight.

They wrote poems and such-like trash in their newspapers just as though John Dawn was finished and done for. The only man left alive on the bay! If his sons had lived, they would sing a different tune. They talked as though ships were done for. It was all steamships now. Dirty low boats full of fire and stink and apt any minute to blow up and send people to Kingdom Come!

Captain John would show them. He wasn't through. Not by a jugful! He had a kick in his hind legs still. He was smarter in his seventies than any of these upstarts in their twenties. He'd make fools of them all.

A man ought not to have to live longer than his sons. It was the worst that could happen to a man.

The hammers had been going for hours in the thin light of the October day. Now the thin light was failing, and they were quickening up. The sun was slipping down into a mass of gray clouds. The shadow of the clouds was coming out over the bay, over the three deserted piers with their sagging sheds, and over the hill that towered above the workmen and the holiday crowd. The red maple leaves that had drifted into the shipyard had taken on a dark hue, like leaves out of another year. The water had grown darker. The frost-struck thatch loomed up more clearly against the dreary color of the waves. A low wind had come up out of the southeast. It made a lonesome sound around the high prow of the *John*

O'Reilly and went off through the bare boughs of the shipyard trees like a sad tune.

A hush had fallen on the people gathered around the ship. Even the children had grown quiet. It was not merely the hush of expectancy. There was something more in it, something that had come out of the going of the low sun and the whole feeling of the short October day. There was something about it, too, that went with seeing a thing happen for the last time. It was more than the end of Summer. Many people there knew, without being able to put it into words, that they were standing in the twilight of a season in the history of America.

Captain Dawn heard the wind sigh around the ship under his feet. He heard the hush that had come over the people below. He had his coat buttoned on him, but he still felt cold all through. It was getting along in the year, and he was getting along in his years, too. That was why.

In a moment more he would go forward and join the selectmen of New Merrymeeting and the editor of the *Record* at the ship's prow. He would raise his hand as he had done it so often in his time, and he would feel the ship begin to come alive under his feet. The crowd would flow back and become merely faces, and the waves would begin to make a clear, mighty sound around the lovely curves of his ship, as they rose and parted to make room for it in their midst. It was the sound that meant most to him. The sound he had loved all the days of his life.

It was time to go forward. The tide was at its tip-top high-water mark. His watch said so. But John Dawn still walked the after deck. He had a feeling that he ought to wait. He could not explain the feeling. It was as though he ought to wait for somebody else to come. Somebody very important. He could not tell what made him feel that way. The important people of New Merrymeeting were all there in their places. There was no one else to stand with him there at the prow.

His sons would have been the ones to wait for. If they had lived. Somehow, his sons seemed very old to him, old, old men now, they had been gone so long. They had been sons so long ago.

Somebody else. As if there were anybody else!

He had picked up no end of loose tackle about the deck for the last hour and more. He liked to have his deck shipshape at a launching. Bits of rope and blocks of wood had been left lying there. He had been doing nothing but pick up after this set of workmen. All along. Carpenters were careless nowadays. Not like the carpenters in the old time.

Well, he would have to go forward now.

A mile away, on the road leading to Merrymeeting, a man was driving as if his life depended on his reaching the shore at once. The wheels of the buggy sent the Autumn leaves eddying and flying, and the frail carriage lurched dangerously behind the racking heels of the horse. The horse was already gray with sweat. The turnout was one from Jones's Livery Stable in New Merrymeeting. The driver was an elderly man, clearly, for his hat had blown off back a piece up the road, and the man's hair was white as driven snow.

John Dawn walked firmly toward the prow of the *John O'Reilly*. As he came abreast of the open well that went down to the bottom of the ship, his foot stumbled into a small coil of rope a workman had dropped there. He lost his balance, went out with his other foot. But the rope whipped up and caught that, too. The man plunged forward. He might have been able even then to save himself with his hands, perhaps, but both hands were hanging wearily at his sides. He pitched headlong into the dark well of the hold.

The selectmen and the editor of the *Record* brought Captain Dawn to the land in a litter made of their coats. They carried him along between them, holding by the sleeves of their coats. He was still breathing when they got him down. The hushed crowd made way for them. A doctor was called out of the throng. He made a hurried examination. The man's back was apparently broken. It was a miracle he was still alive. He might live to reach the house. The four men hoped he would. They bent to lift him and go on.

John Dawn opened his eyes. He spoke in a clear, low voice. Even the people nearby heard what he said.

"Knock away the blocks. . . . Hold me up to see."

The men looked at each other. It was the editor of the *Record* who gave the signal:

"Let the launching go on. Knock away the blocks!"

A man naked to his hairy waist lifted his sledge. There was a sharp report like the snapping of an enormous viol string miles away. The men bent and lifted the head and shoulders of Captain Dawn up so he could watch. The high prow overhead began to move along the sky. Just then the setting sun came out through the clouds, and the low light of it struck full on the moving ship. It turned it into a tower of splendor against the darkened east. The crowd could not help it. They broke into a low cheer, then a louder and louder one. The ship picked up speed. It touched the bay. Two walls of green rose up sheer each side, turned into sheets of crystal and gold, curled over, and let the ship pass through on its way to the sea. The cheers kept up without a break.

The eyes of John Dawn were brimmed with lovely light. Part of it was from the sun. But part of it was from some source of light within himself.

The light was still there as they carried him up the hill to his house. The sun had left the shipyard now, but it was still upon the ship riding proud and high on the bay, and it was still on John Dawn. The face of John Dawn kept pace with the sun as he was borne higher and higher. And John Dawn had a smile on his face now, along with the sunshine.

As often it happened in October, the cloudy ending of the day turned suddenly into one of unspeakable brightness. The air ran liquid gold, trees were swallowed up and lost in a glory. The clouds overhead became golden cloths that reflected a sheen downwards which transfigured everything. Everything swam in a mist of airy flames.

There was a carriage standing on the road by the house, but it was drowned and obscured in the glow. A stranger came down the hill to meet the men ascending. He had hair as white as the man on the litter. It was washed with the glory around it. The man was covered with the sunlight, and the others could not make out his face.

But John Dawn could. For when the man came close to him, John Dawn reached up his arms with all the life left in him and put them about the man's neck.

And the man covered with the sunlight on the edge of night fell on John Dawn's neck and held him in his arms.

"Johnry! Johnry!" said John Dawn. "It was you I was expecting. Brother, see!—Your ship is on the bay!"

John O'Reilly took the whole weight of John Dawn in his arms. He held his brother up in the last of the sunshine. The light went slowly off the world as John O'Reilly held him so. One white head leaned heavier and heavier on the other. The light began to ebb out of John Dawn's eyes.

As he rested there in the arms of his brother, by the rosetrees that had come out of Devon long ago, the years of John Dawn began to flow together and become as one thing. Time ebbed away, and lovely and lost things came back from the depths into the light. The heaviness of long sorrow lifted and moved away. Johnry was with him always, a small boy on his heels and a tall man who held the wheel with him and would not be lost in Devon. John

Dawn stood on a ship he and Johnry had sailed out on the ocean by themselves, and he stood with his strength on him in the midst of his men in his own shipyard. His father was calling him down to breakfast in a drafty old house, a tall ship was making, and John's son Robert, who looked like him, after all, was somewhere about on the hill above. His father loved Robert and held him on his knee and let him write poetry, for he was going to Beaudoin and not to war. John Dawn was going up the hill to his house, and Ruth was coming down to meet him under the morning stars with her toes like apple blossoms under her nightgown. Her voice was coming down to him. Down to him. A girl's. A girl who had two sons, and they were both men as John was, and the three of them worshipping a girl who smiled at them beside a door she had thrown open in a high wall. And the Bristol Channel was shining through the door in the wall. A door in a wall. Thrown open. And Easter came through it, and John's father came through it and let John hold him in his arms as John had always yearned to do, not because his father was wounded by the great explosion behind him but because his father loved him and wanted him to. Ice on the trees in January the day he was born, the day Betsy Holbrook loved to tell him about and her first seeing him naked. And that was the same day Joel was born, for John remembered seeing the ice and the snow then, and John's father came in and said how he was born on that day, too. Three babies with their fists up in a beam of January sunlight coming through a window. Three babies with babies inside them who were really men and could stand on yard-arms across the whole sunset and in the midst of the Winter moon. Four babies, for Johnry had come out of their bodies, too, though you mustn't talk of that when women were around, except only Ruth, and she smiled at your telling it, for she knew how good your body was and helped it to be Joel and Robert, carrying men inside her.

John Dawn was standing on a pitching deck at mid-ocean, and his son Joel was holding the wheel by one side and Johnry by the other, for the door in the wall was open, and Johnry could come through, and the grandfather whose face he couldn't see because of the arrow and the Indians, who were only nothing and melted away. John was standing and looking into a gulf with hot embers, but it wasn't his father's house or a church that had been burned, but a sunrise in Java, and Ruth came up, big with both Joel and Robert, to see. But now it was roses white as the dawn in Devon and peepers in Mast Meadow and a Merrymeeting thrush singing close to twilight. Joel was teaching John to steer a ship, and smacking both Johnry and Johndy on the patches that were alike on both of their seats. A woman who was a stranger he loved, and must be his mother, was taking him and Joel up on her knee. She let him down to run with Ruth to see the new son that had been born to him in the midst of a gray loneliness and albatrosses flying over. They were all running through a January day like a rainbow, beside the dark blue Merrymeeting waves, to see another baby being born. Ruth was under the Spanish mountains, and the evening stars were coming out over the world, but Ruth opened a door in the mountains, and it was a bright sunshiny day through the door. A door. A door in a wall. And years coming through, and years going through. John's father said Robert's butts were the shape of his own, and Sir Robert agreed that they were, and then John's father had to carry John up the hill to the big house because John's legs were so short. And John's father carried Ruth, too, because he could see the strong and handsome men inside her. John O'Reilly's lap was warm under John's head, and the big sails they had set were bellied out overhead. Johnry, Ruth, Robert, and Joel, and all were sliding upside down along the underside of the world in the ship that had just slipped down the Merrymeeting ways. And the masts overhead were tall Merrymeeting pines that brushed on the Summer clouds and played like a thousand harps full of the sound of years growing fainter. And someone opened a door on a room full of babies. A door. A door. And it swayed back and forth. The wind outside whistled through a thousand ropes on a mast. The royal yard swayed back and forth across the sky, like a cradle rocking. And babies in it. A single albatross flying lonely across the sea in the sun. And it swayed, like a cradle. Like a cradle rocking babies. Babies that were sons. Babies that were men. Babies. Rocking. Sons. Sons.

John Dawn's head gave out and sank down. And he died in his brother's arms.

The men of New Merrymeeting did not know how an old man could do it. But the stranger carried the dead captain into the house and laid him down on the sofa in the western parlor. He closed up his eyes with his fingers. He turned to them and thanked them, and sent them away.

John O'Reilly did not ask old Polly Toothaker for a lamp. He wished to sit by his brother in the dark. After a while, the panes were full of high October stars. They moved across the window, and new ones followed them, and the night went by.

Polly Toothaker woke at dawn in the room upstairs. She went to the window and turned her feeble eyes out on the bay. The new ship was there.

And an old one beside it. It had every sail set, the old one, but there was not a sign of any living man on it. As she gazed at it and wondered, the wind took it out to sea. It grew smaller and brighter as the sun pushed up out of the waves and caught its sails. She followed it as long as her old eyes could follow. It seemed like a flake of fire at the last, burning hot like a candle flame set on the edge of the sea.